Foreign Bodies

Foreign Bodies

Edited and Introduced
by Martin Edwards

Poisoned Pen Press

Contents

Introduction

Classic crime fiction is usually associated with authors writing in the English language. Yet in countries as distant from each other, geographically and culturally, as Japan, the Netherlands, and Mexico, foreign language mysteries flourished long, long before the days of Nordic Noir and subtitled TV thriller serials.

Far from the gas-lit streets of Sherlock Holmes' London, far from Miss Marple's peaceful (well, except for the body count) village of St Mary Mead, overseas contemporaries of Conan Doyle and Christie created criminals and detectives in an astonishingly eclectic range of mystery stories. The names of many of those authors are unfamiliar to us today—in most cases, because their work was seldom translated into English.

Foreign Bodies celebrates their achievements. Until now, the British Library's Crime Classics series has focused on home-grown writers, but this book is very different. It will, I hope, offer a new perspective on crime fiction in translation.

This collection brings together vintage crime stories written by authors from Hungary, Japan, Denmark, India, Germany, Mexico, Belgium, the Netherlands, Russia, and France. Several of the stories have been translated into English for the very first time, especially for this anthology.

As a result, present day detective fiction fans have a chance to investigate fictional mysteries which were long unavailable, yet which deserve to be remembered. In one or two cases, the stories are notable primarily for their historic or curiosity value; in other instances, they offer memorable samples of the world's most popular fictional genre.

Most people agree that the first *detective* story was Edgar Allan Poe's 'The Murders in the Rue Morgue', but the *crime* story pre-dates that masterpiece, and its origins are arguably far removed from the Anglo-American tradition of detective fiction. Unfortunately, almost every different historian of the genre has come up with a fresh opinion about precisely where and how the crime story began. Dorothy L. Sayers, for instance, identified elements of the genre in 'The History of Bel' and 'The History of Susanna' from the Apocryphal Scriptures, Virgil's 'The Story of Hercules and Cacus', and 'The Story of Rhampsinitus' Treasure House' by Herodotus. She included each of these pieces in her ground-breaking anthology *Great Stories of Detection, Mystery and Horror* (1928), arguing that they treated, respectively, 'analysis of material evidence', 'analysis of testimony', 'fabrication of false clues', and 'psychological detection'.

Conceivably, Voltaire's *Zadig* (1747) and E.T.A. Hoffmann's novella *Mademoiselle de Scuderi* (1819) influenced Poe when he came to write 'The Murders in the Rue Morgue'. And even Poe's status as a pioneer in the field of classic detection is not beyond dispute. In an article published in the magazine *CADS* in May 2017, Per Bonesmo contended that 'the world's first detective novel was written by a Norwegian', namely Mauritz Hansen, who published *The Murder of Machine-Builder Roolfsen* in 1839/40. Conversely, in *Crime Fiction in German* (2016), Mary Tannert makes a case for Adolph Mullner's *The Caliber* (1828) as 'the first

German-language detective story'. This debate seems certain to run and run.

After Poe, and before the creation of Sherlock Holmes, Emile Gaboriau created the detective Lecoq. Although Holmes brutally dismissed his predecessor as 'a miserable bungler' in *A Study in Scarlet* (1887), Lecoq was popular in his day, and Conan Doyle enjoyed Gaboriau's work. A wide range of books first written in languages other than English influenced the work of British and American writers during the Golden Age of Detective Fiction. A striking example is Gaston Leroux's 'locked room mystery' *The Mystery of the Yellow Room* (1907), which inspired both Agatha Christie and the king of the sealed room puzzle, John Dickson Carr.

Some commentators argue that Anton Chekhov's *The Shooting Party* (1884) is a forerunner of Agatha Christie's *The Murder of Roger Ackroyd* (1926), and that the Belgian writer Stanislas-Andre Steeman's *Six Dead Men* (1931) anticipates key elements of Christie's *And Then There Were None* (1939). These are interesting debating points, but even more thought-provoking is the fact that Hansen, Chekhov, and Steeman were not writing in English, and that consequently, their work in the crime genre (thankfully Chekhov did have more than one string to his bow!) has been under-estimated.

An avalanche of detective novels appeared in Britain during the Golden Age, but hardly any mysteries were translated from other languages. Among the rare exceptions was *Aux Abois* by Tristan Bernard, but even this book was the subject of what was described as 'a free adaptation' by the Americans Virginia and Frank Vernon as *The Diary of a Murderer* (1934). In a review for the *Sunday Times*, Sayers called the story 'interesting' and 'vivid', but it did not make a lasting impression.

The reality is that publishers took the view, rightly or wrongly, that readers of the time had little interest in crime novels by foreign writers, and thus did not go to the trouble of commissioning translations. Extraordinarily, even some of the early novels written by Pierre Boileau and Thomas Narcejac, the gifted authors whose collaborations resulted in superb films such as *Vertigo* and *Les Diaboliques*, have to this day never appeared in English language versions.

If the work of French, German, and other European mystery novelists attracted minimal attention, the lack of interest in crime stories from countries such as Japan and South America was even more conspicuous. Because such books were unavailable, crime readers and critics in Britain and the US often made the assumption that they didn't exist, and that, even if the likes of Conan Doyle and Christie appealed to people all around the world, they lacked foreign counterparts.

Yet even if no other fictional detective surpasses Sherlock, even if no other crime novelist can match Christie's sales, there is much pleasure to be had in discovering the work of long-forgotten examples of 'crime in translation'. The British Library's Crime Classics series is, naturally, focused on the work of authors from or working in Britain, but I have long believed that many fans of the Crime Classics would relish the chance to sample classic crime fiction from overseas. Luckily, my editor Rob Davies agreed, and this book is the outcome.

My interest in 'crime in translation', and in particular in translated short stories, dates back to my teens, when I was given as a Christmas present a hardback copy of *More Rivals of Sherlock Holmes: Cosmopolitan Crimes* (1971), one of a series of four excellent anthologies edited by Sir Hugh Greene. Although most of the authors featured were British or wrote in English, that book introduced me to Baron Palle Rosenkrantz and Balduin Groller, both of whom are represented here. Whilst this book ranges more widely than Greene's anthology, in terms of time as well as in terms of geography and the nationalities of contributing authors, I take this opportunity to pay tribute to the pleasure that his collections afforded me in the 1970s. To this day, they remain worth seeking out.

The stories in *Foreign Bodies* are presented, very approximately, in chronological order of publication. When one reads the stories, the influence of Conan Doyle is often evident, but what is truly captivating, to my mind, is the variety of story-telling styles adopted by writers in different parts of the world at much the same time as Christie and her English-speaking colleagues were debating the so-called 'rules' of the classic whodunit.

In researching this book, I have benefited from a great deal of help from widely-read and multilingual friends who have great insight into foreign crime fiction. I am especially grateful to John Pugmire, whose Locked Room International imprint has revived a range of splendid and unfairly neglected impossible crime novels, and to Josh Pachter, a highly capable crime writer with a particular flair for the short story. John and Josh drew my attention to many hidden gems with which I was unfamiliar, and kindly translated several stories of special interest, as well as checking through my introductions. Josh in turn was assisted by Els Depuydt, Frans de Jong, Piet Schreuders, Hilde Vandermeeren, and especially André Verbrugghen (chairman of the Vriendenkring Jean Ray).

The complexity of this project was increased by the need to trace rights holders in respect of translations as well as authors. Some appealing stories eluded us, but after rather more than two years of work, we are all delighted that this unique book has finally achieved publication. My thanks go to all those who have contributed to *Foreign Bodies*, and especially John, Josh, and Rob and his marvellous team at the British Library.

Martin Edwards
www.martinedwardsbooks.com

The Swedish Match

Anton Chekhov

The great Russian man of letters Anton Chekhov (1860–1904) needs no introduction to readers—except, perhaps, in his guise as a crime writer. It will come as a surprise to many that, during his twenties, Chekhov indulged his enthusiasm for the genre—and made an invaluable contribution to his family's finances—by writing enough stories to fill out an enjoyable book which gathers much of his work in this field, *A Night in the Cemetery: And Other Stories of Crime and Suspense* (2008), translated by Peter Sekerin.

Chekhov also wrote *The Shooting Party* (1884), a full-length mystery which boasts a clever structural ploy. The distinguished critic Julian Symons went so far as to argue that the story represents a landmark in the genre's history, although a British novel utilizing a comparable twist, and published during the Golden Age of Murder between the world wars, is much better known. Chekhov's book did, however, receive the Hollywood treatment, being filmed in 1944 as *Summer Storm,* starring George Sanders and Linda Darnell. 'The Swedish Match' is one of the stories that Chekhov published in magazines such as *Dragonfly*, *Spectator*, and *Alarm Clock*. This light-hearted tale has been reprinted in English from time to time, for instance in *The Mystery Book*, edited by genre historian H. Douglas Thomson, in 1934.

• • ● • •

I

On the morning of October 6, 1885, a well-dressed young man presented himself at the office of the police superintendent of the 2nd division of the S. district, and announced that his employer, a retired cornet of the guards, called Mark Ivanovitch Klyauzov, had been murdered. The young man was pale and extremely agitated as he made this announcement. His hands trembled and there was a look of horror in his eyes.

'To whom have I the honour of speaking?' the superintendent asked him.

'Psyekov, Klyauzov's steward. Agricultural and engineering expert.'

The police superintendent, on reaching the spot with Psyekov and the necessary witnesses, found the position as follows.

Masses of people were crowding about the lodge in which Klyauzov lived. The news of the event had flown round the neighbourhood with the rapidity of lightning, and, thanks to its being a holiday, the people were flocking to the lodge from all the neighbouring villages. There was a regular hubbub of talk. Pale and tearful faces were to be seen here and there. The door into Klyauzov's bedroom was found to be locked. The key was in the lock on the inside.

'Evidently the criminals made their way in by the window,' Psyekov observed, as they examined the door.

They went into the garden into which the bedroom window looked. The window had a gloomy, ominous air. It was covered by a faded green curtain. One corner of the curtain was slightly turned back, which made it possible to peep into the bedroom.

'Has any one of you looked in at the window?' inquired the superintendent.

'No, your honour,' said Yefrem, the gardener, a little, grey-haired old man with the face of a veteran non-commissioned officer. 'No one feels like looking when they are shaking in every limb!'

'Ech, Mark Ivanitch! Mark Ivanitch!' sighed the superintendent, as he looked at the window. 'I told you that you would come to a bad end! I told you, poor dear—you wouldn't listen! Dissipation leads to no good!'

'It's thanks to Yefrem,' said Psyekov. 'We should never have guessed it but for him. It was he who first thought that something was wrong. He came to me this morning and said: "Why is it our master hasn't waked up for so long? He hasn't been out of his bedroom for a whole week!" When he said that to me I was struck all of a heap...The thought flashed through my mind at once. He hasn't made an appearance since Saturday of last week, and today's Sunday. Seven days is no joke!'

'Yes, poor man,' the superintendent sighed again. 'A clever fellow, well-educated, and so good-hearted. There was no one like him, one may say, in company. But a rake; the kingdom of heaven be his! I'm not surprised at anything with him! Stepan,' he said, addressing one of the witnesses, 'ride off this minute to my house and send Andryushka to the police captain's, let him report to him. Say Mark Ivanitch has been murdered! Yes, and run to the inspector—why should he sit in comfort doing nothing? Let him come here. And you go yourself as fast as you can to the examining magistrate, Nikolay Yermolaitch, and tell him to come here. Wait a bit, I will write him a note.'

The police superintendent stationed watchmen round the lodge, and went off to the steward's to have tea. Ten minutes later he was sitting on a stool, carefully nibbling lumps of sugar, and sipping tea as hot as a red-hot coal.

'There it is!…' he said to Psyekov, 'there it is!…a gentleman, and a well-to-do one, too…a favourite of the gods, one may say, to use Pushkin's expression, and what has he made of it? Nothing! He gave himself up to drinking and debauchery, and…here now…he has been murdered!'

Two hours later the examining magistrate drove up. Nikolay Yermolaitch Tchubikov (that was the magistrate's name), a tall, thick-set old man of sixty, had been hard at work for a quarter of a century. He was known to the whole district as an honest, intelligent, energetic man, devoted to his work. His invariable companion, assistant, and secretary, a tall young man of six and twenty, called Dyukovsky, arrived on the scene of action with him.

'Is it possible, gentlemen?' Tchubikov began, going into Psyekov's room and rapidly shaking hands with everyone. 'Is it possible? Mark Ivanitch? Murdered? No, it's impossible! Im-poss-i-ble!'

'There it is,' sighed the superintendent.

'Merciful heavens! Why, I saw him only last Friday. At the fair at Tarabankovo! Saving your presence, I drank a glass of vodka with him!'

'There it is,' the superintendent sighed once more.

They heaved sighs, expressed their horror, drank a glass of tea each, and went to the lodge.

'Make way!' the police inspector shouted to the crowd.

On going into the lodge the examining magistrate, first of all, set to work to inspect the door into the bedroom. The door turned out to be made of deal, painted yellow, and not to have been tampered with. No special traces that might have served as evidence could be found. They proceeded to break open the door.

'I beg you, gentlemen, who are not concerned, to retire,' said the examining magistrate, when, after long banging and cracking, the door yielded to the axe and the chisel. 'I ask this in the interests of the investigation…Inspector, admit no one!'

Tchubikov, his assistant and the police superintendent opened the door and hesitatingly, one after the other, walked into the room. The following spectacle met their eyes. In the solitary window stood a big wooden bedstead with an immense feather bed on it. On the rumpled feather bed lay a creased and crumpled quilt. A pillow, in a cotton pillow-case, also much creased, was on the floor. On a little table beside the bed lay a silver watch, and silver coins to the value of twenty kopecks. Some sulphur matches lay there too. Except the bed, the table, and a solitary chair, there was no furniture in the room. Looking under the bed, the superintendent saw two dozen empty bottles, an old straw hat, and a jar of vodka. Under the table lay one boot, covered with dust. Taking a look round the room, Tchubikov frowned and flushed crimson.

'The blackguards!' he muttered, clenching his fists.

'And where is Mark Ivanitch?' Dyukovsky asked quietly.

'I beg you not to put your spoke in,' Tchubikov answered roughly. 'Kindly examine the floor. This is the second case in my experience, Yevgraf Kuzmitch,' he added to the police superintendent, dropping his voice. 'In 1870 I had a similar case. But no doubt you remember it…The murder of the merchant Portretov. It was just the same. The blackguards murdered him, and dragged the dead body out of the window.'

Tchubikov went to the window, drew the curtain aside, and cautiously pushed the window. The window opened.

'It opens, so it was not fastened…H'm…there are traces on the window-sill. Do you see? Here is the trace of a knee…Some one climbed out…We shall have to inspect the window thoroughly.'

'There is nothing special to be observed on the floor,' said Dyukovsky. 'No stains, nor scratches. The only thing I have found is a used Swedish match. Here it is. As far as I remember, Mark Ivanitch didn't smoke; in a general way he used sulphur ones, never Swedish matches. This match may serve as a clue…'

'Oh, hold your tongue, please!' cried Tchubikov, with a wave of his hand. 'He keeps on about his match! I can't stand these excitable people! Instead of looking for matches, you had better examine the bed!'

On inspecting the bed, Dyukovsky reported:

'There are no stains of blood or of anything else…Nor are there any fresh rents. On the pillow there are traces of teeth. A liquid, having the smell of beer and also the taste of it, has been spilt on the quilt…The general appearance of the bed gives grounds for supposing there has been a struggle.'

'I know there was a struggle without your telling me! No one asked you whether there was a struggle. Instead of looking out for a struggle, you had better be…'

'One boot is here, the other one is not on the scene.'

'Well, what of that?'

'Why, they must have strangled him while he was taking off his boots. He hadn't time to take the second boot off when…'

'He's off again!…And how do you know that he was strangled?'

'There are marks of teeth on the pillow. The pillow itself is very much crumpled, and has been flung to a distance of six feet from the bed.'

'He argues, the chatterbox! We had better go into the garden. You had better look in the garden instead of rummaging about here…I can do that without your help.'

When they went out into the garden their first task was the inspection of the grass. The grass had been trampled down under the windows. The clump of burdock against the wall under the window turned out to have been trodden on too. Dyukovsky succeeded in finding on it some broken shoots, and a little bit of wadding. On the topmost burrs, some fine threads of dark blue wool were found.

'What was the colour of his last suit?' Dyukovsky asked Psyekov.

'It was yellow, made of canvas.'

'Capital! Then it was they who were in dark blue…'

Some of the burrs were cut off and carefully wrapped up in paper. At that moment Artsybashev-Svistakovsky, the police captain, and Tyutyuev, the doctor, arrived. The police captain greeted the others, and at once proceeded to satisfy his curiosity; the doctor, a tall and extremely lean man with sunken eyes, a long nose, and a sharp chin, greeting no one and asking no questions, sat down on a stump, heaved a sigh, and said:

'The Serbians are in a turmoil again! I can't make out what they want! Ah, Austria, Austria! It's your doing!'

The inspection of the window from outside yielded absolutely no result; the inspection of the grass and surrounding bushes furnished many valuable clues. Dyukovsky succeeded, for instance, in detecting a long, dark streak in the grass, consisting of stains, and stretching from the window for a good many yards into the garden. The streak ended under one of the lilac bushes in a big, brownish stain. Under the same bush was found a boot, which turned out to be the fellow to the one found in the bedroom.

'This is an old stain of blood,' said Dyukovsky, examining the stain.

At the word 'blood,' the doctor got up and lazily took a cursory glance at the stain.

'Yes, it's blood,' he muttered.

'Then he wasn't strangled, since there's blood,' said Tchubikov, looking malignantly at Dyukovsky.

'He was strangled in the bedroom, and here, afraid he would come to, they stabbed him with something sharp. The stain under the bush shows that he lay there for a comparatively long time, while they were trying to find some way of carrying him, or something to carry him on out of the garden.'

'Well, and the boot?'

'That boot bears out my contention that he was murdered while he was taking off his boots before going to bed. He had taken off one boot; the other—that is, this boot—he had only managed to get half off. While he was being dragged and shaken the boot that was only half on came off of itself...'

'What powers of deduction: just look at him!' Tchubikov jeered. 'He brings it all out so pat! And when will you learn not to put your theories forward? You had better take a little of the grass for analysis instead of arguing!'

After making the inspection and taking a plan of the locality, they went off to the steward's to write a report and have lunch. At lunch they talked.

'Watch, money, and everything else...are untouched,' Tchubikov began the conversation. 'It is as clear as twice two makes four that the murder was committed not for mercenary motives.'

'It was committed by a man of the educated class,' Dyukovsky put in.

'From what do you draw that conclusion?'

'I base it on the Swedish match, which the peasants about here have not learned to use yet. Such matches are only used by landowners and not by all of them. He was murdered, by the way, not by one but by three, at least: two held him while the third strangled him. Klyauzov was strong and the murderers must have known that.'

'What use would his strength be to him supposing he were asleep?'

'The murderers came upon him as he was taking off his boots. He was taking off his boots, so he was not asleep.'

'It's no good making things up! You had better eat your lunch!'

'To my thinking, your honour,' said Yefrem, the gardener, as he set the samovar on the table, 'this vile deed was the work of no other than Nikolashka.'

'Quite possible,' said Psyekov.

'Who's this Nikolashka?'

'The master's valet, your honour,' answered Yefrem. 'Who else should it be if not he? He's a ruffian, your honour! A drunkard, and such a dissipated fellow! May the Queen of Heaven never bring the like again! He always used to fetch vodka for the master, he always used to put the master to bed...Who should it be if not he? And what's more, I venture to bring to your notice, your honour, he boasted once in the tavern, the rascal, that he would murder his master. It's all on account of Akulka, on account of a woman...He had a soldier's wife...The master took a fancy to her and got intimate with her, and he...was angered by it, to be sure. He's lolling about in the kitchen now, drunk. He's crying... making out he is grieving over the master...'

'And anyone might be angry over Akulka, certainly,' said Psyekov. 'She is a soldier's wife, a peasant woman, but...

Mark Ivanitch might well call her Nana. There is something in her that does suggest Nana…fascinating…'

'I have seen her…I know…' said the examining magistrate, blowing his nose in a red handkerchief.

Dyukovsky blushed and dropped his eyes. The police superintendent drummed on his saucer with his fingers. The police captain coughed and rummaged in his portfolio for something. On the doctor alone the mention of Akulka and Nana appeared to produce no impression. Tchubikov ordered Nikolashka to be fetched. Nikolashka, a lanky young man with a long pock-marked nose and a hollow chest, wearing a reefer jacket that had been his master's, came into Psyekov's room and bowed down to the ground before Tchubikov. His face looked sleepy and showed traces of tears. He was drunk and could hardly stand up.

'Where is your master?' Tchubikov asked him.

'He's murdered, your honour.'

As he said this Nikolashka blinked and began to cry.

'We know that he is murdered. But where is he now? Where is his body?'

'They say it was dragged out of window and buried in the garden.'

'H'm…the results of the investigation are already known in the kitchen then…That's bad. My good fellow, where were you on the night when your master was killed? On Saturday, that is?'

Nikolashka raised his head, craned his neck, and pondered.

'I can't say, your honour,' he said. 'I was drunk and I don't remember.'

'An alibi!' whispered Dyukovsky, grinning and rubbing his hands.

'Ah! And why is it there's blood under your master's window!'

Nikolashka flung up his head and pondered.

'Think a little quicker,' said the police captain.

'In a minute. That blood's from a trifling matter, your honour. I killed a hen; I cut her throat very simply in the usual way, and she fluttered out of my hands and took and ran off...That's what the blood's from.'

Yefrem testified that Nikolashka really did kill a hen every evening and killed it in all sorts of places, and no one had seen the half-killed hen running about the garden, though of course it could not be positively denied that it had done so.

'An alibi,' laughed Dyukovsky, 'and what an idiotic alibi.'

'Have you had relations with Akulka?'

'Yes, I have sinned.'

'And your master carried her off from you?'

'No, not at all. It was this gentleman here, Mr Psyekov, Ivan Mihalitch, who enticed her from me, and the master took her from Ivan Mihalitch. That's how it was.'

Psyekov looked confused and began rubbing his left eye. Dyukovsky fastened his eyes upon him, detected his confusion, and started. He saw on the steward's legs dark blue trousers which he had not previously noticed. The trousers reminded him of the blue threads found on the burdock. Tchubikov in his turn glanced suspiciously at Psyekov.

'You can go!' he said to Nikolashka. 'And now allow me to put one question to you, Mr Psyekov. You were here, of course, on the Saturday of last week?'

'Yes, at ten o'clock I had supper with Mark Ivanitch.'

'And afterwards?'

Psyekov was confused and got up from the table.

'Afterwards...afterwards...I really don't remember,' he muttered. 'I had drunk a good deal on that occasion...I can't remember where and when I went to bed...Why do you all look at me like that? As though I had murdered him!'

'Where did you wake up?'

'I woke up in the servants' kitchen on the stove...They can all confirm that. How I got on to the stove I can't say...'

'Don't disturb yourself...Do you know Akulina?'

'Oh well, not particularly.'

'Did she leave you for Klyauzov?'

'Yes...Yefrem, bring some more mushrooms! Will you have some tea, Yevgraf Kuzmitch?'

There followed an oppressive, painful silence that lasted for some five minutes. Dyukovsky held his tongue and kept his piercing eyes on Psyekov's face, which gradually turned pale. The silence was broken by Tchubikov.

'We must go to the big house,' he said, 'and speak to the deceased's sister, Marya Ivanovna. She may give us some evidence.'

Tchubikov and his assistant thanked Psyekov for the lunch, then went off to the big house. They found Klyauzov's sister, a maiden lady of five and forty, on her knees before a high family shrine of ikons. When she saw portfolios and caps adorned with cockades in her visitors' hands, she turned pale.

'First of all, I must offer an apology for disturbing your devotions, so to say,' the gallant Tchubikov began with a scrape. 'We have come to you with a request. You have heard, of course, already...There is a suspicion that your brother has somehow been murdered. God's will, you know...Death no one can escape, neither Tsar nor ploughman. Can you not assist us with some fact, something that will throw light?'

'Oh, do not ask me!' said Marya Ivanovna, turning whiter still, and hiding her face in her hands. 'I can tell you nothing! Nothing! I implore you! I can say nothing...What can I do? Oh no, no...not a word...of my brother! I would rather die than speak!'

Marya Ivanovna burst into tears and went away into

another room. The officials looked at each other, shrugged their shoulders, and beat a retreat.

'A devil of a woman!' said Dyukovsky, swearing as they went out of the big house. 'Apparently she knows something and is concealing it. And there is something peculiar in the maid-servant's expression too…You wait a bit, you devils! We will get to the bottom of it all!'

In the evening, Tchubikov and his assistant were driving home by the light of a pale-faced moon; they sat in their waggonette, summing up in their minds the incidents of the day. Both were exhausted and sat silent. Tchubikov never liked talking on the road. In spite of his talkativeness, Dyukovsky held his tongue in deference to the old man. Towards the end of the journey, however, the young man could endure the silence no longer, and began:

'That Nikolashka has had a hand in the business,' he said, '*non dubitandum est*. One can see from his mug too what sort of a chap he is…His alibi gives him away hand and foot. There is no doubt either that he was not the instigator of the crime. He was only the stupid hired tool. Do you agree? The discreet Psyekov plays a not unimportant part in the affair too. His blue trousers, his embarrassment, his lying on the stove from fright after the murder, his alibi, and Akulka.'

'Keep it up, you're in your glory! According to you, if a man knows Akulka he is the murderer. Ah, you hot-head! You ought to be sucking your bottle instead of investigating cases! You used to be running after Akulka, too; does that mean that you had a hand in this business?'

'Akulka was a cook in your house for a month, too, but…I don't say anything. On that Saturday night I was playing cards with you, I saw you, or I should be after you too. The woman is not the point, my good sir. The point is the nasty, disgusting, mean feeling…The discreet young man did not like to be cut out, do you see. Vanity, do you see…He longed to be revenged. Then…His thick lips are a strong indication of sensuality. Do you remember how he smacked his lips when he compared Akulka to Nana? That he is burning with passion, the scoundrel, is beyond doubt! And so you have wounded vanity and unsatisfied passion. That's enough to lead to murder. Two of them are in our hands, but who is the third? Nikolashka and Psyekov held him. Who was it smothered him? Psyekov is timid, easily embarrassed, altogether a coward. People like Nikolashka are not equal to smothering with a pillow, they set to work with an axe or a mallet…Some third person must have smothered him, but who?'

Dyukovsky pulled his cap over his eyes, and pondered. He was silent till the waggonette had driven up to the examining magistrate's house.

'Eureka!' he said, as he went into the house, and took off his overcoat. 'Eureka, Nikolay Yermolaitch! I can't understand how it is it didn't occur to me before. Do you know who the third is?'

'Do leave off, please! There's supper ready. Sit down to supper!'

Tchubikov and Dyukovsky sat down to supper. Dyukovsky poured himself out a wine-glassful of vodka, got up, stretched, and with sparkling eyes, said:

'Let me tell you then that the third person who collaborated with the scoundrel Psyekov and smothered him was a woman! Yes! I am speaking of the murdered man's sister, Marya Ivanovna!'

Tchubikov coughed over his vodka and fastened his eyes on Dyukovsky.

'Are you…not quite right? Is your head…not quite right? Does it ache?'

'I am quite well. Very good, suppose I have gone out of my mind, but how do you explain her confusion on our arrival? How do you explain her refusal to give information? Admitting that that is trivial—very good! All right!—but think of the terms they were on! She detested her brother! She is an Old Believer, he was a profligate, a godless fellow... that is what has bred hatred between them! They say he succeeded in persuading her that he was an angel of Satan! He used to practise spiritualism in her presence!'

'Well, what then?'

'Don't you understand? She's an Old Believer, she murdered him through fanaticism! She has not merely slain a wicked man, a profligate, she has freed the world from Antichrist—and that she fancies is her merit, her religious achievement! Ah, you don't know these old maids, these Old Believers! You should read Dostoevsky! And what does Lyeskov say...and Petchersky! It's she, it's she, I'll stake my life on it. She smothered him! Oh, the fiendish woman! Wasn't she, perhaps, standing before the ikons when we went in to put us off the scent? "I'll stand up and say my prayers," she said to herself, "they will think I am calm and don't expect them." That's the method of all novices in crime. Dear Nikolay Yermolaitch! My dear man! Do hand this case over to me! Let me go through with it to the end! My dear fellow! I have begun it, and I will carry it through to the end.'

Tchubikov shook his head and frowned.

'I am equal to sifting difficult cases myself,' he said. 'And it's your place not to put yourself forward. Write what is dictated to you, that is your business!'

Dyukovsky flushed crimson, walked out, and slammed the door.

'A clever fellow, the rogue,' Tchubikov muttered, looking after him. 'Ve-ery clever! Only inappropriately hasty. I shall have to buy him a cigar-case at the fair for a present.'

Next morning a lad with a big head and a hare lip came from Klyauzovka. He gave his name as the shepherd Danilko, and furnished a very interesting piece of information.

'I had had a drop,' said he. 'I stayed on till midnight at my crony's. As I was going home, being drunk, I got into the river for a bathe. I was bathing and what do I see! Two men coming along the dam carrying something black. "Tyoo!" I shouted at them. They were scared, and cut along as fast as they could go into the Makarev kitchen-gardens. Strike me dead, if it wasn't the master they were carrying!'

Towards evening of the same day Psyekov and Nikolashka were arrested and taken under guard to the district town. In the town they were put in the prison tower.

II

Twelve days passed.

It was morning. The examining magistrate, Nikolay Yermolaitch, was sitting at a green table at home, looking through the papers relating to the 'Klyauzov case'; Dyukovsky was pacing up and down the room restlessly, like a wolf in a cage.

'You are convinced of the guilt of Nikolashka and Psyekov,' he said, nervously pulling at his youthful beard. 'Why is it you refuse to be convinced of the guilt of Marya Ivanovna? Haven't you evidence enough?'

'I don't say that I don't believe in it. I am convinced of it, but somehow I can't believe it…There is no real evidence. It's all theoretical, as it were…Fanaticism and one thing and another…'

'And you must have an axe and bloodstained sheets!… You lawyers! Well, I will prove it to you then! Do give up your slipshod attitude to the psychological aspect of the case. Your Marya Ivanovna ought to be in Siberia! I'll prove it. If theoretical proof is not enough for you, I have something material...It will show you how right my theory is! Only let me go about a little!'

'What are you talking about?'

'The Swedish match! Have you forgotten? I haven't forgotten it! I'll find out who struck it in the murdered man's room! It was not struck by Nikolashka, nor by Psyekov, neither of whom turned out to have matches when searched, but a third person, that is Marya Ivanovna. And I will prove it!... Only let me drive about the district, make some inquiries...'

'Oh very well, sit down...Let us proceed to the examination.'

Dyukovsky sat down to the table, and thrust his long nose into the papers.

'Bring in Nikolay Tetchov!' cried the examining magistrate.

Nikolashka was brought in. He was pale and thin as a chip. He was trembling.

'Tetchov!' began Tchubikov. 'In 1879 you were convicted of theft and condemned to a term of imprisonment. In 1882 you were condemned for theft a second time, and a second time sent to prison...We know all about it...'

A look of surprise came up into Nikolashka's face. The examining magistrate's omniscience amazed him, but soon wonder was replaced by an expression of extreme distress. He broke into sobs, and asked leave to go to wash, and calm himself. He was led out.

'Bring in Psyekov!' said the examining magistrate.

Psyekov was led in. The young man's face had greatly changed during those twelve days. He was thin, pale, and wasted. There was a look of apathy in his eyes.

'Sit down, Psyekov,' said Tchubikov. 'I hope that today you will be sensible and not persist in lying as on other occasions. All this time you have denied your participation in the murder of Klyauzov, in spite of the mass of evidence against you. It is senseless. Confession is some mitigation of guilt. Today I am talking to you for the last time. If you don't confess today, tomorrow it will be too late. Come, tell us…'

'I know nothing, and I don't know your evidence,' whispered Psyekov.

'That's useless! Well then, allow me to tell you how it happened. On Saturday evening, you were sitting in Klyauzov's bedroom drinking vodka and beer with him.' (Dyukovsky riveted his eyes on Psyekov's face, and did not remove them during the whole monologue.) 'Nikolay was waiting upon you. Between twelve and one Mark Ivanitch told you he wanted to go to bed. He always did go to bed at that time. While he was taking off his boots and giving you some instruction regarding the estate, Nikolay and you at a given signal seized your intoxicated master and flung him back upon the bed. One of you sat on his feet, the other on his head. At that moment the lady, you know who, in a black dress, who had arranged with you beforehand the part she would take in the crime, came in from the passage. She picked up the pillow, and proceeded to smother him with it. During the struggle, the light went out. The woman took a box of Swedish matches out of her pocket and lighted the candle. Isn't that right? I see from your face that what I say is true. Well, to proceed…Having smothered him, and being convinced that he had ceased to breathe, Nikolay and you dragged him out of window and put him down near the burdocks. Afraid that he might regain consciousness, you struck him with something sharp. Then you carried him, and laid him for some time under a lilac bush. After resting and considering a little, you carried him…lifted him over the hurdle…Then went along the road…Then comes the dam; near the dam you were frightened by a peasant. But what is the matter with you?'

Psyekov, white as a sheet, got up, staggering.

'I am suffocating!' he said. 'Very well...So be it...Only I must go...Please.'

Psyekov was led out.

'At last he has admitted it!' said Tchubikov, stretching at his ease. 'He has given himself away! How neatly I caught him there.'

'And he didn't deny the woman in black!' said Dyukovsky, laughing. 'I am awfully worried over that Swedish match, though! I can't endure it any longer. Good-bye! I am going!'

Dyukovsky put on his cap and went off. Tchubikov began interrogating Akulka.

Akulka declared that she knew nothing about it...

'I have lived with you and with nobody else!' she said.

At six o'clock in the evening Dyukovsky returned. He was more excited than ever. His hands trembled so much that he could not unbutton his overcoat. His cheeks were burning. It was evident that he had not come back without news.

'*Veni, vidi, vici!*' he cried, dashing into Tchubikov's room and sinking into an arm-chair. 'I vow on my honour, I begin to believe in my own genius. Listen, damnation take us! Listen and wonder, old friend! It's comic and it's sad. You have three in your grasp already...haven't you? I have found a fourth murderer, or rather murderess, for it is a woman! And what a woman! I would have given ten years of my life merely to touch her shoulders. But...listen. I drove to Klyauzovka and proceeded to describe a spiral round it. On the way I visited all the shopkeepers and innkeepers, asking for Swedish matches. Everywhere I was told "No." I have been on my round up to now. Twenty times I lost hope, and as many times regained it. I have been on the go all day long, and only an hour ago came upon what I was looking for. A couple of miles from here they gave me a packet of a dozen boxes of matches. One box was missing...I asked at once: "Who bought that box?" "So-and-so. She took a fancy to them...They crackle." My dear fellow! Nikolay Yermolaitch! What can sometimes be done by a man who has been expelled from a seminary and studied Gaboriau is beyond all conception! From today I shall begin to respect myself!...Ough...Well, let us go!'

'Go where?'

'To her, to the fourth...We must make haste, or...or I shall explode with impatience! Do you know who she is? You will never guess! The young wife of our old police superintendent, Yevgraf Kuzmitch, Olga Petrovna; that's who it is! She bought that box of matches!'

'You...you...Are you out of your mind?'

'It's very natural! In the first place she smokes, and in the second she was head over ears in love with Klyauzov. He rejected her love for the sake of an Akulka. Revenge. I remember now, I once came upon them behind the screen in the kitchen. She was cursing him, while he was smoking her cigarette and puffing the smoke into her face. But do come along; make haste, for it is getting dark already...Let us go!'

'I have not gone so completely crazy yet as to disturb a respectable, honourable woman at night for the sake of a wretched boy!'

'Honourable, respectable...You are a rag then, not an examining magistrate! I have never ventured to abuse you, but now you force me to it! You rag! You old fogey! Come, dear Nikolay Yermolaitch, I entreat you!'

The examining magistrate waved his hand in refusal and spat in disgust.

'I beg you! I beg you, not for my own sake, but in the interests of justice! I beseech you, indeed! Do me a favour, if only for once in your life!'

Dyukovsky fell on his knees.

'Nikolay Yermolaitch, do be so good! Call me a scoundrel, a worthless wretch, if I am in error about that woman! It is such a case, you know! It is a case! More like a novel than a case. The fame of it will be all over Russia. They will make you examining magistrate for particularly important cases! Do understand, you unreasonable old man!'

The examining magistrate frowned and irresolutely put out his hand towards his hat.

'Well, the devil take you!' he said. 'Let us go.'

It was already dark when the examining magistrate's waggonette rolled up to the police superintendent's door.

'What brutes we are!' said Tchubikov, as he reached for the bell. 'We are disturbing people.'

'Never mind, never mind, don't be frightened. We will say that one of the springs has broken.'

Tchubikov and Dyukovsky were met in the doorway by a tall, plump woman of three and twenty, with eyebrows as black as pitch and full red lips. It was Olga Petrovna herself.

'Ah, how very nice,' she said, smiling all over her face. 'You are just in time for supper. My Yevgraf Kuzmitch is not at home…He is staying at the priest's. But we can get on without him. Sit down. Have you come from an inquiry?'

'Yes…We have broken one of our springs, you know,' began Tchubikov, going into the drawing-room and sitting down in an easy-chair.

'Take her by surprise at once and overwhelm her,' Dyukovsky whispered to him.

'A spring…er…yes…We just drove up…'

'Overwhelm her, I tell you! She will guess if you go drawing it out.'

'Oh, do as you like, but spare me,' muttered Tchubikov, getting up and walking to the window. 'I can't! You cooked the mess, you eat it!'

'Yes, the spring,' Dyukovsky began, going up to the superintendent's wife and wrinkling his long nose. 'We have not come in to...er-er-er...to supper, nor to see Yevgraf Kuzmitch. We have come to ask you, madam, where is Mark Ivanovitch, whom you have murdered?'

'What? What Mark Ivanovitch?' faltered the superintendent's wife, and her full face was suddenly in one instant suffused with crimson. 'I...don't understand.'

'I ask you in the name of the law! Where is Klyauzov? We know all about it!'

'Through whom?' the superintendent's wife asked slowly, unable to face Dyukovsky's eyes.

'Kindly inform us where he is!'

'But how did you find out? Who told you?'

'We know all about it. I insist in the name of the law.'

The examining magistrate, encouraged by the lady's confusion, went up to her:

'Tell us and we will go away. Otherwise we...'

'What do you want with him?'

'What is the object of such questions, madam? We ask you for information. You are trembling, confused...Yes, he has been murdered, and if you will have it, murdered by you! Your accomplices have betrayed you!'

The police superintendent's wife turned pale.

'Come along,' she said quietly, wringing her hands. 'He is hidden in the bath-house. Only, for God's sake, don't tell my husband! I implore you! It would be too much for him.'

The superintendent's wife took a big key from the wall, and led her visitors through the kitchen and the passage into the yard. It was dark in the yard. There was a drizzle of fine rain. The superintendent's wife went on ahead. Tchubikov and Dyukovsky strode after her through the long grass, breathing in the smell of wild hemp and slops, which made a squelching sound under their feet. It was a big yard. Soon there were no more pools of slops, and their feet felt ploughed land. In the darkness they saw the silhouette of trees, and among the trees a little house with a crooked chimney.

'This is the bath-house,' said the superintendent's wife, 'but, I implore you, do not tell anyone.'

Going up to the bath-house, Tchubikov and Dyukovsky saw a large padlock on the door.

'Get ready your candle-end and matches,' Tchubikov whispered to his assistant.

The superintendent's wife unlocked the padlock and let the visitors into the bath-house. Dyukovsky struck a match and lighted up the entry. In the middle of it stood a table. On the table, beside a podgy little samovar, was a soup tureen with some cold cabbage-soup in it, and a dish with traces of some sauce on it.

'Go on!'

They went into the next room, the bath-room. There, too, was a table. On the table there stood a big dish of ham, a bottle of vodka, plates, knives and forks.

'But where is he...where's the murdered man?'

'He is on the top shelf,' whispered the superintendent's wife, turning paler than ever and trembling.

Dyukovsky took the candle-end in his hand and climbed up to the upper shelf. There he saw a long, human body, lying motionless on a big feather bed. The body emitted a faint snore...

'They have made fools of us, damn it all!' Dyukovsky cried. 'This is not he! It's some living blockhead lying here. Hi! Who are you, damnation take you!'

The body drew in its breath with a whistling sound and moved. Dyukovsky prodded it with his elbow. It lifted up its arms, stretched, and raised its head.

'Who is that poking?' a hoarse, ponderous bass voice inquired. 'What do you want?'

Dyukovsky held the candle-end to the face of the unknown and uttered a shriek. In the crimson nose, in the ruffled uncombed hair, in the pitch-black moustaches, of which one was jauntily twisted and pointed insolently towards the ceiling, he recognized Cornet Klyauzov.

'You…Mark…Ivanitch! Impossible!'

The examining magistrate looked up and was dumbfounded.

'It is I, yes…And it's you, Dyukovsky! What the devil do you want here? And whose ugly mug is that down there? Holy saints, it's the examining magistrate! How in the world did you come here?'

Klyauzov hurriedly got down and embraced Tchubikov. Olga Petrovna whisked out of the door.

'However did you come? Let's have a drink!—dash it all! Tra-ta-ti-to-tom…Let's have a drink! Who brought you here, though? How did you get to know I was here? It doesn't matter, though! Have a drink!'

Klyauzov lighted the lamp and poured out three glasses of vodka.

'The fact is, I don't understand you,' said the examining magistrate, throwing out his hands. 'Is it you, or not you?'

'Stop that…Do you want to give me a sermon? Don't trouble yourself! Dyukovsky boy, drink up your vodka! Friends, let us pass the…What are you staring at…? Drink!'

'All the same, I can't understand,' said the examining magistrate, mechanically drinking his vodka. 'Why are you here?'

'Why shouldn't I be here, if I am comfortable here?' Klyauzov sipped his vodka and ate some ham.

'I am staying with the superintendent's wife, as you see. In the wilds among the ruins, like some house goblin. Drink! I felt sorry for her, you know, old man! I took pity on her, and, well, I am living here in the deserted bath-house, like a hermit…I am well fed. Next week I am thinking of moving on…I've had enough of it…'

'Inconceivable!' said Dyukovsky.

'What is there inconceivable in it?'

'Inconceivable! For God's sake, how did your boot get into the garden?'

'What boot?'

'We found one of your boots in the bedroom and the other in the garden.'

'And what do you want to know that for? It is not your business. But do drink, dash it all. Since you have waked me up, you may as well drink! There's an interesting tale about that boot, my boy. I didn't want to come to Olga's. I didn't feel inclined, you know, I'd had a drop too much…She came under the window and began scolding me…You know how women…as a rule…Being drunk, I up and flung my boot at her…Ha-ha!…Don't scold, I said. She clambered in at the window, lighted the lamp, and gave me a good drubbing, as I was drunk. I have plenty to eat here…Love, vodka, and good things! But where are you off to? Tchubikov, where are you off to?'

The examining magistrate spat on the floor and walked out of the bath-house. Dyukovsky followed him with his head hanging. Both got into the waggonette in silence and drove off. Never had the road seemed so long and dreary. Both were silent. Tchubikov was shaking with anger all the way. Dyukovsky hid has face in his collar as though he were afraid the darkness and the drizzling rain might read his shame on his face.

On getting home the examining magistrate found the doctor, Tyutyuev, there. The doctor was sitting at the table and heaving deep sighs as he turned over the pages of the *Neva*.

'The things that are going on in the world,' he said, greeting the examining magistrate with a melancholy smile. 'Austria is at it again…and Gladstone, too, in a way…'

Tchubikov flung his hat under the table and began to tremble.

'You devil of a skeleton! Don't bother me! I've told you a thousand times over, don't bother me with your politics! It's not the time for politics! And as for you,' he turned upon Dyukovsky and shook his fist at him, 'as for you…I'll never forget it, as long as I live!'

'But the Swedish match, you know! How could I tell…'

'Choke yourself with your match! Go away and don't irritate me, or goodness knows what I shall do to you. Don't let me set eyes on you.'

Dyukovsky heaved a sigh, took his hat, and went out.

'I'll go and get drunk!' he decided, as he went out of the gate, and he sauntered dejectedly towards the tavern.

When the superintendent's wife got home from the bath-house she found her husband in the drawing-room.

'What did the examining magistrate come about?' asked her husband.

'He came to say that they had found Klyauzov. Only fancy, they found him staying with another man's wife.'

'Ah, Mark Ivanitch, Mark Ivanitch!' sighed the police superintendent, turning up his eyes. 'I told you that dissipation would lead to no good! I told you so—you wouldn't heed me!'

A Sensible Course of Action

Palle Rosenkrantz

Baron Palle Adam Vilhelm Rosenkrantz (1867–1941) was descended from a seventeenth century Danish nobleman, also called Palle Rosenkrantz, who was an envoy to the court of King James I. He was accompanied by a colleague called Gyldenstierne, and it does not take a Sherlock Holmes to deduce that Shakespeare borrowed their names (but not their life histories) for two characters in *Hamlet*.

The Baron was a lawyer who—like many other lawyers before and since—took up writing to supplement his income. He became both prolific and successful, publishing novels, plays, non-fiction books, and radio plays, as well as translating *Pygmalion* and other plays by George Bernard Shaw into Danish. Of his detective fiction, *The Magistrate's Own Case* was translated into English in 1908. Sir Hugh Greene described that book as 'readable and ingenious', and included Michael Meyer's translation of 'A Sensible Course of Action', first published in 1909, in *More Rivals of Sherlock Holmes*. In 1973, Meyer's version of the story was televised, with a glittering cast including John Thaw in his pre-Inspector Morse days, and Philip Madoc, best known for playing the title role in *The Life and Times of David Lloyd George*. Greene's description of the story as 'rather charmingly cynical' is apt.

• ● ● ● •

She was very pretty; indeed, she was beautiful. Twenty-six at most, slim, very smart in a foreign style; unpretentious, but the real thing. She turned to Holst as he entered, and her grey dress rustled with the light whisper of silk. It sat as though moulded to her fine body, almost as though cast and not yet set. Her cheeks flushed, a little too redly, and her eyes flickered nervously.

Holst bowed to the Inspector. His eyes rested on her for no more than a second; but he saw much in a glance.

The Inspector asked him to sit. He sounded somewhat embarrassed. He sat at his desk facing the lady, restless as always, toying with a paper-knife, which he put down to scratch his sparse reddish hair.

Holst seated himself and looked at the lady.

'Lieutenant Holst, my assistant,' explained the Inspector in French. Holst bowed slightly.

The Inspector broke into Danish. He was not very fluent in French.

'A ridiculous business, Holst,' he said. 'I'm damned if I know what course of action we should take. This lady says her name is Countess Wolkonski, and that she is from Russia. Her papers are in order.'

He tapped the desk with some documents which had been lying in front of him.

'Countess Wolkonski from Volhynien, to be precise from Shitomir in the district of Kiev. She is a widow. Her husband died in a Russian prison. He was a naval officer who was implicated in the Odessa mutiny—she says. Her only son died too, not long after his father—she says. She is passing through Copenhagen and is staying at the Hotel Phoenix. She arrived the day before yesterday. But, and this is the point, she asserts that her husband's brother, who is also named Count Wolkonski, is trailing her and intends to murder her, because he believes she betrayed her husband to the Russian authorities. She went into a long rigmarole about it, all straight out of a novelette. To cut a long story short, she wants me to protect her. A charming person, as you can see, but I'm damned if I know what to do about her.'

'I am handing this case over to Mr Holst,' he added in French to the lady.

She inclined her head and looked at Holst, as though seeking his help. Her eyes were at the same time searching and pleading. She was very beautiful.

'I have checked,' continued the Inspector, 'that there is a Count Wolkonski staying at the Phoenix. He arrived a few hours ago from Malmö, and asked to see the Countess. When the porter sent up to her she was out, but as soon as she returned and learned that the Count was there she came along here like a scalded cat. I've tried to explain to her that there's really nothing I can do. She practically fell around my neck, which would have been delightful, but how can I possibly help her? We can't arrest the man, for we've nothing against him, we can't take her into custody, and she genuinely seems too terrified to go back to her cab. I've promised her I'll send a man down to the hotel. You must have a word with this Russian fellow and find what it's all about. Of course we could send her papers along to the Embassy, but I can't keep her here. You take her along and do what you can. I know I can rely on you to take a sensible course of action.'

Holst said nothing, but rose and bowed.

'Please go with this gentleman,' explained the Inspector, thinking how much more charming the words sounded in French: *'voulez-vous aller avec ce monsieur?'*

The lady protested. She would not go.

'Madame,' said Holst. 'You need have no fear. No harm can befall you if you come with me.' He looked impressively heroic as he said it. He was much better-looking than the Inspector, and spoke much better French. His appearance radiated reliability. He was a handsome man.

She accepted his hand a little timidly and looked at him with two deep black eyes in a way that would have bothered Holst's wife Ulla if she could have seen it. He noticed a small movement at the corners of her mouth, a faint tremor of emotion. She looked very unhappy.

The Inspector seemed impatient.

Eventually the lady agreed to go with Holst; and as they walked through the offices, all the station clerks almost audibly craned their necks.

The Inspector muttered something to himself and, most uncharacteristically, bit one of his nails.

• • ● • •

Holst drove with the lady towards Vimmelskaftet. As soon as she realized where they were going, she became very nervous.

'Monsieur Olst,' she said. 'You must not take me to the hotel. He will kill me. He has sworn to kill me, and he will do it, at whatever cost. I am innocent, but he is a traitor, a very great traitor. He has killed my little Ivan—do you hear, they murdered my little Ivan!' She was totally distraught, and began a long story which lasted until they reached the corner of Pilestraede. It was a strange story, involving Dimitri Ivanovitch and Nicolai and the police and an Admiral Skrydlov and a Lieutenant Schmidt and others besides.

But she would not return to the Hotel Phoenix, and at the corner of Ny Ølstergade she tried to get out of the cab. Is she mad, wondered Holst. But she looked, no, sensible. Hysterical, yes, afraid certainly; this Dimitri Ivanovitch wanted to shoot her, of that she was sure.

Holst did not get many words in. He leaned out of the cab and told the man to drive down St Kongensgade to Marmorpladsen. At least that would provide a temporary respite. Then he explained to her what he had in mind, and that calmed her somewhat. She continued her narrative about Odessa, Lieutenant Schmidt, and several Admirals.

Her voice was deep and rich. When she was calm, her face revealed a certain strength. But she was plainly very frightened, and it seemed unlikely to Holst that these fears could be wholly without foundation. Unless of course, she was mad.

The cab stopped at Holst's house, and he led the lady up the stairs and rang the bell. His wife was at home. It was lunchtime, and he introduced the Russian lady with a brief explanation of her presence. 'Either she is mad,' he said, 'in which case I must get a doctor to her, or she is in genuine trouble, in which case we must try to help her. Talk French to her, and see if you can make anything of her. I'll be back in half an hour.'

So Ulla Holst found herself alone with the lady. It was the first time her husband had asked her to do anything like this. However, it seemed to her that if one member of the family had to have a tête-à-tête with so extraordinarily beautiful a woman, it was just as well that it should be she.

The lady accepted a cup of coffee, sat down, and began to talk in a more ordered and logical manner. Gradually but visibly, she regained her self-composure. Ulla Holst sat and listened, blonde and calm, and found the Russian lady's story by no means incredible. As she listened to its ramifications,

Holst drove to the Hotel Phoenix and asked to see Count Dimitri Ivanovitch Wolkonski.

He was in his room, and the porter took Holst up.

The Count was a tall man, of military appearance, rather short-sighted, very swarthy, and far from attractive. A real Tartar, thought Holst. But he was courteous, and spoke exquisite French.

'Count Wolkonski?' asked Holst. The man nodded.

'I am from the city police,' continued Holst. 'A lady residing in this hotel has come to us and asked for protection against you, on the grounds that you have designs upon her life.'

Holst smiled politely and shrugged his shoulders. 'The lady was in a very excited frame of mind—'

'Where is she?' interrupted the Russian, looking sharply at Holst.

Holst didn't like his eyes.

'She struck us as mentally confused,' replied Holst. 'So we are keeping her under observation. Her story was so involved and improbable that we felt unable to regard it as anything but a—a hallucination.'

The Russian said nothing.

Holst went on: 'I should appreciate it if you could tell me the truth of the matter. We naturally thought of approaching your Embassy—'

'There is no need for that,' interrupted the Russian quickly. 'No need whatever. My sister-in-law is—not mentally ill—certainly not insane. But my brother's unhappy fate upset her balance. Then her only child died. In my house, unfortunately, and she is convinced that I was to blame. That is the situation—as you have seen. I followed her here. She sold her estates in Russia; she had a fortune—she is very wealthy and spoiled. I traced her in Stockholm. She has made insane dispositions of her property, involving considerable sums that concern me. *Enfin.* I must speak to her, to try to bring her to her senses. Where is she?'

Holst looked closely at the Russian. He thought the fellow was talking jerkily and a little hectically. But he might be telling the truth, and the lady's behaviour had certainly been curious.

'If you could accompany me to the Embassy it is possible that by discussing the matter with His Excellency and the Embassy doctor we might be able to arrange matters to your satisfaction. We cannot possibly take any action in this affair except through the authorities.'

The Russian nibbled his lip.

'You realize, officer, that our position in Russia is not easy. My brother was deeply compromised in a naval mutiny. He died in prison. I myself—God knows, I have been guilty of no crime, but I neither can nor will deal with the representative in your country of a ruler whom I regard as a tyrant. I hope you understand. Yours is a free country. Such political differences of opinion as may exist between the Tsarist régime and myself are no concern of yours, as I think you will agree. But I do not wish to have any intercourse with the Ambassador, or anything whatever to do with our Embassy.'

Holst reflected.

'It is unfortunate,' he said. 'But I appreciate your point of view. I have no official cause to take action against you. We do not perform political errands for foreign governments. I have received no orders in this affair and have no desire to take any step on my own initiative. Your sister-in-law asserts that you have designs on her life, but we cannot act on so vague a charge. But I must warn you that we shall be compelled to contact the Embassy, and it is possible that their reaction may alter the position.'

'Will you arrest me?' asked the Russian sharply.

'Certainly not,' replied Holst. 'I have not the slightest ground or justification for that. But if you feel that any unpleasantness may result for you, my advice is that you should leave immediately. We shall have to speak to the Embassy and—well, I don't know, but it is always possible that—. By leaving you will avoid any disagreeable consequences.'

'I shall not leave without my sister-in-law,' replied the Count.

Holst was silent.

'Where is she?'

'At the police station,' said Holst. 'If you care to go there, you can see her there.'

'And meanwhile you will contact the Embassy?'

'My superior has probably already done so,' replied Holst. The Russian's face pleased him less and less.

'Very well. Then I shall come at once with you to the police station. When my sister-in-law has seen me and spoken with me, I hope she may come to her senses, unless—'

He shrugged his shoulders.

Holst felt unhappy. Now the Inspector would have another Russian on his hands. But what could be done? If this sinister character was really at odds with the Tsar, his position was hardly of the kind that could justify any action against him in Denmark. The newspapers had their eyes open, and the government would hardly be anxious to stretch itself to assist the present Russian régime. The main danger was for the Countess, if her brother-in-law really—but that was unthinkable. He scarcely suggested a mad nihilist with a revolver in his pocket; indeed, she seemed rather the less balanced of the two. Besides, he was under the eye of the police, and if the worst came to the worst Holst could help her to get out of the country while the Count discussed the matter with the Chief of Police, who would have to be brought in where such international issues were involved. Then the two could work out their problems in Malmö or Berlin, which were not in Holst's district.

To gain time, however, he prepared a long report giving the Count's explanation of why he was trailing his sister-in-law. It read very plausibly. She had fled after somewhat precipitately disposing of her estates, to which he apparently had some legal claim; she was in a highly nervous and distraught state. His political opinions made it impossible for him to seek the assistance of the Russian Embassy; he therefore appealed to the police for assistance and, if necessary, medical aid, and undertook to present himself before the Chief of Police that day.

Holst pocketed this paper and returned to his apartment.

Ulla Holst had become quite friendly with the Countess. She had a kind heart, and the Countess's story was of the kind to bring two sensitive ladies close together. Countess Helena Wolkonski was the daughter of a Lithuanian landowner; at an early age she had married a naval officer, Count Nicolai Wolkonski, with whom she had spent six happy years. Then her husband, who was attached to the marine depot at Odessa, had become addicted to drink and cards. Marital infidelity had followed, and their home had broken up. The Count had allied himself to the forces of political discontent, thereby threatening the safety of his wife and child. In her despair the young wife had gone to his commanding officer and—she did not deny it—had betrayed him and his brother, who were hostile to the existing régime and were deeply implicated in the revolutionary movement. Count Wolkonski, by now in a state of physical degeneration, had been arrested and shortly afterwards had died in prison. His brother had saved himself by flight, taking with him her son, a boy of seven. Before long he had written to her demanding that she visit him in Vienna, whither he had betaken himself. She had no other relatives to turn to, and had therefore sold her estates. These realized a considerable sum. In Vienna she learned that her son was dead and—she declared—an old woman who had accompanied her brother-in-law on his flight had warned her that he was planning revenge. She said he had sworn to kill her to repay her for her treachery.

Such was her story.

She had fled, and he had followed her. She dared not return to Russia, for fear of the revolutionaries, so had gone to Stockholm, where he had traced her. Now she was fleeing southwards.

Ulla Holst believed her story, and Holst had no evidence to contradict it. He briefly summarized his meeting with the Count and advised the Countess to leave the country with all speed, since she could produce no evidence for her charges against her brother-in-law. Her son's death had been caused by pneumonia, and although it was not impossible that the Count was responsible there could be no means of proving this, or of taking any action against him.

Ulla deplored the masculine indifference of the police, but Holst had to explain that there was nothing they could do in this case.

'And if he murders her?' she asked.

'Well, then we must arrest him,' said Holst. 'But let us hope he won't.'

'And you call that police work?'

Holst shrugged his shoulders. 'We can't put people in custody for things they might do.'

Ulla could not understand that; but women do not understand everything, least of all matters relating to the police. Countess Wolkonski despaired; however, her despair did not express itself in any violent outburst. Holst explained to her that the police could not take her into custody, since she had not committed any unlawful act, nor could they act against her brother-in-law, for the same reason. But he was willing to help her to leave the country.

'To be hunted to death like a wild beast?' was all she replied.

She calmed down, however. It was almost as though she had conceived some plan. She thanked Ulla warmly for all her kindness, kissed Holst's son, and wept as she patted his curls. Holst got her a cab. She refused his offer to accompany her, and drove away.

Ulla was very angry, and Holst not altogether at ease. He hurried back to the police station to keep an eye on the Russian.

At three o'clock the police station in Antoniestraede received a report that an elegantly dressed foreign lady had been arrested in a jeweller's shop on Købmagergade while attempting to steal a diamond ring. Holst was in his office: the Russian had not yet arrived. Holst had told him that the Chief of Police was unlikely to be available before three-thirty, since there was a parade at three.

A police van arrived, and Holst stood at the window as it rolled into the gloomy yard. A plain-clothes policeman stepped out, followed by a lady in grey.

It was Countess Wolkonski, arrested for attempted theft. Holst was slowly beginning to believe her story.

When she was brought into the station he went to meet her. She greeted him with a melancholy smile. 'Now you will have to take care of me,' she said.

Holst bowed.

As he did so, he noticed through the window the figure of the Russian standing in the gateway of the yard. At once, with a quick word to the astonished desk sergeant, he ordered the Countess to be taken to the Inspector's office.

A few moments later Count Wolkonski entered and asked in German for the Chief of Police.

He was asked to take a seat.

Holst withdrew into his office to formulate a plan. If Countess Wolkonski had resorted to so desperate a measure as shoplifting to get taken into custody, her fears could not lightly be dismissed. In any case, it would be unpardonable under the circumstances to leave her to her own devices. There was no knowing what she might do next. Besides, now she was under arrest she could be placed under observation; the magistrate would certainly order this, and in the meantime one might, through official channels, obtain at any rate some information which might throw light on this complicated affair. And the Count was sitting outside. He would certainly demand to be allowed to see her.

A cold shiver ran down Holst's spine. It was a momentary thought, a stupid, crazy, insane notion, but if—if that Russian was a fanatical revolutionary, an avenger—God knows, the whole business might have come out of a Russian novel, but in Russia, as one knew from the newspapers, anything was possible. Certainly a Copenhagen police officer had no right to believe all that is in the newspapers; he has no right to believe that novels can come to life; he must act soberly and professionally. But—Russia is, when all is said and done, Russia, and it cannot all be lies. Suppose that Count Wolkonski before the very eyes of the Chief of Police were to draw a pistol from his pocket and shoot his sister-in-law, or—suppose he took out a bomb, a bomb, that might blow the whole police station with its lord and master into the air?

Of course it was totally impossible, idiotic, crazy, insane. This was Copenhagen, a.d. 1905. But the notion had got inside Holst's head, and was beating away with impish hammers in a way to drive any man from his wits.

He could not possibly say all this to anyone. The Inspector would think he had lost his reason. And so he had; it was an obsession, a foolish obsession from which he could not free himself. In ten minutes the parade would be over, and the case would be on the carpet. The Countess, now a shoplifter caught red-handed, would be confronted with the Count. A flash, an explosion, and the Chief of Police himself might be flying skywards.

Then Lieutenant Eigil Holst, of the Copenhagen police force, on his own responsibility, and at his own risk took a decision which branded him not as a sober, reliable and trained officer but as a man of dangerous fantasy.

He summoned one of the youngest and most slavishly obedient of the station's constables, went to the window where Count Wolkonski was seated correctly on a bench, formally charged him with being implicated in an attempted robbery committed at a shop in Købmagergade by a woman calling herself his sister-in-law, had the amazed Count marched into an adjacent room, had him, despite some considerable resistance, searched, and found in his right trouser pocket a small American revolver containing six sharp bullets.

Holst drafted a stylish report to his Chief of Police, with the result that the sun set that evening over a cell at Nytorv in which Count Dimitri Ivanovitch Wolkonski sat sadly with sunken head, following a highly suspicious interrogation. And, it must be added, when the sun rose over the same cell, Count Dimitri Ivanovitch Wolkonski was found hanging by his braces dead on a gas bracket.

It is well known that it is easier to enter the clutches of the law than escape from them. Countess Wolkonski had found great difficulty in persuading the police to put her under their protection. She had resorted to a radical method. She had succeeded; but she remained in custody. The Chief of Police dared not set her at liberty. Her theft had been barefaced and her explanation, however truthful it might seem, buttressed by Holst's evidence and a quantity of bonds and jewels in her possession valued at a considerable fortune, at the least required a closer investigation.

She was arrested, to Holst's distress, and Ulla Holst was less than respectful in her comments upon her husband's superior. The Countess spent the night in a cell, not far from the place where her enemy had met his death. The next day she was freed, Count Wolkonski's suicide having weighed powerfully in her favour.

Not everything that was written in the newspapers about this affair was untrue, but the full facts of what happened have not previously been revealed. The Embassy bestirred itself and obtained further details concerning the background of the case. Countess Wolkonski had in fact betrayed her husband. She was not a heroine, and could never be one.

But she was certainly beautiful, and now she had found peace of mind. Count Dimitri Wolkonski was a revolutionary, and as such was entitled to his due share of sympathy from all good and peace-loving Danish citizens who cannot bear to think of a butcher slaughtering a calf but support with all their hearts the bomb-throwing barricade heroes of darkest Russia. In truth, this Dimitri Wolkonski was one of the blackest villains upon whom the sun of Russia has ever shone. His conscience was so heavy with evil deeds that it is a wonder that the gas bracket in the cell at Nytorv did not break beneath his weight.

This must serve as some excuse for the pretty Countess, and may explain why her brother-in-law, once he found himself in the hands of justice, settled his account with his Maker, whether the bill was right or no.

Yet Holst had a lingering suspicion that the Countess's life had never in fact been in danger, nor that of the Chief of Police; and that the Count had been carrying the pistol only in case his own life was threatened by his enemies. And he shared the doubts later drily expressed by the coroner as to whether his arrest and search of the Count had been justified.

Countess Helena stayed for some time in Copenhagen and was a frequent visitor at Ulla Holst's. Ulla enjoyed her company, and refused to believe that she had behaved wrongly in any way regarding those revolutionaries. Ulla was, after all, a policeman's wife, and was therefore opposed to any movement whose activities threatened the lives of policemen anywhere. When the Countess finally left Denmark, accompanied by Ulla's best wishes, the latter expressed her opinion of the affair to her husband. 'It may well be, Eigil,' she said, 'that you had no right to search that Russian, and that as you say it was a stupid idea you got into your head that afternoon in the station. But if you want my opinion, I think you took a very sensible course of action.'

Strange Tracks

Balduin Groller

Balduin Groller was the pen-name of Adalbert Goldscheider (1848–1916). He was born in Arad, which then belonged to Hungary but became part of Romania four years after his death. He studied philosophy and law in Vienna, worked as a journalist, founded a magazine which failed and resulted in his bankruptcy, and even had a spell as a magician. This versatile man is one of the few crime writers to have enjoyed a career as a senior sports official, with an organization that was the forerunner of the Austrian Olympic Committee.

Groller's reputation as a crime writer rests on the creation of Detective Dagobert, whose cases were recorded in half a dozen short volumes from 1910–12. As Sir Hugh Greene said, Groller 'somehow managed to preserve in his usually rather gay little stories something of the overblown charm of Vienna on the edge of the precipice'. His story 'Anonymous Letters' was televised in 1973, with a cast including Ronald Lewis as Dagobert, Nicola Pagett, and Francis De Wolff. This story, translated by N.L. Lederer, also features Dagobert. Like 'The Swedish Match', it merited inclusion in a famous early crime anthology, *The Great Detective Stories* (1927) edited by W.H. Wright, better known as the then best-seller S.S. Van Dine. Whilst it does not present an 'impossible crime' puzzle, the storyline foreshadows that of 'Footprint in the Sky' by impossible crime specialist Carter Dickson, aka John Dickson Carr.

• • ● • •

At six o'clock on a beautiful Saturday morning in September Dagobert was roused by his valet. His friend, Andreas Grumbach, President of the Industrial Club, had sent an urgent message asking him to come with all possible speed. A murder had been committed.

Immediately Dagobert leaped out of bed, and rushed into the bathroom. No matter how urgent the occasion he would never forget his matutinal routine. He took his usual cold shower, had his customary rub-down by his valet, and then went through the gymnastic exercises with which he always started his day. As he hurriedly drew on his clothes, with the able assistance of his valet, the messenger, Grumbach's chauffeur Marius, reported the details of the murder.

A trifle pale from fright and excited by his mad rush, he poured forth the following facts: The Grumbachs were spending their vacation at their château on the Danube, near the old historical city of Pöchlarn. The château was part of an estate so extensive that it embraced the villages of Palting, Hiersau, Eichgraben—

'Go on, go on,' Dagobert interrupted. He knew these details better even than did the chauffeur.

'Yesterday evening,' continued the messenger, 'Mathias Diwald, the forester, came to the château, as he did every Friday, to receive the money for the game-keepers and wood-cutters and take it to the estate office for the Saturday pay-roll. But Diwald never returned to the office. They waited for him there until eleven p.m., and then the head game-keeper and two assistants went out to search for him. At three o'clock in the morning he was found at the edge of the forest, murdered and robbed of the money. The head keeper then hurried to the château and informed his master.'

'Did Frau Grumbach hear the details?' asked Dagobert. He was anxious that the gruesome details should be kept from her.

'Yes. She rose at once, and it was she who asked Herr Grumbach to send immediately for Herr Dagobert. I do not know, of course, how the murder happened, but I believe the circumstances were—'

Dagobert stopped him. He did not wish to hear any more. It was an old principle of his never to listen to second-hand testimony before beginning an investigation.

'When did you leave?' he asked the chauffeur.

'Four o'clock, sharp, Herr Dagobert. And I was here at six to the minute.'

'What is the distance?'

'Ninety-six kilometres.'

'In two hours. Not so bad. Of course, we'll have to do better on the way back.'

'But, Herr Dagobert—'

'Do better, I said. That is hardly asking too much of a sixty-horse-power Mercedes. I am taking a stop-watch along, and shall time you. Listen, Marius: for every minute under two hours in your running time back to the château, I will give you two kronen. If ever time is money, it is in these cases.'

Marius, from his own standpoint, agreed with this view; and they reached Palting castle in one hour and thirty-two minutes. Marius, with undisguised satisfaction, collected his merited reward of fifty-six kronen.

Frau Grumbach, who was waiting on the terrace, ran down the wide stairway when she saw Dagobert's patriarchal head rise from the big car, welcoming her old friend even more cordially than usual. She was pale and very much upset by the terrible occurrence. Dagobert's presence calmed her somewhat,—she knew that now everything would be done to exact full atonement for the crime.

'I have waited breakfast for you,' she began. 'But we have only twenty minutes in which to eat. At half past eight the Judicial Commission will meet here to begin the investigation. My husband has gone to get the Commission together now.'

Dagobert enjoyed his breakfast. He had not taken time for such trifles before leaving home.

The Commission, led by the master of the house, arrived punctually. Grumbach made the necessary introductions, and immediately the proceedings were begun. There were present: the District Judge with his secretary; the District Attorney's representative; the County Surgeon, Dr Ramsauer; the chief of the local gendarmes; and the head game-keeper.

The District Attorney's representative was not a state dignitary. He was the local barber, who merely functioned by proxy at such occasions and made the necessary motions for the instigation of the judiciary proceedings. The case under investigation, on account of its gravity, would not come under the jurisdiction of the District Court, but would be brought before the Circuit Court. The District Attorney and the Examining Magistrate would not arrive until the following day; and it was the duty of those assembled to prepare the report as accurately as possible so as to give a clear presentation of the case. Also, it was incumbent on the Commission to take any precaution to preserve intact all the circumstances that might tend toward a solution of the crime.

The preliminaries of the meeting occupied but a short time. The Commission had met at the château merely that they might approach the site of the crime together. Their preliminary examination was to take place at the actual scene of the murder, and the minutes were to be drawn up afterwards in accordance with their findings. There had, however, already been considerable activity in connection with the case. The head game-keeper, when he had found the body, had placed his two assistants near the corpse to prevent anyone from approaching it before the Commission arrived. He had then summoned the District Judge and the chief gendarme; and, after some discussion, two gendarmes and two armed foresters had been sent out to search the woods.

Grumbach had informed the members of the Commission that a famous detective had been called upon to take charge of the investigation, and now they were eager to know if Dagobert approved of their preliminary methods.

'So far, all's in order,' Dagobert said. 'But now we must get to the scene of the crime as quickly as possible. Every minute counts.'

The outskirts of the wood where Diwald had been murdered were a quarter of an hour's walk from the château. Grumbach asked if they should ride or go on foot. In any event the carriage stood ready; but it was suggested that if they walked they might discover some clues on the way. Dagobert decided, however, that they should ride, announcing that the investigation was to begin only after they had inspected the body.

The Commission drove off in two carriages. Frau Grumbach and Dagobert took the automobile, which, driven by Marius, brought up the rear of the procession. They had been on their way scarcely two minutes when Frau Grumbach halted the car and, descending, threw a few coins into the hat of a beggar sitting at the side of the road.

'You might have thrown the money without getting out,' Dagobert objected, when she returned to the car.

'No, Dagobert. Look at him. What would he do if I should miss the hat? He can hardly move.'

Dagobert looked. The cripple was of monstrous and loathsome physique. He had an ugly, abnormally large head which showed every sign of hydrocephaly. His shoulders were powerful, and his arms abnormally long and strong, though the lower part of his body was terribly stunted, the legs being like those of a child of four years, and strangely twisted and crippled. It was difficult to imagine how he could move at all.

'Drive on, Marius,' ordered Dagobert when Frau Grumbach had resumed her seat in the car. 'We must be the first to arrive.'

In a short time they had caught up the others. Frau Grumbach reverted to the subject of the cripple.

'He was the only beggar in our district,' she said, and added by way of excuse: 'We would have placed him in an institution so that he would not have had to beg, but I've always felt that it would be cruel to deprive him of his profession. As he is, he can sit at the roadside, and at least he can see the world about him. Since he cannot move, it would be heartless, I think, to lock him up in a room. Now if he shows himself at the roadside every passerby gives him something.'

The well-kept road led to the edge of the woods. When they came within sight of the foresters guarding the corpse, Dagobert stopped the car.

'You, Frau Violet, stay here in the car. The dead man will be no sight for your eyes. I will report to you later if I find out anything.'

With these words he walked to the place where the body lay. The two foresters had done their duty,—it could be immediately seen that no unauthorized person had approached the murdered man. A number of peasants, in awed silence, formed a wide circle about the spot. Dagobert did not touch the body, but looked around for possible clues with which to begin his investigation.

When the Commission arrived the surgeon was permitted to approach first. He knelt down and, with some exertion, turned over the body which had been lying face downward. His findings, given at intervals during the examination, were:

'Suicide or accident out of the question...Murder beyond a doubt...The man was strangled...Finger-prints are plainly visible...*Pomum Adami* crushed. Moreover, the thyroid cartilage and the Santorian cartilage are broken...Death must have been instantaneous...The murder was committed eight or ten hours ago—probably before midnight.'

'Permit me, doctor,' said Dagobert; 'the exact time might be of some importance. I believe we have the necessary data at hand.'

'I do not think so, Herr Dagobert,' replied the surgeon. 'Science does not make it possible for us to fix the time of death to the hour or minute.'

'In that case, then, we will have to try without science. It rained last evening or last night. Though the road is now dry, one can see that it has been raining recently, especially here where the body was lying. The wet clothes of the victim, now almost dry, have left a moist rim on the ground. We will surely be able to ascertain when the rain began.'

'I can state that to the minute,' put in the head gamekeeper. 'From a quarter to eight until eight we had quite a downpour, with thunder and lightning.'

'So we have a start anyway,' said Dagobert. 'I maintain that the murder was committed before the rain fell. See for yourselves. The ground under the body is dusty, whereas the road is dry but not dusty. There is also evidence that the rain began falling immediately after the murder,—but of this more later: the indications may prove to be misleading, and we will not go into that point at present. However, the dust does not lie. So, then, Diwald was killed before a quarter to eight. We know that he received the money at the château at half past six, and that he put the linen bag containing it into his pocket.

'Furthermore, it has been ascertained that he went from the château to the village tavern, drank two pints of wine, and started on his way home shortly after the seven-o'clock Angelus bell tolled. After this, however, the time does not seem to jibe; but the difference is only a matter of minutes.—I am convinced that he got here shortly before the rain began. But walking here should have taken him at most a quarter of an hour. We do not know why he took at least twice as long; but we have succeeded in fixing the time within a quarter of an hour.'

The members of the Commission continued to discuss the various matters relating to the crime, and exchanged opinions and advice as to the proper methods of procedure. Dagobert did not disturb them. He returned to Frau Grumbach; and Marius was told to drive slowly back to the château.

'Well Dagobert,' asked Frau Grumbach, 'have you hopes?'

Dagobert briefly related the facts and continued to inspect the side of the road with great interest. He then lapsed into silence and appeared to be considering the case.

'It was an ordinary matter of robbery,' he said after a while. 'And yet it has certain peculiar features. The indications contradict one another in a seemingly incomprehensible way. One is led to the belief that the murderer is a native of these parts—some one who was familiar with local conditions. One does not attack a poor forest guard unless one is pretty certain that he is carrying a large sum of his master's money.'

'For a miserable 450 kronen!' said Frau Grumbach, tears coming into her eyes. 'We would rather have lost ten or even a hundred times that amount than the life of a loyal and devoted servant.'

'Only a local person could have known of Diwald's regular Friday mission to the château. And yet the signs all point to a stranger.—Tell me, Frau Violet, has there been, within the past few days, any circus with acrobats or tumblers in the village?'

'Surely not, Dagobert.'

'Or gypsies?'

'Neither.'

'Has there been a fete of any kind in the neighbourhood?'

'Not within miles.'

'It's very strange—and something quite new to me. I would have sworn the murderer was an acrobat.'

'Why an acrobat, of all men?'

'Or have you in the village somebody who is known to do acrobatic tricks?'

'No, Dagobert.'

'It's enough to drive one insane. I can prove to you that it was a native who killed Diwald; and I can prove, just as conclusively, that it could not have been a native.'

They had now arrived at the place where the cripple was sitting. Dagobert suddenly threw him two pieces of silver with one gesture. The coins flew apart, and neither of them dropped into the extended hat. Both fell upon the roadway several yards from the beggar. Dagobert descended from the car, but was in no haste to help retrieve the money. Instead, with somewhat cruel indifference, he watched the cripple move along on his hands to collect the coins. Then he reentered the car and drove to the château, arriving there simultaneously with the Commission.

The members immediately busied themselves with the drawing up of their report. Dagobert, apparently not wishing to disturb them, retired. He would, he said, take a short walk and look at the scenery until they had finished.

The secretary was occupied for a little over an hour drawing up the minutes which had been dictated to him by the District Judge; and the finished report was just about to be read over to the Commission, preparatory to its being signed by the members present, when Dagobert arrived. Grumbach was very much pleased that he had returned, and asked him to listen to the reading of the minutes so that, if they were in accord with his views, he, too, could sign them.

'I don't think that will be necessary,' replied Dagobert, taking a seat. 'I rather fancy we will have to draw up a new report.—Here is the stolen money.'

He came forward and placed on the table the little linen bag that Diwald had always used. The amount of the money, as was immediately ascertained, was complete. The members of the Commission were greatly excited. Frau Grumbach threw Dagobert a look of pride and gratitude: she knew— and had always said—that they could rely on Dagobert.

At once the questions began to fly. Since he had recovered the money, he must be in possession of clues pointing to the actual culprit.

'As far as the culprit is concerned,' said Dagobert, 'I have taken the liberty of apprehending him myself and delivering him to the local jail.'

'Who, in Heaven's name—who is it?'

'Permit me to proceed in order. The surgeon had determined two things with certainty—the impossibility of suicide, and death by strangulation. He did not add, however—and anyhow it was no concern of his—that the circumstances showed that the attack had been made from behind. This fact is proved by the plainly visible finger-prints on the throat, and by the position of the body—which was face downward. There were no signs of a fight or a struggle; and from this arose the first difficulty in analysing the situation. It was hard to conceive that the attack had been made so quickly and suddenly that the victim had had no time even to turn round.—The second difficulty was still more bewildering. Indeed, I was confronted by something entirely new—something that perhaps had never happened before. The chief of gendarmes, you recall, had conscientiously looked for footprints. Conditions for such a search were partly advantageous, partly disadvantageous. Disadvantageous, because any footprints made before the storm would have been obliterated by the rain. Advantageous, because any footprints made after the rain had fallen would be, after drying, all the plainer, since the soil at the scene of the crime contained lime.

'Now, there were no footprints visible aside from those made by Diwald himself. But there was something that was not at first observed—something that presented an extraordinary riddle. Hand prints! I was able to follow these strange tracks easily and I came to the conclusion that the crime had been committed by an acrobat who, in order that he should make no footprints, had left the place standing on his hands and with his feet in the air.

'This conclusion, however, was wrong, although the murder was certainly done by someone who walks on his hands. In the whole district there is only one man who does this—the beggar Lipp. And he is the murderer.'

'Impossible! Quite impossible!' came the unanimous opposition. 'The man cannot move.'

'Be calm, gentlemen. He is unquestionably the criminal. And the crime was all the more repulsive because it was the reward of an act of charity on Diwald's part. Lipp had asked

Diwald to carry him part of the way home. Diwald took the cripple on his back and carried him, thereby sealing his own fate. This also explains the difference in time, which I previously noted. With his burden Diwald took half an hour for a trip which otherwise would have required only a quarter of an hour.

'My investigations are complete. Besides, I have here Lipp's confession signed before me and the chauffeur Marius as witnesses. When I left you I took Marius along and told him to put a strong rope in his pocket. I also borrowed from your gendarme a pair of handcuffs. We went to Lipp's hut. His housekeeper, an old hag, was there, and she was in a towering rage. Last night, she complained, Lipp had been late again in coming home; he had stayed at the tavern until ten o'clock. I straightway found out that he had not been at the tavern at all; and I also ascertained that, with his slow method of locomotion, it would require at least two hours for him to get home from the *situs criminis*.

'The rest is obvious. I searched his hut, and found the money under a loose board in the floor. Then I went to the road where Lipp was stationed, and accused him point-blank of murdering Diwald. At first he attempted to deny it; but when I showed him the money he collapsed and, tremblingly, admitted having done it.

'At a sign from me Marius threw the rope over his shoulders from behind, pinioning his arms to his body. Lipp raised his hands in an instinctive gesture of self-defence, and so presented them to me for the manacles. Marius and I then lifted him into the car and drove to the jail.—As far as I am concerned this closes the case. The final word will rest with his judges. It is they who will decide whether or not he is fully responsible for his acts…I must now ask your permission to go, as I am very busy on another unusually difficult case.'

Dagobert bowed to the commission, kissed Frau Grumbach's hand with his usual courtesy, and two minutes later was on his way back in the car with Marius at the wheel.

The Kennel

Maurice Level

Maurice Level was the pseudonym of Jeanne Mareteux-Levelle (1875–1926) who worked as a doctor before earning success as a playwright and author of popular fiction. He demonstrated a particular flair for writing macabre tales, melodramatic but often very powerful; some were performed at the legendary Le Theatre du Grand Guignol in his native Paris. H.P. Lovecraft described this type of story as 'the so-called *conte cruel*, in which the wrenching of the emotions is accomplished through dramatic tantalizations, frustrations and gruesome physical horrors.'

Level's fiction was evidently influenced by that of Guy de Maupassant and Edgar Allan Poe, and film versions of his work include *The Roadhouse Murder* (1932). His reputation has not survived the passage of time, and he is—especially in comparison to Lovecraft—now essentially a forgotten writer. Perhaps he is due for a revival. This grim little story comes from Level's *Tales of Mystery and Horror* (1920), translated by Alys Eyre Macklin.

• • ● • •

As ten o'clock struck, M. de Hartevel emptied a last tankard of beer, folded his newspaper, stretched himself, yawned, and slowly rose.

The hanging-lamp cast a bright light on the table-cloth, over which were scattered piles of shot and cartridge wads. Near the fireplace, in the shadow, a woman lay back in a deep arm-chair.

Outside the wind blew violently against the windows, the rain beat noisily on the glass, and from time to time deep bayings came from the kennel where the hounds had struggled and strained since morning.

There were forty of them: big mastiffs with ugly fangs, stiff-haired griffons of Vendée, that flung themselves with ferocity on the wild boar on hunting days. During the night their sullen bayings disturbed the country-side, evoking response from all the dogs in the neighbourhood.

M. de Hartevel lifted a curtain and looked out into the darkness of the park. The wet branches shone like steel blades; the autumn leaves were blown about like whirligigs and flattened against the walls. He grumbled.

'Dirty weather!'

He walked a few steps, his hands in his pockets, stopped before the fireplace, and with a kick broke a half-consumed log. Red embers fell on the ashes; a flame rose, straight and pointed.

Madame de Hartevel did not move. The light of the fire played on her face, touching her hair with gold, throwing a rosy glow on her pale cheeks and, dancing about her, cast fugitive shadows on her forehead, her eyelids, her lips.

The hounds, quiet for a moment, began to growl again; and their bayings, the roaring of the wind and the hiss of the rain on the trees made the quiet room seem warmer, the presence of the silent woman more intimate.

Subconsciously this influenced M. de Hartevel. Desires stimulated by those of the beasts and by the warmth of the room crept through his veins. He touched his wife's shoulders.

'It is ten o'clock. Are you going to bed?'

She said 'yes,' and left her chair, as if regretfully.

'Would you like me to come with you?'

'No—thank you—'

Frowning, he bowed.

'As you like.'

His shoulders against the mantelshelf, his legs apart, he watched her go. She walked with a graceful, undulating movement, the train of her dress moving on the carpet like a little flat wave. A surge of anger stiffened his muscles.

In this chateau where he had her all to himself he had in bygone days imagined a wife who would like living in seclusion with him, attentive to his wishes, smiling acquiescence to all his desires. She would welcome him with gay words when he came back from a day's hunting, his hands blue with cold, his strong body tired, bringing with him the freshness of the fields and moors, the smell of horses, of game and of hounds, would lift eager lips to meet his own. Then, after the long ride in the wind, the rain, the snow, after the intoxication of the crisp air, the heavy walking in the furrows, or the gallop under branches that almost caught his beard, there would have been long nights of love, orgies of caresses of which the thrill would be mutual.

The difference between the dream and the reality!

When the door had shut and the sound of steps died away in the corridor, he went to his room, lay down, took a book and tried to read.

The rain hissed louder than ever. The wind roared in the chimney; out in the park, branches were snapping from the trees; the hounds bayed without ceasing, their howlings sounded through the creaking of the trees, dominating the roar of the storm; the door of the kennel strained under their weight.

He opened the window and shouted:

'Down!'

For some seconds they were quiet. He waited. The wind that drove the rain on his face refreshed him. The barkings began again. He banged his fist against the shutter, threatening:

'Quiet, you devils!'

There was a singing in his ears, a whistling, a ringing; a desire to strike, to ransact, to feel flesh quiver under his fists took possession of him. He roared: 'Wait a moment!' slammed the window, seized a whip, and went out.

He strode along the corridors with no thought of the sleeping house till he got near his wife's room, when he walked slowly and quietly, fearing to disturb her sleep. But a ray of light from under her door caught his lowered eyes, and there was a sound of hurried footsteps that the carpet did not deaden. He listened. The noise ceased, the light went out...He stood motionless, and suddenly, impelled by a suspicion, he called softly:

'Marie Therése...'

No reply. He called louder. Curiosity, a doubt that he dared not formulate, held him breathless. He gave two sharp little taps on the door; a voice inside asked:

'Who is there?'

'I—open the door—'

A whiff of warm air laden with various perfumes and a suspicion of other odours passed over his face.

The voice asked:

'What is it?'

He walked in without replying. He felt his wife standing close in front of him; her breath was on him, the lace of her dress touched his chest. He felt in his pocket for matches. Not finding any, he ordered:

'Light the lamp!'

She obeyed, and as his eyes ran over the room he saw the curtains drawn closely, a shawl on the carpet, the open bed, white and very large; and in a corner, near the fireplace, a man lying across a long rest-chair, his collar unfastened, his head drooping, his arms hanging loosely, his eyes shut.

He gripped his wife's wrist:

'Ah, you…filth!…Then this is why you turn your back on me!…'

She did not shrink from him, did not move. No shadow of fear passed over her pallid face. She only raised her head, murmuring:

'You are hurting me!—'

He let her go, and bending over the inert body, his fist raised, cried:

'A lover in my wife's bedroom!…And…what a lover! A friend…Almost a son…Whore!—'

She interrupted him:

'He is not my lover…'

He burst into a laugh.

'Ah! Ah! You expect me to believe that!'

He seized the collar of the recumbent man, and lifted him up towards him. But when he saw the livid face, the half-opened mouth showing the teeth and gums, when he felt the strange chill of the flesh that touched his hands, he started and let go. The body fell back heavily on the cushions, the forehead beating twice against a chair. His fury turned upon his wife.

'What have you to say?…Explain!…'

'It is very simple,' she said. 'I was just going to bed when I heard the sound of footsteps in the corridor…uncertain steps…faltering…and a voice begging, "Open the door…

open the door"...I thought you might be ill. I opened the door. Then he came, or rather, fell into the room...I knew he was subject to heart-attacks...I laid him there...I was just going to bring you when you knocked...That's all...'

Bending over the body, and apparently quite calm again, he asked, every word pronounced distinctly:

'And it does not surprise you that no one heard him come in?...'

'The hounds bayed...'

'And why should he come here at this hour of the night?'

She made a vague gesture:

'It does seem strange...But...I can only suppose that he felt ill and that...quite alone in his own house...he was afraid to stay there...came here to beg for help...In any case, when he is better...as soon as he is able to speak...he will be able to explain...'

M. de Hartevel drew himself up to his full height, and looked into his wife's eyes.

'It appears we shall have to accept your supposition, and that we shall never know exactly what underlies his being here tonight...for he is dead.'

She held out her hands and stammered, her teeth chattering:

'It's not possible...He is...'

'Yes—dead...'

He seemed to be lost in thought for a moment, then went on in an easier voice:

'After all, the more I think of it, the more natural it seems...Both his father and his uncle died like this, suddenly...Heart disease is hereditary in his family...A shock... a violent emotion...too keen a sensation...a great joy...We are weak creatures at best...'

He drew an arm-chair to the fire, sat down, and, his hands stretched out to the flames, continued:

'But however simple and natural the event in itself may be, nothing can alter the fact that a man has died in your bedroom during the night...Is that not so?'

She hid her face in her hands and made no reply.

'And if your explanation satisfies me, I am not able to make others accept it. The servants will have their own ideas, will talk...That will be dishonour for you, for me, for my family...That is not possible...We must find a way out of it...and I have already found it...With the exception of you and me, no one knows, no one will ever know what has happened in this room...No one saw him come in...Take the lamp and come with me...'

He seized the body in his arms and ordered:

'Walk on first...'

She hesitated as they went out at the door.

'What are you going to do?...'

'Leave it to me...Go on...'

Slowly and very quietly they went towards the staircase, she holding high the lamp, its light flickering on the walls, he carefully placing his feet on stair after stair. When they got to the door that led to the garden, he said:

'Open it without a sound.'

A gust of wind made the light flare up. Beaten on by the rain, the glass burst and fell in pieces on the threshold. She placed the extinguished lamp on the soil. They went into the park. The gravel crunched under their steps and the rain beat upon them. He asked:

'Can you see the walk?...Yes?...Then come close to me... hold the legs...the body is heavy...'

They went forward in silence. M. de Hartevel stopped near a low door, saying:

'Feel in my right-hand pocket...There is a key there... That's it...Give it to me...Now let the legs go...It is as dark as a grave…Feel about till you find the key-hole…Have you got it?—Turn…'

Excited by the noise, the hounds began to bay. Madame de Hartevel started back.

'You are frightened?…Nonsense…Another turn…That's it!—Stand out of the way…'

With a thrust from his knee he pushed open the door. Believing themselves free, the hounds bounded against his legs. Pushing them back with a kick, suddenly, with one great effort, he raised the body above his head, balanced it there a moment, flung it into the kennel, and shut the door violently behind him.

Baying at full voice, the beasts fell on their prey. A frightful death-rattle: 'Help!' pierced their clamour, a terrible cry, superhuman. It was followed by violent growlings.

An unspeakable horror took possession of Madame de Hartevel; a quick flash of understanding dominated her fear, and, her eyes wild, she flung herself on her husband, digging her nails in his face as she shrieked:

'Fiend!…He wasn't dead!…'

M. de Hartevel pushed her off with the back of his hand, and standing straight up before her, jeered:

'Did you think he was!'

Footprints in the Snow

Maurice Leblanc

Maurice Leblanc (1864–1941) was born in Rouen, and combined journalism with a career as an industrious but low-profile writer of crime fiction until in 1905 he was commissioned to contribute a story to a new journal called *Je Sais Tout*. For this project, Leblanc created a new character, heavily influenced by E.W. Hornung's amateur cracksman A.J. Raffles. Thus was born Arsène Lupin. Leblanc's stories about Lupin enjoyed immediate success and were gathered in a collection published in 1907, which had many successors. Lupin was a rogue, but his daring thrilled readers—including Jean-Paul Sartre, who wrote: 'In 1912…I adored the Cyrano of the Underworld, Arsène Lupin…his herculean strength, his shrewd courage, his typically French intelligence…' Leblanc continued to write stories about Lupin for the rest of his life. His attempts to introduce Sherlock Holmes into the Lupin canon foundered on the rock of copyright law; his not especially cunning solution was to pit Lupin against characters with such names as Herlock Sholmes and Holmlock Shears.

This story appeared in Leblanc's collection *The Eight Strokes of the Clock* (1923) which he prefaced with a note: 'These adventures were told to me in the old days by Arsène Lupin, as though they had happened to a friend of his, named Prince Rénine. As for me, considering the way in which they were conducted, the actions, the behaviour and the very character of the hero, I find it very difficult not to identify the two friends as one and the same person. Arsène Lupin is gifted with a powerful imagination and is quite capable of attributing to himself adventures which are not his at all and of disowning those which are really his...'

• • ● • •

To Prince Serge Rénine
Boulevard Haussmann
Paris

La Roncière
near Bassicourt
14 November

My Dear Friend—
You must be thinking me very ungrateful. I have been here three weeks; and you have had not one letter from me! Not a word of thanks! And yet I ended by realizing from what terrible death you saved me and understanding the secret of that terrible business! But indeed, indeed I couldn't help it! I was in such a state of prostration after it all! I needed rest and solitude so badly! Was I to stay in Paris? Was I to continue my expeditions with you? No, no, no! I had had enough adventures! Other people's are very interesting, I admit. But when one is oneself the victim and barely escapes with one's life?...Oh, my dear friend, how horrible it was! Shall I ever forget it?...

Here, at la Roncière, I enjoy the greatest peace. My old spinster cousin Ermelin pets and coddles me like an invalid. I am getting back my colour and am very well, physically...so much so, in fact, that I no longer ever think of interesting myself in other people's business. Never again! For instance (I am only telling you this because you are incorrigible, as inquisitive as any old charwoman, and always ready to busy yourself with things that don't concern you), yesterday I was present at a rather curious meeting. Antoinette had taken me to the inn at Bassicourt, where we were having tea in the public room, among the peasants (it was market-day), when the arrival of three people, two men and a woman, caused a sudden pause in the conversation.

One of the men was a fat farmer in a long blouse, with a jovial, red face, framed in white whiskers. The other was younger, was dressed in corduroy, and had lean, yellow, cross-grained features. Each of them carried a gun slung over his shoulder. Between them was a short, slender young woman, in a brown cloak and a fur cap, whose rather thin and extremely pale face was surprisingly delicate and distinguished-looking.

'Father, son and daughter-in-law,' whispered my cousin.

'What! Can that charming creature be the wife of that clodhopper?'

'And the daughter-in-law of Baron de Gorne.'

'Is the old fellow over there a baron?'

'Yes, descended from a very ancient, noble family which used to own the château in the old days. He has always lived like a peasant: a great hunter, a great drinker, a great litigant, always at law with somebody, now very nearly ruined. His son Mathias was more ambitious and less attached to the soil and studied for the bar. Then he went to America. Next, the lack of money brought him back to the village, whereupon he fell in love with a young girl in the nearest town. The poor girl consented, no one knows why, to marry him; and for five years past she has been leading the life of a hermit, or rather of a prisoner, in a little manor-house close by, the Manoir-au-Puits, the Well Manor.'

'With the father and the son?' I asked.

'No, the father lives at the far end of the village, on a lonely farm.'

'And is Master Mathias jealous?'

'A perfect tiger!'

'Without reason?'

'Without reason, for Natalie de Gorne is the straightest woman in the world, and it is not her fault if a handsome young man has been hanging around the manor-house for the past few months. However, the de Gornes can't get over it.'

'What, the father neither?'

'The handsome young man is the last descendant of the people who bought the château long ago. This explains old de Gorne's hatred. Jérôme Vignal—I know him and am very fond of him—is a good-looking fellow and very well off; and he has sworn to run off with Natalie de Gorne. It's the old man who says so, whenever he has had a drop too much. There, listen!'

The old chap was sitting among a group of men who were amusing themselves by making him drink and plying him with questions. He was already a little bit 'on' and was holding forth with a tone of indignation and a mocking smile which formed the most comic contrast.

'He's wasting his time, I tell you, the coxcomb! It's no manner of use his poaching round our way and making sheep's-eyes at the wench…The coverts are watched! If he comes too near, it means a bullet, eh, Mathias?'

He gripped his daughter-in-law's hand.

'And then the little wench knows how to defend herself too,' he chuckled. 'Eh, you don't want any admirers, do you Natalie?'

The young wife blushed, in her confusion at being addressed in these terms, while her husband growled: 'You'd do better to hold your tongue, father. There are things one doesn't talk about in public.'

'Things that affect one's honour are best settled in public,' retorted the old one. 'Where I'm concerned, the honour of the de Gornes comes before everything; and that fine spark, with his Paris airs, shan't…'

He stopped short. Before him stood a man who had just come in and who seemed to be waiting for him to finish his sentence. The newcomer was a tall, powerfully-built young fellow, in riding-kit, with a hunting-crop in his hand. His strong and rather stern face was lighted up by a pair of fine eyes in which shone an ironical smile.

'Jérôme Vignal,' whispered my cousin.

The young man seemed not at all embarrassed. On seeing Natalie, he made a low bow; and, when Mathias de Gorne took a step forward, he eyed him from head to foot, as though to say: 'Well, what about it?'

And his attitude was so haughty and contemptu-
ous that the de Gornes unslung their guns and took
them in both hands, like sportsmen about to shoot.
The son's expression was very fierce.

Jérôme was quite unmoved by the threat. After a
few seconds, turning to the inn-keeper, he remarked:
'Oh, I say! I came to see old Vasseur. But his shop
is shut. Would you mind giving him the holster of
my revolver? It wants a stitch or two.'

He handed the holster to the inn-keeper and
added, laughing: 'I'm keeping the revolver, in case
I need it. You never can tell!'

Then, still very calmly, he took a cigarette from a
silver case, lit it and walked out. We saw him through
the window vaulting on his horse and riding off at
a slow trot.

Old de Gorne tossed off a glass of brandy, swearing most horribly.

His son clapped his hand to the old man's mouth
and forced him to sit down. Natalie de Gorne was
weeping beside them…

That's my story, dear friend. As you see, it's not
tremendously interesting and does not deserve your
attention. There's no mystery in it and no part for
you to play. Indeed, I particularly insist that you
should not seek a pretext for any untimely interfer-
ence. Of course, I should be glad to see the poor
thing protected: she appears to be a perfect martyr.
But, as I said before, let us leave other people to get
out of their own troubles and go no farther with our
little experiments…

Rénine finished reading the letter, read it over again and
ended by saying: 'That's it. Everything's right as right can be.

She doesn't want to continue our little experiments, because this would make the seventh and because she's afraid of the eighth, which under the terms of our agreement has a very particular significance. She doesn't want to…and she does want to…without seeming to want to.'

He rubbed his hands. The letter was an invaluable witness to the influence which he had gradually, gently and patiently gained over Hortense Daniel. It betrayed a rather complex feeling, composed of admiration, unbounded confidence, uneasiness at times, fear and almost terror, but also love: he was convinced of that. His companion in adventures which she shared with a good fellowship that excluded any awkwardness between them, she had suddenly taken fright; and a sort of modesty, mingled with a certain coquetry, was impelling her to hold back.

That very evening, Sunday, Rénine took the train.

And, at break of day, after covering by diligence, on a road white with snow, the five miles between the little town of Pompignat, where he alighted, and the village of Bassicourt, he learnt that his journey might prove of some use: three shots had been heard during the night in the direction of the Manoir au-Puits.

'Three shots, sergeant. I heard them as plainly as I see you standing before me,' said a peasant whom the gendarmes were questioning in the parlour of the inn which Rénine had entered.

'So did I,' said the waiter. 'Three shots. It may have been twelve o'clock at night. The snow, which had been falling since nine, had stopped…and the shots sounded across the fields, one after the other: bang, bang, bang.'

Five more peasants gave their evidence. The sergeant and his men had heard nothing, because the police-station backed on the fields. But a farm-labourer and a woman arrived, who said that they were in Mathias de Gorne's service, that they had been away for two days because of the intervening Sunday and that they had come straight from the manor-house, where they were unable to obtain admission.

'The gate of the grounds is locked, sergeant,' said the man. 'It's the first time I've known this to happen. M. Mathias comes out to open it himself, every morning at the stroke of six, winter and summer. Well, it's past eight now. I called and shouted. Nobody answered. So we came on here.'

'You might have enquired at old M. de Gorne's,' said the sergeant. 'He lives on the high-road.'

'On my word, so I might! I never thought of that.'

'We'd better go there now,' the sergeant decided. Two of his men went with him, as well as the peasants and a locksmith whose services were called into requisition. Rénine joined the party.

Soon, at the end of the village, they reached old de Gorne's farmyard, which Rénine recognized by Hortense's description of its position.

The old fellow was harnessing his horse and trap. When they told him what had happened, he burst out laughing.

'Three shots? Bang, bang, bang? Why, my dear sergeant, there are only two barrels to Mathias' gun!'

'What about the locked gate?'

'It means that the lad's asleep, that's all. Last night, he came and cracked a bottle with me…perhaps two…or even three; and he'll be sleeping it off, I expect…he and Natalie.'

He climbed on to the box of his trap—an old cart with a patched tilt—and cracked his whip.

'Goodbye, gentlemen all. Those three shots of yours won't stop me from going to market at Pompignat, as I do every Monday. I've a couple of calves under the tilt; and they're just fit for the butcher. Good-day to you!'

The others walked on. Rénine went up to the sergeant and gave him his name.

'I'm a friend of Mlle Ermelin, of La Roncière; and, as it's too early to call on her yet, I shall be glad if you'll allow me to go round by the manor with you. Mlle Ermelin knows Madame de Gorne; and it will be a satisfaction to me to relieve her mind, for there's nothing wrong at the manor-house, I hope?'

'If there is,' replied the sergeant, 'we shall read all about it as plainly as on a map, because of the snow.'

He was a likeable young man and seemed smart and intelligent. From the very first he had shown great acuteness in observing the tracks which Mathias had left behind him the evening before on returning home, tracks which soon became confused with the footprints made in going and coming by the farm-labourer and the woman. Meanwhile they came to the walls of a property of which the locksmith readily opened the gate.

From here onward, a single trail appeared upon the spotless snow, that of Mathias; and it was easy to perceive that the son must have shared largely in the father's libations, as the line of footprints described sudden curves which made it swerve right up to the trees of the avenue.

Two hundred yards farther stood the dilapidated two-storeyed building of the Manoir-au-Puits. The principal door was open.

'Let's go in,' said the sergeant.

And, the moment he had crossed the threshold, he muttered: 'Oho! Old de Gorne made a mistake in not coming. They've been fighting in here.'

The big room was in disorder. Two shattered chairs, the overturned table and much broken glass and china bore witness to the violence of the struggle. The tall clock, lying on the ground, had stopped at twenty past eleven.

With the farm-girl showing them the way, they ran up to the first floor. Neither Mathias nor his wife was there. But the door of their bedroom had been broken down with a hammer which they discovered under the bed.

Rénine and the sergeant went downstairs again. The living-room had a passage communicating with the kitchen, which lay at the back of the house and opened on a small yard fenced off from the orchard. At the end of this enclosure was a well near which one was bound to pass.

Now, from the door of the kitchen to the well, the snow, which was not very thick, had been pressed down to this side and that, as though a body had been dragged over it. And all around the well were tangled traces of trampling feet, showing that the struggle must have been resumed at this spot. The sergeant again discovered Mathias' footprints, together with others which were shapelier and lighter.

These latter went straight into the orchard, by themselves. And, thirty yards on, near the footprints, a revolver was picked up and recognized by one of the peasants as resembling that which Jérôme Vignal had produced in the inn two days before.

The sergeant examined the cylinder. Three of the seven bullets had been fired.

And so the tragedy was little by little reconstructed in its main outlines; and the sergeant, who had ordered everybody to stand aside and not to step on the site of the footprints, came back to the well, leant over, put a few questions to the farm-girl and, going up to Rénine, whispered: 'It all seems fairly clear to me.'

Rénine took his arm.

'Let's speak out plainly, sergeant. I understand the business pretty well, for, as I told you, I know Mlle Ermelin, who is a friend of Jérôme Vignal's and also knows Madame de Gorne. Do you suppose...?'

'I don't want to suppose anything. I simply declare that someone came there last night…'

'By which way? The only tracks of a person coming towards the manor are those of M. de Gorne.'

'That's because the other person arrived before the snowfall, that is to say, before nine o'clock.'

'Then he must have hidden in a corner of the living-room and waited for the return of M. de Gorne, who came after the snow?'

'Just so. As soon as Mathias came in, the man went for him. There was a fight. Mathias made his escape through the kitchen. The man ran after him to the well and fired three revolver-shots.'

'And where's the body?'

'Down the well.'

Rénine protested.

'Oh, I say! Aren't you taking a lot for granted?'

'Why, sir, the snow's there, to tell the story; and the snow plainly says that, after the struggle, after the three shots, one man alone walked away and left the farm, one man only, and his footprints are not those of Mathias de Gorne. Then where can Mathias de Gorne be?'

'But the well…can be dragged?'

'No. The well is practically bottomless. It is known all over the district and gives its name to the manor.'

'So you really believe…?'

'I repeat what I said. Before the snowfall, a single arrival, Mathias, and a single departure, the stranger.'

'And Madame de Gorne? Was she too killed and thrown down the well like her husband?'

'No, carried off.'

'Carried off?'

'Remember that her bedroom was broken down with a hammer.'

'Come, come, sergeant! You yourself declare that there was only one departure, the stranger's.'

'Stoop down. Look at the man's footprints. See how they sink into the snow, until they actually touch the ground. Those are the footprints of a man, laden with a heavy burden. The stranger was carrying Madame de Gorne on his shoulder.'

'Then there's an outlet this way?'

'Yes, a little door of which Mathias de Gorne always had the key on him. The man must have taken it from him.'

'A way out into the open fields?'

'Yes, a road which joins the departmental highway three quarters of a mile from here…And do you know where?'

'Where?'

'At the corner of the château.'

'Jérôme Vignal's château?'

'By Jove, this is beginning to look serious! If the trail leads to the château and stops there, we shall know where we stand.'

The trail did continue to the château, as they were able to perceive after following it across the undulating fields, on which the snow lay heaped in places. The approach to the main gates had been swept, but they saw that another trail, formed by the two wheels of a vehicle, was running in the opposite direction to the village.

The sergeant rang the bell. The porter, who had also been sweeping the drive, came to the gates, with a broom in his hand. In answer to a question, the man said that M. Vignal had gone away that morning before anyone else was up and that he himself had harnessed the horse to the trap.

'In that case,' said Rénine, when they had moved away, 'all we have to do is to follow the tracks of the wheels.'

'That will be no use,' said the sergeant. 'They have taken the railway.'

'At Pompignat station, where I came from? But they would have passed through the village.'

'They have gone just the other way, because it leads to the town, where the express trains stop. The procurator-general has an office in the town. I'll telephone; and, as there's no train before eleven o'clock, all that they need do is to keep a watch at the station.'

'I think you're doing the right thing, sergeant,' said Rénine, 'and I congratulate you on the way in which you have carried out your investigation.'

They parted. Rénine went back to the inn in the village and sent a note to Hortense Daniel by hand.

> My very dearest Friend,
>   I seemed to gather from your letter that, touched as always by anything that concerns the heart, you were anxious to protect the love-affair of Jérôme and Natalie. Now there is every reason to suppose that these two, without consulting their fair protectress, have run away, after throwing Mathias de Gorne down a well.
>   Forgive me for not coming to see you. The whole thing is extremely obscure; and, if I were with you, I should not have the detachment of mind which is needed to think the case over.

It was then half-past ten. Rénine went for a walk into the country, with his hands clasped behind his back and without vouchsafing a glance at the exquisite spectacle of the white meadows. He came back for lunch, still absorbed in his thoughts and indifferent to the talk of the customers of the inn, who on all sides were discussing recent events.

He went up to his room and had been asleep some time when he was awakened by a tapping at the door. He got up and opened it.

'Is it you?...Is it you?' he whispered.

Hortense and he stood gazing at each other for some seconds in silence, holding each other's hands, as though nothing, no irrelevant thought and no utterance, must be allowed to interfere with the joy of their meeting. Then he asked: 'Was I right in coming?'

'Yes,' she said, gently, 'I expected you.'

'Perhaps it would have been better if you had sent for me sooner, instead of waiting…Events did not wait, you see, and I don't quite know what's to become of Jérôme Vignal and Natalie de Gorne.'

'What, haven't you heard?' she said, quickly. 'They've been arrested. They were going to travel by the express.'

'Arrested? No,' Rénine objected. 'People are not arrested like that. They have to be questioned first.'

'That's what's being done now. The authorities are making a search.'

'Where?'

'At the château. And, as they are innocent…For they are innocent, aren't they? You don't admit that they are guilty, any more than I do?'

He replied: 'I admit nothing, I can admit nothing, my dear. Nevertheless, I am bound to say that everything is against them…except one fact, which is that everything is too much against them. It is not normal for so many proofs to be heaped up one on top of the other and for the man who commits a murder to tell his story so frankly. Apart from this, there's nothing but mystery and discrepancy.'

'Well?'

'Well, I am greatly puzzled.'

'But you have a plan?'

'None at all, so far. Ah, if I could see him, Jérôme Vignal, and her, Natalie de Gorne, and hear them and know what they are saying in their own defence! But you can understand that I shan't be permitted either to ask them any questions or to be present at their examination. Besides, it must be finished by this time.'

'It's finished at the château,' she said, 'but it's going to be continued at the manor-house.'

'Are they taking them to the manor-house?' he asked eagerly.

'Yes…at least, judging by what was said to the chauffeur of one of the procurator's two cars.'

'Oh, in that case,' exclaimed Rénine, 'the thing's done! The manor-house! Why, we shall be in the front row of the stalls! We shall see and hear everything; and, as a word, a tone of the voice, a quiver of the eyelids will be enough to give me the tiny clue I need, we may entertain some hope. Come along.'

He took her by the direct route which he had followed that morning, leading to the gate which the locksmith had opened. The gendarmes on duty at the manor-house had made a passage through the snow, beside the line of footprints and around the house. Chance enabled Rénine and Hortense to approach unseen and through a side-window to enter a corridor near a back-staircase. A few steps up was a little chamber which received its only light through a sort of bull's-eye, from the large room on the ground-floor. Rénine, during the morning visit, had noticed the bull's-eye, which was covered on the inside with a piece of cloth. He removed the cloth and cut out one of the panes.

A few minutes later, a sound of voices rose from the other side of the house, no doubt near the well. The sound grew more distinct. A number of people flocked into the house. Some of them went upstairs to the first floor, while the sergeant arrived with a young man of whom Rénine and Hortense were able to distinguish only the tall figure.

'Jérôme Vignal,' said she.

'Yes,' said Rénine. 'They are examining Madame de Gorne first, upstairs, in her bedroom.'

A quarter of an hour passed. Then the persons on the first floor came downstairs and went in. They were the procurator's deputy, his clerk, a commissary of police and two detectives.

Madame de Gorne was shown in and the deputy asked Jérôme Vignal to step forward.

Jérôme Vignal's face was certainly that of the strong man whom Hortense had depicted in her letter. He displayed no uneasiness, but rather decision and a resolute will. Natalie, who was short and very slight, with a feverish light in her eyes, nevertheless produced the same impression of quiet confidence.

The deputy, who was examining the disordered furniture and the traces of the struggle, invited her to sit down and said to Jérôme: 'Monsieur, I have not asked you many questions so far. This is a summary enquiry which I am conducting in your presence and which will be continued later by the examining-magistrate; and I wished above all to explain to you the very serious reasons for which I asked you to inter-rupt your journey and to come back here with Madame de Gorne. You are now in a position to refute the truly distress-ing charges that are hanging over you. I therefore ask you to tell me the exact truth.'

'Mr Deputy,' replied Jérôme, 'the charges in question trouble me very little. The truth for which you are asking will defeat all the lies which chance has accumulated against me. It is this.'

He reflected for an instant and then, in clear, frank tones, said: 'I love Madame de Gorne. The first time I met her, I conceived the greatest sympathy and admiration for her. But my affection has always been directed by the sole thought of her happiness. I love her, but I respect her even more.

Madame de Gorne must have told you and I tell you again that she and I exchanged our first few words last night.'

He continued, in a lower voice: 'I respect her the more inasmuch as she is exceedingly unhappy. All the world knows that every minute of her life was a martyrdom. Her husband persecuted her with ferocious hatred and frantic jealousy. Ask the servants. They will tell you of the long suffering of Natalie de Gorne, of the blows which she received and the insults which she had to endure. I tried to stop this torture by resorting to the rights of appeal which the merest stranger may claim when unhappiness and injustice pass a certain limit. I went three times to old de Gorne and begged him to interfere; but I found in him an almost equal hatred towards his daughter-in-law, the hatred which many people feel for anything beautiful and noble. At last I resolved on direct action and last night I took a step with regard to Mathias de Gorne which was…a little unusual, I admit, but which seemed likely to succeed, considering the man's character. I swear, Mr Deputy, that I had no other intention than to talk to Mathias de Gorne. Knowing certain particulars of his life which enabled me to bring effective pressure to bear upon him, I wished to make use of this advantage in order to achieve my purpose. If things turned out differently, I am not wholly to blame…So I went there a little before nine o'clock. The servants, I knew, were out. He opened the door himself. He was alone.'

'Monsieur,' said the deputy, interrupting him, 'you are saying something—as Madame de Gorne, for that matter, did just now—which is manifestly opposed to the truth. Mathias de Gorne did not come home last night until eleven o'clock. We have two definite proofs of this: his father's evidence and the prints of his feet in the snow, which fell from a quarter past nine o'clock to eleven.'

'Mr Deputy,' Jérôme Vignal declared, without heeding the bad effect which his obstinacy was producing, 'I am relating things as they were and not as they may be interpreted. But to continue. That clock marked ten minutes to nine when I entered this room. M. de Gorne, believing that he was about to be attacked, had taken down his gun. I placed my revolver on the table, out of reach of my hand, and sat down: "I want to speak to you, monsieur," I said. "Please listen to me." He did not stir and did not utter a single syllable. So I spoke. And straightway, crudely, without any previous explanations which might have softened the bluntness of my proposal, I spoke the few words which I had prepared beforehand: "I have spent some months, monsieur," I said, "in making careful enquiries into your financial position. You have mortgaged every foot of your land. You have signed bills which will shortly be falling due and which it will be absolutely impossible for you to honour. You have nothing to hope for from your father, whose own affairs are in a very bad condition. So you are ruined. I have come to save you."…He watched me, still without speaking, and sat down, which I took to mean that my suggestion was not entirely displeasing. Then I took a sheaf of bank-notes from my pocket, placed it before him and continued: "Here is sixty thousand francs, monsieur. I will buy the Manoir-au-Puits, its lands and dependencies and take over the mortgages. The sum named is exactly twice what they are worth."… I saw his eyes glittering. He asked my conditions. "Only one," I said, "that you go to America."…Mr Deputy, we sat discussing for two hours. It was not that my offer roused his indignation—I should not have risked it if I had not known with whom I was dealing—but he wanted more and haggled greedily, though he refrained from mentioning the name of Madame de Gorne, to whom I myself had not once alluded. We might have been two men engaged in a dispute and seeking an agreement on common ground, whereas it was the happiness and the whole destiny of a woman that were at stake. At last, weary of the discussion, I accepted a compromise and we came to terms, which I resolved to make definite then and there. Two letters were exchanged between us: one in which he made the Manoir-au-Puits over to me for the sum which I had paid him; and one, which he pocketed immediately, by which I was to send him as much more in America on the day on which the decree of divorce was pronounced...So the affair was settled. I am sure that at that moment he was accepting in good faith. He looked upon me less as an enemy and a rival than as a man who was doing him a service. He even went so far as to give me the key of the little door which opens on the fields, so that I might go home by the short cut. Unfortunately, while I was picking up my cap and greatcoat, I made the mistake of leaving on the table the letter of sale which he had signed. In a moment, Mathias de Gorne had seen the advantage which he could take of my slip: he could keep his property, keep his wife...and keep the money. Quick as lightning, he tucked away the paper, hit me over the head with the butt-end of his gun, threw the gun on the floor and seized me by the throat with both hands. He had reckoned without his host. I was the stronger of the two; and after a sharp but short struggle, I mastered him and tied him up with a cord which I found lying in a corner...Mr Deputy, if my enemy's resolve was sudden, mine was no less so. Since, when all was said, he had accepted the bargain, I would force him to keep it, at least in so far as I was interested. A very few steps brought me to the first floor...I had not a doubt that Madame de Gorne was there and had heard the sound of our discussion. Switching on the light of my pocket-torch, I looked into three bedrooms. The fourth was locked. I knocked at the door. There was no reply. But this was one of the moments in which a man allows no obstacle to stand in his way. I had seen a hammer in one of the rooms. I picked it up and smashed in the door...Yes, Natalie was lying there, on the floor, in a dead faint. I took her in my arms, carried her downstairs and went through the kitchen. On seeing the snow outside, I at once realized that my footprints would be easily traced. But what did it matter? Was there any reason why I should put Mathias de Gorne off the scent? Not at all. With the sixty thousand francs in his possession, as well as the paper in which I undertook to pay him a like sum on the day of his divorce, to say nothing of his house and land, he would go away, leaving Natalie de Gorne to me. Nothing was changed between us, except one thing: instead of awaiting his good pleasure, I had at once seized the precious pledge which I coveted. What I feared, therefore, was not so much any subsequent attack on the part of Mathias de Gorne, but rather the indignant reproaches of his wife. What would she say when she realized that she was a prisoner in my hands?...The reasons why I escaped reproach Madame de Gorne has, I believe, had the frankness to tell you. Love calls forth love. That night, in my house, broken by emotion, she confessed her feeling for me. She loved me as I loved her. Our destinies were henceforth mingled. She and I set out at five o'clock this morning...not foreseeing for an instant that we were amenable to the law.'

Jérôme Vignal's story was finished. He had told it straight off the reel, like a story learnt by heart and incapable of revision in any detail.

There was a brief pause, during which Hortense whispered: 'It all sounds quite possible and, in any case, very logical.'

'There are the objections to come,' said Rénine. 'Wait till you hear them. They are very serious. There's one in particular...'

The deputy-procurator stated it at once.

'And what became of M. de Gorne in all this?'

'Mathias de Gorne?' asked Jérôme.

'Yes. You have related, with an accent of great sincerity, a series of facts which I am quite willing to admit. Unfortunately, you have forgotten a point of the first importance: what became of Mathias de Gorne? You tied him up here, in this room. Well, this morning he was gone.'

'Of course, Mr Deputy, Mathias de Gorne accepted the bargain in the end and went away.'

'By what road?'

'No doubt by the road that leads to his father's house.'

'Where are his footprints? The expanse of snow is an impartial witness. After your fight with him, we see you, on the snow, moving away. Why don't we see him? He came and did not go away again. Where is he? There is not a trace of him...or rather...'

The deputy lowered his voice.

'Or rather, yes, there are some traces on the way to the well and around the well...traces which prove that the last struggle of all took place there...And after that there is nothing...not a thing...' Jérôme shrugged his shoulders.

'You have already mentioned this, Mr Deputy, and it implies a charge of homicide against me. I have nothing to say to it.'

'Have you anything to say to the fact that your revolver was picked up within fifteen yards of the well?'

'No.'

'Or to the strange coincidence between the three shots heard in the night and the three cartridges missing from your revolver?'

'No, Mr Deputy, there was not, as you believe, a last struggle by the well, because I left M. de Gorne tied up, in this room, and because I also left my revolver here. On the other hand, if shots were heard, they were not fired by me.'

'A casual coincidence, therefore?'

'That's a matter for the police to explain. My only duty is to tell the truth and you are not entitled to ask more of me.'

'And if that truth conflicts with the facts observed?'

'It means that the facts are wrong, Mr Deputy.'

'As you please. But, until the day when the police are able to make them agree with your statements, you will understand that I am obliged to keep you under arrest.'

'And Madame de Gorne?' asked Jérôme, greatly distressed.

The deputy did not reply. He exchanged a few words with the commissary of police and then, beckoning to a detective, ordered him to bring up one of the two motor-cars. Then he turned to Natalie.

'Madame, you have heard M. Vignal's evidence. It agrees word for word with your own. M. Vignal declares in particular that you had fainted when he carried you away. But did you remain unconscious all the way?'

It seemed as though Jérôme's composure had increased Madame de Gorne's assurance. She replied: 'I did not come to, monsieur, until I was at the château.'

'It's most extraordinary. Didn't you hear the three shots which were heard by almost everyone in the village?'

'I did not.'

'And did you see nothing of what happened beside the well?'

'Nothing did happen. M. Vignal has told you so.'

'Then what has become of your husband?'

'I don't know.'

'Come, madame, you really must assist the officers of the law and at least tell us what you think. Do you believe that there may have been an accident and that possibly M. de Gorne, who had been to see his father and had more to drink than usual, lost his balance and fell into the well?'

'When my husband came back from seeing his father, he was not in the least intoxicated.'

'His father, however, has stated that he was. His father and he had drunk two or three bottles of wine.'

'His father is not telling the truth.'

'But the snow tells the truth, madame,' said the deputy, irritably. 'And the line of his footprints wavers from side to side.'

'My husband came in at half-past-eight, monsieur, before the snow had begun to fall.'

The deputy struck the table with his fist.

'But, really, madame, you're going right against the evidence!...That sheet of snow cannot speak false!...I may accept your denial of matters that cannot be verified. But these footprints in the snow...in the snow...'

He controlled himself.

The motor-car drew up outside the windows. Forming a sudden resolve, he said to Natalie: 'You will be good enough to hold yourself at the disposal of the authorities, madame, and to remain here, in the manor-house...'

And he made a sign to the sergeant to remove Jérôme Vignal in the car.

The game was lost for the two lovers. Barely united, they had to separate and to fight, far away from each other, against the most grievous accusations.

Jérôme took a step towards Natalie. They exchanged a long, sorrowful look. Then he bowed to her and walked to the door, in the wake of the sergeant of gendarmes.

'Halt!' cried a voice. 'Sergeant, right about...turn!... Jérôme Vignal, stay where you are!'

The ruffled deputy raised his head, as did the other people present. The voice came from the ceiling. The bull's-eye window had opened and Rénine, leaning through it, was waving his arms.

'I wish to be heard!...I have several remarks to make... especially in respect of the zigzag footprints!...It all lies in that!...Mathias had not been drinking!...'

He had turned round and put his two legs through the opening, saying to Hortense, who tried to prevent him.

'Don't move...No one will disturb you.'

And, releasing his hold, he dropped into the room.

The deputy appeared dumbfounded.

'But, really, monsieur, who are you? Where do you come from?'

Rénine brushed the dust from his clothes and replied: 'Excuse me, Mr Deputy. I ought to have come the same way as everybody else. But I was in a hurry. Besides, if I had come in by the door instead of falling from the ceiling, my words would not have made the same impression.'

The infuriated deputy advanced to meet him.

'Who are you?'

'Prince Rénine. I was with the sergeant this morning when he was pursuing his investigations, wasn't I, sergeant? Since then I have been hunting about for information. That's why, wishing to be present at the hearing, I found a corner in a little private room...'

'You were there? You had the audacity?...'

'One must needs be audacious, when the truth's at stake. If I had not been there, I should not have discovered just the one little clue which I missed. I should not have known that Mathias de Gorne was not the least bit drunk. Now that's the key to the riddle. When we know that, we know the solution.'

The deputy found himself in a rather ridiculous position. Since he had failed to take the necessary precautions to ensure the secrecy of his enquiry, it was difficult for him to take any steps against this interloper. He growled: 'Let's have done with this. What are you asking?'

'A few minutes of your kind attention.'

'And with what object?'

'To establish the innocence of M. Vignal and Madame de Gorne.'

He was wearing that calm air, that sort of indifferent look which was peculiar to him in moments of actions when the crisis of the drama depended solely upon himself. Hortense felt a thrill pass through her and at once became full of confidence.

'They're saved,' she thought, with sudden emotion. 'I asked him to protect that young creature; and he is saving her from prison and despair.'

Jérôme and Natalie must have experienced the same impression of sudden hope, for they had drawn nearer to each other, as though this stranger, descended from the clouds, had already given them the right to clasp hands.

The deputy shrugged his shoulders.

'The prosecution will have every means, when the time comes, of establishing their innocence for itself. You will be called.'

'It would be better to establish it here and now. Any delay might lead to grievous consequences.'

'I happen to be in a hurry.'

'Two or three minutes will do.'

'Two or three minutes to explain a case like this!'

'No longer, I assure you.'

'Are you as certain of it as all that?'

'I am now. I have been thinking hard since this morning.'

The deputy realized that this was one of those gentry who stick to you like a leech and that there was nothing for it but to submit. In a rather bantering tone, he asked: 'Does your thinking enable you to tell us the exact spot where M. Mathias de Gorne is at this moment?'

Rénine took out his watch and answered: 'In Paris, Mr Deputy.'

'In Paris? Alive then?'

'Alive and, what is more, in the pink of health.'

'I am delighted to hear it. But then what's the meaning of the footprints around the well and the presence of that revolver and those three shots?'

'Simply camouflage.'

'Oh, really? Camouflage contrived by whom?'

'By Mathias de Gorne himself.'

'That's curious! And with what object?'

'With the object of passing himself off for dead and of arranging subsequent matters in such a way that M. Vignal was bound to be accused of the death, the murder.'

'An ingenious theory,' the deputy agreed, still in a satirical tone. 'What do you think of it, M. Vignal?'

'It is a theory which flashed through my own mind, Mr Deputy,' replied Jérôme. 'It is quite likely that, after our struggle and after I had gone, Mathias de Gorne conceived a new plan by which, this time, his hatred would be fully gratified. He both loved and detested his wife. He held me in the greatest loathing. This must be his revenge.'

'His revenge would cost him dear, considering that, according to your statement, Mathias de Gorne was to receive a second sum of sixty thousand francs from you.'

'He would receive that sum in another quarter, Mr Deputy. My examination of the financial position of the de Gorne family revealed to me the fact that the father and son had taken out a life-insurance policy in each other's favour. With the son dead, or passing for dead, the father would receive the insurance-money and indemnify his son.'

'You mean to say,' asked the deputy, with a smile, 'that in all this camouflage, as you call it, M. de Gorne the elder would act as his son's accomplice?'

Rénine took up the challenge.

'Just so, Mr Deputy. The father and son are accomplices.'

'Then we shall find the son at the father's?'

'You would have found him there last night.'

'What became of him?'

'He took the train at Pompignat.'

'That's a mere supposition.'

'No, a certainty.'

'A moral certainty, perhaps, but you'll admit there's not the slightest proof.'

The deputy did not wait for a reply. He considered that he had displayed an excessive goodwill and that patience has its limits and he put an end to the interview.

'Not the slightest proof,' he repeated, taking up his hat. 'And, above all,…above all, there's nothing in what you've said that can contradict in the very least the evidence of that relentless witness, the snow. To go to his father, Mathias de Gorne must have left this house. Which way did he go?'

'Hang it all, M. Vignal told you: by the road which leads from here to his father's!'

'There are no tracks in the snow.'

'Yes, there are.'

'But they show him coming here and not going away from here.'

'It's the same thing.'

'What?'

'Of course it is. There's more than one way of walking. One doesn't always go ahead by following one's nose.'

'In what other way can one go ahead?'

'By walking backwards, Mr Deputy.'

These few words, spoken very simply, but in a clear tone which gave full value to every syllable, produced a profound silence. Those present at once grasped their extreme significance and, by adapting it to the actual happenings, perceived in a flash the impenetrable truth, which suddenly appeared to be the most natural thing in the world.

Rénine continued his argument. Stepping backwards in the direction of the window, he said: 'If I want to get to that window, I can of course walk straight up to it; but I can just as easily turn my back to it and walk that way. In either case I reach my goal.'

And he at once proceeded in a vigorous tone: 'Here's the gist of it all. At half-past eight, before the snow fell, M. de Gorne comes home from his father's house. M. Vignal arrives twenty minutes later. There is a long discussion and a struggle, taking up three hours in all. It is then, after M. Vignal has carried off Madame de Gorne and made his escape, that Mathias de Gorne, foaming at the mouth, wild with rage, but suddenly seeing his chance of taking the most terrible revenge, hits upon the ingenious idea of using against his enemy the very snowfall upon whose evidence you are now relying. He therefore plans his own murder, or rather the appearance of his murder and of his fall to the bottom of the well and makes off backwards, step by step, thus recording his arrival instead of his departure on the white page.'

The deputy sneered no longer. This eccentric intruder suddenly appeared to him in the light of a person worthy of attention, whom it would not do to make fun of. He asked: 'And how could he have left his father's house?'

'In a trap, quite simply.'

'Who drove it?'

'The father. This morning the sergeant and I saw the trap and spoke to the father, who was going to market as usual. The son was hidden under the tilt. He took the train at Pompignat and is in Paris by now.'

Rénine's explanation, as promised, had taken hardly five minutes. He had based it solely on logic and the probabilities of the case. And yet not a jot was left of the distressing mystery in which they were floundering. The darkness was dispelled. The whole truth appeared.

Madame de Gorne wept for joy and Jérôme Vignal thanked the good genius who was changing the course of events with a stroke of his magic wand.

'Shall we examine those footprints together, Mr Deputy?' asked Rénine. 'Do you mind? The mistake which the sergeant and I made this morning was to investigate only the footprints left by the alleged murderer and to neglect Mathias de Gorne's. Why indeed should they have attracted our attention? Yet it was precisely there that the crux of the whole affair was to be found.'

They stepped into the orchard and went to the well. It did not need a long examination to observe that many of the footprints were awkward, hesitating, too deeply sunk at the heel and toe and differing from one another in the angle at which the feet were turned.

'This clumsiness was unavoidable,' said Rénine. 'Mathias de Gorne would have needed a regular apprenticeship before his backward progress could have equalled his ordinary gait; and both his father and he must have been aware of this, at least as regards the zigzags which you see here since old de Gorne went out of his way to tell the sergeant that his son had had too much drink.' And he added, 'Indeed it was the detection of this falsehood that suddenly enlightened me. When Madame de Gorne stated that her husband was not drunk, I thought of the footprints and guessed the truth.'

The deputy frankly accepted his part in the matter and began to laugh.

'There's nothing left for it but to send detectives after the bogus corpse.'

'On what grounds, Mr Deputy?' asked Rénine. 'Mathias de Gorne has committed no offence against the law. There's nothing criminal in trampling the soil around a well, in shifting the position of a revolver that doesn't belong to you, in firing three shots or in walking backwards to one's father's house. What can we ask of him? The sixty thousand francs? I presume that this is not M. Vignal's intention and that he does not mean to bring a charge against him?'

'Certainly not,' said Jérôme.

'Well, what then? The insurance-policy in favour of the survivor? But there would be no misdemeanour unless the father claimed payment. And I should be greatly surprised if he did...Hullo, here the old chap is! You'll soon know all about it.'

Old de Gorne was coming along, gesticulating as he walked. His easy-going features were screwed up to express sorrow and anger.

'Where's my son?' he cried. 'It seems the brute's killed him!...My poor Mathias dead! Oh, that scoundrel of a Vignal!'

And he shook his fist at Jérôme.

The deputy said, bluntly: 'A word with you, M. de Gorne. Do you intend to claim your rights under a certain insurance-policy?'

'Well, what do *you* think?' said the old man, off his guard.

'The fact is...your son's not dead. People are even saying that you were a partner in his little schemes and that you stuffed him under the tilt of your trap and drove him to the station.'

The old fellow spat on the ground, stretched out his hand as though he were going to take a solemn oath, stood for an instant without moving and then, suddenly, changing his mind and his tactics with ingenuous cynicism, he relaxed his features, assumed a conciliatory attitude and burst out laughing.

'That blackguard Mathias! So he tried to pass himself off as dead? What a rascal! And he reckoned on me to collect the insurance-money and send it to him? As if I should be capable of such a low, dirty trick!…You don't know me, my boy!'

And, without waiting for more, shaking with merriment like a jolly old fellow amused by a funny story, he took his departure, not forgetting, however, to set his great hob-nail boots on each of the compromising footprints which his son had left behind him.

· ● ● ● ·

Later, when Rénine went back to the manor to let Hortense out, he found that she had disappeared.

He called and asked for her at her cousin Ermelin's. Hortense sent down word asking him to excuse her: she was feeling a little tired and was lying down.

'Capital!' thought Rénine. 'Capital! She avoids me, therefore she loves me. The end is not far off.'

The Return of Lord Kingwood

Ivans

Jakob van Schevichaven (1866–1935), like so many writers during the Golden Age, chose to publish his detective fiction under a pseudonym. He chose the name Ivans (i.e. J + van + S), and between 1917 and 1935, he produced no fewer than 44 detective novels. He argued in an interview in 1926 that there was a strong public demand for 'light literature', and that the best way of satisfying it was by supplying detective stories in the Sherlock Holmes tradition. Like so many others of his era, in Britain and elsewhere, Ivans borrowed from Conan Doyle (who had in turn borrowed from Poe) in creating a sleuthing duo. This comprised the English detective Geoffrey Gill and his Dutch friend Willy Hendriks, who regularly confronted mysteries involving international crime and espionage.

'The Return of Lord Kingwood', originally published in 1926, is characteristic of Ivans' output, and features a Great Detective called Mr Monk (a name that would be given many years later to the detective in an enjoyable American television series). This is a new translation by Josh Pachter, who has long combined translating work with a career as a writer of highly engaging short stories, many of which have been published in *Ellery Queen's Mystery Magazine*.

• • ● • •

I

It was 10:30 in the evening. Outside, it was raining.

Mr Monk sat in his office at Scotland Yard: a little, unattractive, sloppy man in a little, unattractive, sloppy room, and yet...the axis around which the Yard revolved, as his admirers were wont to put it.

The few dilapidated chairs and the large circular desk were piled high with newspapers and documents, a chaos through which Mr Monk, guided apparently by some sixth sense, seemed able to find his way. At any rate, he worked zealously, consulting various papers from time to time, papers he deftly plucked as needed from amidst the chaos.

His telephone shrilled.

Mr Monk raised the receiver to his ear and listened for some seconds. Then he made an impatient gesture. 'You'd better come here, Higgins', he said. 'It will be easier for me to understand what you're saying if we're eye to eye'.

There was a hint of sarcasm in this utterance, but when Inspector Higgins stepped into the room a moment later there was no slightest indication on his face that he was aware of it. He was dressed in uniform, and he saluted.

'I regret, Inspector, that there's nowhere for you to sit', said the little man, with a glance at the overflowing chairs, 'but fortunately we human beings can converse while standing. Will you be so good as to repeat the information you presented by 'phone? You said something about Kingwood

Manor and Lord Kingwood, and also a caretaker. But I'm unclear what the one has to do with the other'.

'The case is quite simple', responded Inspector Higgins. 'We've just been contacted by Lord Kingwood's caretaker, who rang us from Kingwood Manor near Bridgetown. After an absence of many years, Lord Kingwood returned home earlier this evening, and the caretaker—whose name seems to be John Perkins—has requested the assistance of the Yard as quickly as possible, as he claims to have made a discovery of the utmost importance'.

'And what discovery would that be?'

'He was unwilling to explain over the telephone, sir'.

'How, then, Inspector, do you know that the case is a simple one?'

Inspector Higgins looked rather helpless, so he chose the wisest course of action and said nothing.

Mr Monk also chose the wisest course of action and declined to repeat his question. 'What did you tell him, Inspector?' he said instead.

'I asked him why Lord Kingwood hadn't placed the call himself, if the matter had something to do with His Lordship's return. The man replied that His Lordship knew nothing about it, and that we must in no event inform Lord Kingwood that Perkins had requested our presence until after first speaking privately with Perkins himself'.

'Perhaps not so simple, after all, Inspector', said Mr Monk.

And Inspector Higgins again appeared quite helpless.

Mr Monk, on the other hand, held his head high. He reminded one of a hunting dog whose nostrils have just inhaled the distant scent of game.

'At what time does the first morning train depart for Bridgetown?' he enquired.

'Sharp on eight', said the inspector without any hesitation. He was often referred to as a walking timetable, and the man had indeed a remarkable memory, though it was not always—and certainly not in this case—paired with an equally remarkable store of common sense.

'Then that's the train I shall take', said Mr Monk, and gestured that the inspector's presence was no longer required. But Higgins appeared to have something else to ask. 'Will you go alone?' he said. 'Or perhaps you'd like me to...?'

'No, thank you, Higgins, I'll be fine on my own. After all, if your judgement is correct, it's quite a simple matter!' The inspector saluted and left.

Mr Monk then ferreted a number of newspaper clippings and other papers out from an assortment of nooks and crannies. Each made some reference to Lord Kingwood. How the little man managed to locate them so quickly, after they had spent years tucked away and forgotten, was impossible to explain. But it was generally acknowledged that there were certain secret passages through the wilderness of documents strewn both within and without the office's many cabinets, passages that were known only to Mr Monk, passages that invariably led him directly to whatever information he sought.

And again on this occasion, the conventional wisdom seemed to hold true. For, half an hour after Inspector Higgins had taken his leave, Mr Monk was in possession of the following facts:

William Henry, Marquis of Kingwood, had left Kingwood Manor almost 20 years previously, after the sudden death of his wife. He had in fact left the country, with his 10-year-old daughter in tow. After some years spent travelling half the world, they had ultimately settled in Florence. But even there they were rarely in residence, for the lure of travel seemed to hold Lord Kingwood still in its power. The death of his wife had made such an impact upon him that he never wished to see Kingwood Manor again, and he had so declared himself on many occasions. Lady Mary, his daughter, now some 30 years of age and unmarried, had however often expressed a wish that they might return to England. She now seemed to have gotten her way at last, and Lord Kingwood had determined that they should pay a visit to the Manor—apparently a quite unexpected decision, since their arrival had not been announced in the press, as would normally have happened in such cases. His former butler, John Perkins, had with his wife served as caretakers of the property for all these intervening years.

This was the essence of what Mr Monk had learned from his researches. There was nothing out of the ordinary to it, nothing that had not been seen before amongst the British aristocracy.

And yet...

Once again, Mr Monk raised his head and sniffed at the stuffy air of his sanctum sanctorum.

What could the old caretaker have to communicate to the police—on the exact day of Lord Kingwood's return—that His Lordship himself must not know?

No, this was *not* a simple case. Most assuredly not.

II

Mr Monk stepped onto the platform at Bridgetown at nine the following morning to find a beautiful summer day awaiting him. The air was rich with the scents of roses and lilacs.

The little man took several deep breaths. He gazed longingly at the hills that lay off to his left: how deeply would he have relished the opportunity to climb them, to while away the morning in the forests that blanketed them. The little man in the untidy clothes had, occasionally, a poetic turn of mind. But that seldom lasted for long, and the duty that now called him brought him back to the prosaic reality of his life. The hills lay off to his left, but to his right Kingwood Manor beckoned.

A friendly gentlewoman lounging in the doorway of her simple home gave him directions to 'the Manor', as the locals referred to it. As she did so, she examined him with an expression Mr Monk did not entirely comprehend. She was, though he did not realize it, considering whether or not this little, slovenly man with the broad necktie might be an artist who had fallen on hard times, and whether it would offend him were she to offer him a bite to eat. She might well have done so, until she observed the bright look in Mr Monk's eyes; those eyes were much too lively, she decided, to belong to a man who had fallen on hard times. Such a poor soul must instead appear sorrowful…or unintelligent.

Mr Monk strolled along the wide and well maintained road, which would bring him to Kingwood Manor within an hour of walking. He was lost in a whirl of thoughts that had no bearing whatsoever on the task that awaited him. He focused on the singing of the birds, followed with his aging but still sharp gaze the rising flight of a merry lark, and inhaled with great pleasure the smells of a warm, ripe summer.

Yes, England was indeed a wonderful country!

How could someone like Lord Kingwood have turned his back on it for so long?

But the Prodigal Son had at last returned! There at Kingwood Manor, he could once again enjoy an English summer, for the first time in many years!

Mr Monk spotted the Manor's two small towers in the distance, jutting up above the thick green canopy of beeches and oaks.

At the same moment, he saw a boy bicycling toward him from the direction of the house. The lad pedalled as if his life depended upon it, and, as he approached, Mr Monk saw that his face was deathly pale and there were beads of sweat on his forehead.

The little man's police persona immediately took command of his posture and expression.

'Has something happened?' he shouted.

'I'm going for the constable in Bridgetown!' the boy cried in response. 'There's been a murder at the Manor!' And, like the wind, he blew off down the country lane.

A murder?

Mr Monk stood still for a moment, and wiped the perspiration from his own forehead with his handkerchief.

Then he continued on his way.

A murder?…

It seemed an act of Providence that he should have arrived so promptly at the scene of the crime.

Or should his presence not be credited to old John Perkins, the caretaker, who had summoned him?

But why had the man not explained himself more fully, with such an awful occurrence hanging over his head?…

Mr Monk increased his pace. The matter would become clearer on his arrival at the Manor.

As the little man turned into the broad driveway and approached the ivy-draped house—which was in fact an agglomeration of sections representing various periods of English architectural history—it was apparent that *something* extraordinary had occurred. The massive front door stood open and—immediately before it—a large number of servants stood clustered in groups on the grass, busily chattering amongst themselves and gesticulating. Under ordinary circumstances, they would surely be elsewhere, not gathered together on the lawn.

When they spotted Mr Monk, a silence descended upon them.

One of their number, a young man in simple livery, came toward him. 'May I assist you?' he asked.

'I should like to speak with the butler, John Perkins', the little man replied.

The servant went pale and took a step back. 'This—person wishes to speak with John Perkins!' he cried to the others. Turning back to Mr Monk, he said, 'Who are you, and what do you want with Mr Perkins?'

'You will perhaps forgive me if I discuss my business with him and not with you', came the rather cutting reply.

'Not so fast', the servant returned. 'Mr Perkins seems to be missing'.

'And Mrs Perkins?'

'Mrs Perkins…Mrs Perkins…' The young man swallowed repeatedly. 'Mrs Perkins was found murdered in her bed this morning'.

Mr Monk was accustomed to remaining calm in the face of sudden surprises. But this time his usual equanimity failed him.

The servant saw that his announcement had shaken the little man. 'You're not related to the poor woman, are you?' he enquired.

'I am a close friend', said Mr Monk, who had come to the conclusion that it would be wise to conceal his true occupation for as long as was feasible. 'What you have told me, young man, is most distressing'.

'We're all at sixes and sevens', the servant confided. 'His Lordship and his daughter returned to the Manor last night after an absence of many years. And now, today, they have been welcomed home by this terrible event'.

'Can you tell me what precisely has happened?'

Pacing back and forth along the side of the house, Mr Monk was made privy to the following:

The unusual absence of the butler had that morning been remarked. He had been seen for the last time on the previous evening, when he had returned from a walk in the delightful summer air.

Mr Monk reminded himself that the man had telephoned from Bridgetown to Scotland Yard at 10:30 p.m. So it seemed likely that it was from *that* excursion that he had been seen to return.

This morning, it was noted that the door to the Perkins' bedroom was standing open. On peeking inside, the dead body of Mrs Perkins had been discovered in their communal bed; her throat had been cut by a sharp blade, probably a razor. And the staff—always ready to believe the worst of each other—had jumped to the conclusion that the crime had been committed by her husband, who had then fled the scene.

Yet the little man wondered if that view of the events was in fact accurate. The various male and female servants had only been engaged by the butler less than 24 hours previously, upon the unanticipated arrival of Lord Kingwood and his daughter. None of them reported having observed the slightest discord between Mr and Mrs Perkins, and the butler had been thought of as a good-natured, friendly man by all and sundry.

How, they marvelled, could such a kindly soul be driven to such a terrible deed?

And above all else, Mr Monk asked himself, why would a man on the verge of committing an act of violence place a call to Scotland Yard, inviting their presence at the scene of his impending crime?

'How is Lord Kingwood holding up under these tragic circumstances?' asked Mr Monk with visible concern.

'Bravely', replied the servant, rather enthusiastically. 'He made very little fuss and sent immediately for the constable'.

'Well done', said Mr Monk, with matching enthusiasm. 'And do you expect the constable soon?'

'Jimmy, the gardener's son, has gone off to fetch him on his bicycle'.

'Yes, I met him on the road. He cried out that there had been a murder at the Manor, but I thought he was only sporting with me'.

'Will detectives come?' asked the servant, with evident trepidation in his voice.

'I hope not', said Mr Monk shamelessly. 'I can't stand those stuffed shirts!'

III

Ten minutes later, Mr Monk—who had freed himself with some difficulty from the young servant's company—waved the gardener's boy Jimmy and the constable, both on bicycles, to a stop in the lane just outside Kingwood Manor's wide gate.

The constable seemed at first about to take some action, as he suspected that the unimposing man who had flagged him down was perhaps either guilty of or at the least an accomplice to the crime he had been summoned to investigate. But when Mr Monk drew a sheaf of well thumbed papers from his pocket and presented them to the officer, that worthy converted his aggressive posture to one of deferential politeness.

'Your name, my good man?' enquired Mr Monk.

'O'Leigh, at your service, sir. Patrick O'Leigh', said the constable, whose red hair, blue eyes and rasping brogue conspired to indicate his Irish ancestry.

'Very well, Patrick O'Leigh, I shall accompany you up to the Manor. You may test your mettle against the challenging

case that awaits you there, but any instructions I may give
you, you must follow without question'.

'Indeed I will, Your Honour'.

'I see you understand my position. And now I must
consult with my good friend Jimmy here'.

Jimmy examined the little man with a mistrustful gaze.
'I ain't your friend', he said roughly.

'But I am yours, Jimmy, for I intend to allow you to earn
six shillings', came the response. 'And the constable will
assure you that you would do well to obey me'.

'The gennelman's a mucky muck with the secret police',
the constable whispered, his attitude fawning.

'So you now understand', said Mr Monk, 'but you must
keep that knowledge to yourself'.

The boy said nothing, but stuck out his hand for the
promised payment.

'I shall give you three shillings in advance', said Mr Monk,
laying the silver on the lad's palm. 'You will receive the balance when this case has been satisfactorily concluded and
you have kept my confidence'.

'When will the case be concluded?' asked young Jimmy.

'When it is no longer necessary for you to hold your
tongue', the little man replied. 'Now attend me closely.
You will find the tracks of an automobile on the east side
of the Manor. There was considerable rain last night, so the
tracks will be easy to see. They curve around to the rear of
the house. Is there a back gate?'

The boy nodded.

'Then you will find that the tracks go through it. You
must follow them on your bicycle until you lose them…or
until you discover where they lead. When you bring me a
useful report, then—'

The boy kept silent, but his eyes spoke volumes.

'—then instead of receiving three additional shillings, you shall have six!'

'Rather!' said the boy, and he clambered aboard his machine and hastened off along the path.

'Where are you off to?' Mr Monk called after him.

'The back gate!' cried Jimmy, and he disappeared from sight behind a stand of shubbery.

'A clever lad', remarked the little man, nodding approvingly. 'Now be off with you, Patrick O'Leigh, and do your best to be just as clever'.

A moment later, the constable passed through the gate into the park. Mr Monk followed him, then veered off onto a narrow side path through the bushes, a path he suspected would ultimately lead him to the east side of the house. This suspicion proved well founded, as he soon stood before a side entrance to Kingwood Manor, at the precise spot where, as the servants paced to and fro, he had noted the ruts of an automobile's wheels baked into the previous night's mud.

Just then he heard loud voices and footsteps from within. He scurried around to the front of the house and slipped through the door—which still stood open—into a marble foyer, from which a broad staircase led to the upper floors.

At the foot of the stairs stood a man and a woman, and the respectful posture of the servants in the foyer made it clear that they must be Lord Kingwood and his daughter.

As Mr Monk made his entrance, the lord of the manor was addressing those of his people who stood there assembled. 'It is impossible to understand what has occurred here', said Lord Kingwood, 'and I urge you all to suspend your judgements for the time being. All we know for certain is that John Perkins, my old butler, has disappeared and that his wife has been murdered, and that two valuable canvases have been cut from their frames in the painting gallery'.

His Lordship, who understandably seemed quite upset with these facts, paused briefly and then demanded, 'Which of you was the last to enter the gallery?'

The servants, men and women alike, stared at each other in bewilderment. Then the young man with whom Mr Monk had previously spoken stepped forward.

'Mr Perkins forbade us to go into that room', said he. 'Only *he* had the key. And the rest of us were only engaged last evening'.

'So John Perkins was the only one who could have had access to the gallery?' said Lord Kingwood, shaking his head in perplexity. Then he glanced sharply around the foyer and asked, 'Have the police not yet arrived?'

The Bridgetown constable stepped forward and introduced himself, and Lord Kingwood and his daughter led the man upstairs to the second floor, where the painting gallery was situated. The servants remained in the foyer, whispering amongst themselves.

Mr Monk had observed these proceedings in silence, half concealed behind one of the columns which supported the foyer's ceiling. He had admired the thin, aristocratic appearance of Lord Kingwood, unbent despite the man's advanced age, and the sympathetic face with its high forehead and a full moustache that extended to the corners of his mouth. His daughter was almost as tall as her father, and possessed the same regular features.

When the two of them and the constable had ascended out of sight, Mr Monk approached the young servant, who seemed surprised to see him still there. The little man led him off to a corner and engaged him in a conversation which seemed to be of no little significance, for the servant's face revealed increasing concern as the exchange unfolded.

• • ● • •

Not half an hour later, Mr Monk slipped outside. The first human creature he encountered was the lad he had set on the trail of the automobile that appeared to have left Kingwood Manor via the back gate on the previous evening.

'I followed the tracks to the banks of the Thames', the boy reported, 'and there they ended'.

'Was there a boat landing at that point?'

'A narrow wooden dock, sir, yes. And now...'

Jimmy held out his hand, and Mr Monk dropped six shillings upon it. 'That makes nine shillings in all', he said. 'Would you like to try for twelve?'

'Indeed, sir!' came the rejoinder.

'Then get back on your bicycle and deliver this sealed envelope to the telegraph office in Bridgetown. Here is the money to send it off, but you must tell no one, do you understand?'

The boy nodded, and eyed Mr Monk—who had delivered these instructions in a tone that did indeed suggest him to be a 'mucky muck' with the police—fearfully.

An instant later, the young messenger was on his way, pedalling furiously.

And Mr Monk planted himself on a bench in a corner of the foyer to await the constable's return.

IV

The manly Patrick O'Leigh descended the staircase alone; Lord Kingwood and his daughter had remained upstairs.

He brought with him a message for the servants from their employer—that they should go on with their duties as if nothing out of the ordinary had occurred—and then stepped outside.

Mr Monk accompanied him.

'What will you do now, my good fellow?' the little man enquired.

'At His Lordship's request, I am off to notify the coroner and the doctor', Patrick replied.

'If I am not incorrect', said Mr Monk, 'the coroner is Sir Francis Foreman, who resides in Willow Court?' When the constable nodded his agreement, the little man went on: 'That is quite some distance from here'.

'Three quarters of an hour by bicycle', said Patrick.

'If Sir Francis steps immediately into his automobile', Mr Monk remarked, 'then it will be at least an hour before he reaches us'.

'Longer than that, sir', said the constable. 'Sir Francis lives quite simply. He has no automobile. But His Lordship will drive over to fetch him at mid-day. Meanwhile, he will notify Scotland Yard. The telephone in the Manor is out of service, so he will have to go to Bridgetown to place the call'.

'You did not inform him of my presence?'

'Certainly not! You specifically instructed me not to do so'.

'Good man! It would not have been so terrible if you had. But then the servants would have learned the truth, and I would have been sorry of that: it is better that I remain unidentified, which will allow me to hear things that might be concealed from an officer of the police'.

'Is there anything else you have to say to me, sir?'

'Nothing, my friend. You may hop onto your bicycle and set off for Sir Francis Foreman'.

The constable departed, and Mr Monk strolled slowly back to the house. As he neared the front door, the servant with whom he had already spoken several times that morning came out to meet him.

'Lord Kingwood wishes to see you', said he.

'Lord Kingwood? Me? How does he know that I am here?'

'Perhaps he was informed by one of the other servants', came the reply. 'I have, of course, not mentioned that someone was looking for John Perkins'.

These words were accompanied by an expression of some mistrust.

Mr Monk grinned: it seemed as if these people were somehow connecting him with the unhappy events of the last 24 hours. Perhaps they even suspected him of the murder! The little man had always been appreciative of comic developments.

A minute later, he was in Lord Kingwood's study, face to face with the man himself.

He had long since reached the conclusion that he must preserve his incognito as best he could, even after the eventual arrival of other functionaries from the Yard. What he referred to as 'silent observation' had often helped him to unravel a difficult puzzle.

Lord Kingwood invited him to take a chair.

'I have been informed', said he, 'that you have come here to see my old butler, John Perkins. You have, I trust, been told that present circumstances have made your request impossible to accommodate. Those same circumstances force me to pose several pressing questions to you'.

Without rising from his chair, Mr Monk made a silent bow.

'What is your name?'

'Monk, my Lord, James Monk', the little man replied, knowing full well that his name was not well enough known to the general public to reveal his occupation.

'And what did you want with Perkins, James Monk?'

'Nothing, my Lord. We have known each other for many years, but it has been a very long time since last we met. I came here merely to renew our acquaintance'.

'And how do you know him?'

'We were born in the same town: Durham', replied
Mr Monk, laughing to himself, for he had obtained his
knowledge of John Perkins' birthplace from the talkative
manservant that very morning.

'You have heard what has happened here, the tragic death
of Perkins' wife?'

'The servants have told me all they know'.

'And it has not occurred to you that your unexpected
presence on the scene might be cause for some suspicion?'

'Suspicion, my Lord? How do you—?' Mr Monk's face
was an innocent question mark.

'You must agree that it is rather coincidental, your arrival
at the very time of these sad events'.

Mr Monk now looked quite distressed. 'I thought that the
explanation of the events which have taken place here was
quite clear, my Lord: Perkins has run off with the paintings,
and his wife has been murdered. As I have said, I have not
seen him for years…and a man may change greatly over such
a period of time. It seems to me that one wouldn't need to
be a detective to understand what has occurred'.

'And what leads you to these conclusions?'

'Perkins must have decided to commit this theft long ago',
said Mr Monk. 'Perhaps his wife was opposed to that plan.
Your unexpected arrival, my Lord, must have been quite a
shock to him, forcing him to accelerate his timetable—and,
when his wife continued to object to his scheme, he had no
choice but to cut her throat'.

'What a terrible scenario!' exclaimed Lord Kingwood.
'But I acknowledge that it seems to take all of the facts as
we know them into account. I am eager to hear the coroner's
opinion'.

He fell silent, and Mr Monk said nothing further.

'You will oblige me', said the aristocrat at last, 'by remaining until the coroner has completed his investigation. As

an old friend of John Perkins, you may perhaps be of some assistance'.

'At what hour is the coroner expected, my Lord?'

'It has been agreed that I shall fetch him from his residence with my automobile this afternoon'.

'I shall be sure that I am here, my Lord'.

When Mr Monk descended the broad staircase, he saw before him the tall figure of Lady Mary, Lord Kingwood's daughter, poised on the bottom step and about to cross the hall in the direction of the front door. Just outside the door, a stableboy in livery held two horses by their bridles.

The little man followed in her footsteps and came to a stop on the inside of the doorway. From that vantage point, he heard Lady Mary inform the stableboy that it would be unnecessary for him to accompany her. She was accustomed to riding alone and had no fear of losing her way.

Shortly thereafter, she galloped across the park in the direction of the road. The boy watched her go, shook his head, and led his own mount back toward the stables.

There was a smile on Mr Monk's face, as if he had seen something that had mightily amused him.

He wandered now through the park, following the path in the same direction Lady Mary had taken. Not many minutes passed before he espied Jimmy coming toward him on foot.

'I've been back for ages', exclaimed that worthy young man. 'I couldn't find you'.

And, according to his new custom, he held out his hand, palm upward.

'Here are the three shillings I promised you', said Mr Monk. 'But you remain obliged to keep your knowledge of my true identity to yourself. Otherwise you will forfeit the next three'.

'The *next* three! But that would make fifteen in all', Jimmy calculated, his face beaming with delight.

'Indeed, we are well on our way to a pound', confirmed Mr Monk.

'I'd bite my tongue off, sir, before I'd tell a soul that you're—'

'Be still, lad! The trees and bushes have ears. You don't need to shout your promise for me to believe it. Now back to the house with you, and keep your mouth shut tight!'

The boy continued on his way, hands in his pockets and whistling a tune that could not be deemed exactly musical.

The little man consulted his pocket watch.

'They should be here within half an hour', he murmured. 'That will be just in time'.

He stretched out on the grass by the side of the path, in the shade of a tree, took a sandwich wrapped in paper from one of his pockets and began to eat.

For as yet that day he had had no time for breakfast.

V

The rumble of an automobile's engine could be heard in the distance. It approached at top speed but came to an abrupt halt when Mr Monk arose and revealed his presence.

'Good morning', said the little man. 'Have you found anything?'

The figure behind the wheel—who, despite his civilian clothes, was none other than Inspector Higgins—replied, 'We've fished a body out of the Thames, a little south of the point where you instructed us to begin the search. There were heavy stones tied to its feet'.

'Then good fortune has been with us', said Mr Monk, taking the empty place beside the inspector and nodding at the pair of plainclothes officers who occupied the automobile's rear seat. 'What was the condition of the body?'

'The skull had been smashed in. The man must have already been dead when he was cast into the water'.

Monk nodded. 'As I expected', said he. 'And now, Inspector, there is a side road just ahead. Turn in there, out of sight, and reverse your direction. Unless I am much mistaken, Lord Kingwood will be coming this way rather soon. When he goes by, follow him until'—he paused for a moment, then went on—'until the loving father catches up with his daughter. Quickly, Inspector, we haven't much time!'

Twenty minutes later, Lord Kingwood left Kingwood Manor at the wheel of his own automobile, apparently off to fetch the coroner as planned. Five minutes later, Inspector Higgins and his passengers were on his tail, far enough behind to stay out of sight.

At the junction where Lord Kingwood should have turned right to reach the coroner's home, he instead carried straight on.

Mr Monk chuckled aloud.

He chuckled again when, fifteen minutes later, Lady Mary came into view around a curve in the road, still on horseback. Lord Kingwood slowed down as he drew abreast of her.

'Now, Inspector, with all possible speed! Weapons at the ready!'

The police car streaked forward.

Within moments, they had closed the gap which separated them from the other vehicle, and four revolvers were aimed directly at father and daughter.

'Hands up!' shouted Mr Monk.

At the same instant, one of the plainclothesmen leapt deftly into the front seat of Lord Kingwood's automobile and took command of the wheel.

'I say hands up, Your Lordship!'

Both automobiles came to a halt, and both father and daughter raised their hands. The second plainclothesman climbed out of the back seat and grabbed the horse by its bridle.

'What is the meaning of this?' demanded Lord Kingwood with some difficulty.

'The meaning', replied Mr Monk, 'is that this is the very last time I shall address you as Your Lordship'.

With his revolver steady in his hand, he approached Lord Kingwood, whose face had now gone pale, and with a quick jerk of his free hand ripped off the man's moustache and grey wig, revealing in the place of the elderly aristocrat an attractive young man with a clean-shaven face and short black hair.

There was a brief struggle, the click of a pair of handcuffs, and Mr Monk gave a sigh of relief.

'Inspector Higgins', he said, 'it is my great pleasure to introduce to you Mr and Mrs Reckart, whose names will not be unfamiliar to you: they are the notorious art thieves we have been pursuing for the last several months'.

The unmasked captive swore violently.

'Such language won't help you, Mr Reckart', said the little man. 'It is unfortunate that you didn't keep to your usual profession—and, as a consequence, two innocent people have lost their lives. What that will mean for the two of you is—'

He finished his sentence with a gesture whose import was unmistakable.

The paintings which had been cut from their frames in the gallery at Kingwood Manor were found hidden beneath the automobile's rear seat.

'How I tumbled to it?' replied Mr Monk that evening to Inspector Higgins' question. 'There were a number of small indications, but first and foremost was the fact that it went against all the rules of logic for a thief and murderer to call in the police himself, even before he had committed his theft or murder. Last night, Mr Perkins was still alive, and the paintings were still in their frames'.

'How do you know that, sir?'

'I know it because the servant, with whom I spoke several times at Kingwood Manor this morning and with whom I had a further conversation after I learned of the theft, told me that Mr Perkins had been in the painting gallery last night'.

'But couldn't he have cut the paintings from their frames himself?'

'No, Inspector, as Lord Kingwood—for the present I shall continue to refer to Reckart by that name—only obtained the gallery key from him afterwards and made no mention of any missing paintings. Why would he have kept such a discovery secret until the following day?'

'But why would the *thief* announce the theft at all?'

'Because it had the advantage of explaining Perkins' disappearance. His acceptance of my most improbable explanation of the case spoke eloquently against him!'

Mr Monk continued: 'None of the members of the household had ever actually *met* Lord Kingwood before, with the exception of the butler and his wife. And the man *did* rather resemble the occasionally published portraits of His Lordship. But is it not reasonable to conclude that Perkins and his wife were not fooled by the attempted deception? That would explain the man's telegram to Scotland Yard: he had no idea how to handle the remarkable appearance of an impostor at the Manor'.

'And how do you believe the subsequent events unfolded?'

'The Reckarts had to work quickly, as there were certainly many in the surrounding area who *had* known Lord Kingwood personally. I suspect that Perkins must have failed to conceal his suspicion, and that failure cost him his life. The Reckarts then had to get rid of the body. The false

Lord dealt with the matter himself, drove it to the Thames in the middle of the night and consigned it to the water, weighted down with stones, in the hope that this would prevent its discovery until well after he and his "daughter" had made their escape. But Perkins' wife, shocked by the disappearance of her husband, was also careless enough to reveal her suspicion that "His Lordship" was not who he said he was, so she too had to die. And the murderer made a clumsy attempt to lay the blame for her murder—and for the theft which was committed later last night—at the feet of the missing butler. Reckart may be an experienced art thief, but he is an amateur murderer'.

'Were there further clues?'

'The automobile tracks leading to the Thames, which I reported in my telegram to the Yard and which led to the immediate dispatch of yourself, Inspector, and your two men. And then of course the false Lord Kingwood's mad offer to fetch the coroner himself, but not 'til this afternoon.

'Then there was the unexpected nature of Lord Kingwood and Lady Mary's return, in addition to Perkins' strange request that we not speak to His Lordship until he had first been consulted. And yet another inexplicable point: why did Lord Kingwood not summon Scotland Yard himself, the moment Mrs Perkins' body was discovered? Not until the following day did he send for assistance…and then for the local constable, not the Yard!

'Finally, don't forget the coincidence of the Manor's telephone, suddenly out of order at the very moment Lord Kingwood returned from abroad. Does that not indicate a desire to isolate himself and his household for the time being, in order to avoid any intervention from the outside world?

'All of my suspicions would be proven valid should His Lordship and his supposed daughter attempt to flee—with their ill-gotten gains, of course. Lady Mary's ride, which she insisted on taking without the company of the stableboy across unfamiliar terrain—for you will recall that she was but a child at the time of her supposed departure—was another indication, as was her "father's" automobile journey to fetch the coroner. The intention was that Reckart would rendezvous with his wife, and they would make their getaway and lay low in some far-off place until the storm of publicity to which their crimes would surely give rise should pass. He would obviously have promptly divested himself of his disguise, and the automobile in which they had arrived was not known hereabouts. As soon as I had snatched away his moustache and wig, I knew who we had: we have Reckart's photograph on file at the Yard. His wife's picture is unfortunately not a good likeness, else I would have recognized her much sooner'.

Inspector Higgins sat for a moment in silence. 'There was a great deal of guesswork involved in this case', he said at last, a trifle disparagingly.

'A pity you didn't indulge in such guesswork yourself, Inspector', replied Mr Monk drily. 'But at least this matter has left *one* person happy. Our young friend Jimmy has benefited to the tune of a pound sterling!'

The Stage Box Murder

Paul Rosenhayn

Paul Rosenhayn (1877–1929), born in Hamburg, and the son of a seafarer, led a cosmopolitan life. He was educated in Britain as well as Germany, and studied law prior to concentrating on journalism. He travelled extensively, settling for some years in India. He was also a prolific writer of screenplays prior to his death at the age of 51. Once the Nazis came to power, his reputation faded rapidly, and today he is a forgotten author. Many of the films he scripted have been lost, and he did not even rate a mention in the wide-ranging *Crime Fiction in Germany* (2016).

In terms of crime writing, Rosenhayn was really an exponent of pulp fiction. He created the American detective Joe Jenkins, who enjoyed considerable popularity during the First World War—at least until the United States entered the conflict. Several of the Jenkins stories were filmed. Jenkins was a Great Detective in the Sherlock Holmes mould, with a reputation for deductive genius and a fondness for disguise. Admittedly, he was much less memorable than Sherlock, and Rosenhayn's writing lacked Conan Doyle's sparkle. But the stories were pacy, by the standards of their time, and Rosenhayn's use of international locations helped to give them a veneer of sophistication. Two collections of Joe Jenkins stories were translated into English by June Head; this story appeared in *Joe Jenkins: Detective*, published in Britain in the year of Rosenhayn's death.

• • ● • •

(Berlin)
November 3rd.

My dear Clara,

I have given up hope of ever finding another engagement. Everything is full up…no one seems to have any use for an out-of-work actor in these hard times. The agents merely laugh at you when you talk about getting something. Anyone who's fortunate enough to get taken on at all, works for next to no salary. It's absolutely hopeless.

I don't know what to do. I've set myself a limit of time. If I don't have any luck by a certain date—then I'll give you back your promise. You'll be free then, Clara darling, to find someone else more worthy to be your husband…and I shall send you my blessing.

Till then, ever your
Kurt.

• • ● • •

November 6th.

My darling Clara,

This morning I went to the last theatre I haven't so far tried. It was the Rembrandt Theatre, and I saw the director, Mr Valoni. He was very nice, but told me quite firmly that there were no vacancies. Not even a walking-on part.

This was my last hope. I shall wait until the fifteenth, and then…

Kurt.

• • ● • •

November 9th.

Dearest Clara,

A miracle has happened overnight! But I mustn't be too optimistic, for it's all still quite in the air, and it has nothing to do with my real profession. However, necessity, as you know, is said to be the mother of invention. I'll tell you all about it.

Through an advertisement in the papers I made the acquaintance of a very rich man. I suggested an idea to him which pleased him immensely. It is this. There is at the moment no newspaper here which deals exclusively with local news and events. The big papers are given over almost exclusively to politics. It occurred to me that a paper devoted entirely to the interesting happenings of the town should be a great success. My wealthy friend was delighted with the idea. He is going to give it a three months' trial. If it makes good, there'll be a proper contract and a real job for me. And then, sweetheart…

The first number will appear as soon as anything exciting happens to justify it. We want to start with a splash. But—isn't it like life? There's absolutely nothing happening. Can you beat it! Every burglar, thief, and murderer seems to have packed up business.

Perhaps you are doubting my capability for the job I have taken on? No need to worry. I used to earn extra pocket money while I was still at college, writing little articles. You just wait, it'll turn out all right. The only thing I want is copy…Copy!

Kurt.

• • ● • •

November 15th.

Darling,

Our paper was born today. We brought out the first number and christened it *The Sensation*, though nothing has happened to justify the title. Just a few minor sensations. But we are still hoping. I enclose a copy for you. I am being perfectly indefatigable. I interviewed a foreign diplomat yesterday. This evening I went to the Rembrandt Theatre. It was a first night, a famous Viennese actor is giving a season there, and he played Romeo. I managed to get hold of the director's son in the first interval, and ask him for an introduction to the actor. He was very nice, and took me round behind to see him. I got a long interview, which has already gone to Press. I am writing this at the office, though it is long past midnight.

My love, *Kurt.*

● ● ● ● ●

November 16th,
Early in the morning.

I've got it! Got it at last! Copy, I mean.

Something startling has happened, far sooner than I dared to hope. Mr Valoni, the director of the Rembrandt Theatre, was murdered in his stage box during the performance last night.

Of course, I'm terribly sorry about him, but it is marvellous copy. What is even more marvellous—I am the only journalist who was on the spot when the tragedy occurred. You'll read all about it in the copy of *The Sensation* which I enclose. My partner is more than satisfied.

Kurt.

Special Edition

The Sensation
November 16th

MYSTERY CRIME

Director of Rembrandt Theatre Murdered in his Box

A terrible tragedy occurred yesterday evening between ten and eleven o'clock at the Rembrandt Theatre. Herr Sch…the celebrated Viennese actor, was playing Romeo before a crowded house. While the audience was intent upon the drama on the stage, a far more realistic and gruesome tragedy was being enacted in the auditorium itself.

Mr Valoni, the director of the theatre, entered his box punctually at eight o'clock, and took a seat in the shadow at the back of the box, as it was his custom to do. He had for some days past been feeling indisposed, so gave orders to the attendant not to tell anyone that he was present at the performance, and to allow no one to enter his box. He remained in his seat throughout the whole performance, breaking his customary rule of going on to the stage in the intervals.

At about ten o'clock Herr Ernst Valoni, the director's son, entered the box and remained sitting beside his father watching the play until about ten-thirty, when he left the theatre and went home.

At eleven o'clock, after the curtain had fallen for the last time, the man who attended the boxes noticed that the director had not moved. He knocked several times, but receiving no answer, decided to enter the box. The director's coat was thrown across the back of one of the chairs. The attendant took it up and approached the old gentleman, but even then he did not move. On looking more closely the attendant discovered to his horror that Mr Valoni was dead. Further examination disclosed a piece of cord knotted tightly about his throat. He had been strangled.

The attendant was confident that no one except Mr Valoni, junior, had entered the box. It is fitted with a trick lock, which can only be opened from the outside with a special key, and there are only two of these keys in existence. The box attendant had one, and the other was found in the dead man's pocket.

• • ● • •

November 18th.

My dear Clara,

Many thanks for your long letter, which arrived yesterday. No wonder you are interested in the Valoni case. Here is the latest news.

The box attendant has been arrested. That was a foregone conclusion, for he is the most obvious person on whom suspicion would fall.

I have just been to see the police commissioner who questioned him. He was very puzzled, for he had proved that the man had absolutely no motive for committing the murder. He had been in his job for six years, and in spite of bad times, was making quite a good living because he worked in the richest part of the house, and did very well on tips. He has a clean record, and his private life is unimpeachable. The murdered man's son testified to the fact that his father never carried more than a few odd marks about with him. A search of the attendant's house revealed nothing suspicious—certainly no money, though that in itself proves nothing. I asked the commissioner if he suspected anyone else. He looked grave for a moment, but said he did not.

Here I said something I am afraid I very much regretted afterwards. I'll confess to you. It is a well-known fact in theatrical circles that young Valoni could never get on with his father. In the excitement of the moment I let slip a few words on this subject. The next minute I could have bitten out my tongue. I saw the commissioner grow instantly alert. I did my best to wash out the effect of my rash words, I told him I knew the son personally, that he was a peaceable, good-natured fellow. I hope it's all right. Still, I shall keep a check on my tongue in future!

With love,
Kurt.

• • ● • •

November 20th.

Dearest Clara,

Fresh excitement! Events are tumbling over one another. Young Valoni was arrested today on the suspicion of having killed his father.

The box attendant protested his innocence, and witnesses were called in the shape of fellow-members of the theatre staff who were able to establish his alibi. They proved that he had been under observation practically the whole evening, and had not entered the director's box during the performance that night. The only person besides the dead man who had set foot inside the box was his son. The attendant was pronounced not guilty and dismissed.

A number of fresh witnesses were then called, among them the box-office cashier, who gave evidence to prove that young Valoni had taken sums of money from the cash-box far larger than he had any right to. On the evening of the murder he presented a draft to the value of 15,000 marks, which he demanded should be cashed from his father's account.

Later, two actors who were waiting to see the director, heard high words coming from his office. They recognized the voices of father and son, and could hear old Valoni taking the young man to task. One of them heard the son say: 'If you go on being so dam' close-fisted, I shall do something I'll be sorry for afterwards.' Immediately after this he rushed out of the room, slamming the door behind him. The two actors, who had come to ask for an advance on their salaries, thought better of it, and went away!

The Sensation is doing very well. Tomorrow I have to go to the police station and give evidence. I shall try and get an article for tomorrow's number. Good-night!

Kurt.

• • ● • •

The Sensation
November 22nd
Valoni Case

Son Detained on Suspicion of Murdering Father

The mystery of the Rembrandt Theatre murder grows daily more and more baffling. A number of witnesses who had seen and spoken to young Valoni on the night of the fifteenth were called to give evidence. Our special representative, Herr Kurt Harsfeld, who was present at the theatre on the night of the tragedy, and who has been called as a witness, writes the following description of the proceedings:

The last witness to be called was Ernst Valoni. He is tall and handsome, a well-known figure about town, whose charm of face and manner have caused sleepless nights to more than one middle-aged husband—it will be remembered he played a conspicuous part in the Frau von R—case two years ago. His face as he entered the box today was grave and pale.

The following cross-examination took place:

Police Commissioner: 'I want you to tell us what you saw on the evening of the murder.'

Valoni: 'I'm afraid I shan't be able to tell you very much.'

Com: 'Why not?'

Val: 'Because I left the theatre at half-past nine.'

Com: 'Where did you go?'

Val: 'I went to see a lady at her house.'

Com: 'Who was the lady?'

Val: 'Fräulein M., the Soubrette at the Stadttheater.'

Com: 'Then the lady can prove that you spent the evening with her?'

Val (hesitating): 'No…'

Com: 'Come, speak the truth. You did not see the lady because she was at the Stadttheater the whole evening from eight to eleven o'clock.'

Val: 'That's quite true. I went to her house, but I didn't see her.'

Com: 'Surely you knew beforehand that she would be occupied at the theatre the whole evening?'

Val: 'Yes, I did know that. But…I had reason to believe that she would not go to the theatre.'

Com: 'Did Fräulein M. express any such intention?'

Val: 'No.'

Com: 'Then perhaps you will explain why you had this strange idea?'

Val (hesitating): 'If you insist—I had reason to be jealous, that is, suspicious. I kept a watch on her villa that evening.'

Com: 'Hm...Has Fräulein M. ever given you cause for jealousy?'

Val: 'No, but—'

Com: 'Well, what?'

Val: 'I was rung up on the telephone that evening and informed that Fräulein M. intended to entertain a gentleman in her villa.'

Com: 'Who gave you this information?'

Val: 'I don't know. It was a man's voice that I did not recognize.'

Com: 'What time was it when you had this telephone call?'

Val: 'Shortly after nine o'clock.'

Com: 'At the theatre?'

Val: 'Yes.'

Com: 'Your statement agrees with the evidence in one respect. It is true that you left the theatre at half-past nine. Herr Harsfeld, of *The Sensation*, told us that he spoke to you at the theatre and requested you to obtain an interview for him with the principal actor. He interviewed the gentleman in your presence, and then at nine-thirty you said you had to leave, whereupon Herr Harsfeld accompanied you to the door and saw you enter your car and drive off.'

Val: 'That is so.'

Com: 'Whereabouts is Fräulein M.'s villa?'

Val: 'In the Kirschenallee.'

Com: 'Your chauffeur can verify that he took you there?'

Val: 'I drove the car myself.'

Com: 'When you reached the Kirschenallee what did you do?'

Val: 'I parked my car in a little wood at the back of the road. Then I walked round and hid in the shadow of some houses opposite Fräulein M.'s villa. I waited there for about two hours.'

Com: 'Did you see anything that confirmed your suspicions?'

Val: 'No.'

Com: 'You say you waited there for two hours. What did you do then?'

Val: 'I got the car out and drove home.'

Com: 'Therefore your car remained standing in the street for a period of two hours. How is it that no one noticed it?'

Val: 'There are only two houses near the wood where I parked it. Naturally no one saw it; that was my object in putting it there. And I switched off the headlights.'

Com: 'Very good. What time did you reach your home?'

Val: 'It was about midnight. My servant informed me of the dreadful news about my father...'

The Commissioner stood up. 'Herr Valoni,' he said gravely, 'six impartial witnesses have given evidence which disagrees entirely with what you say. You left the theatre at nine-thirty, everyone is unanimous on that point. But the rest of your statement does not fit in. You returned to the theatre again at ten o'clock.'

At these words Valoni sprang to his feet, pale and trembling. 'It's not true!' he cried excitedly. 'I left the theatre at half-past nine and did not return again.'

'The actors on the stage saw you sitting in the back of the box beside your father.'

'I never went into his box!'

'There is another point which deserves our attention. Your father was found sitting peacefully in his chair, with his face still turned to the stage. A proof that there was no struggle, and that he must have known who the person was who entered the box and sat beside him for half an hour. There is no doubt whatsoever that this person and the murderer were one and the same.'

'I never went into the box.'

'Herr Valoni, you are arrested on the suspicion of having murdered your father.'

News of the arrest spread like wildfire through the town. The general public, who have been following the case with the greatest interest, are openly divided into two camps; those who are convinced that Ernst Valoni is the murderer, and the others who hold him to be innocent of the whole affair. We shall continue to report further developments from an entirely unbiased angle.

• • ● • •

November 24th.

Dearest Clara,

The Sensation continues to flourish. We sold over a thousand copies in the streets alone today.

There are no further developments in the Valoni case, except that public opinion is veering round in young Valoni's favour. I heard an open hint at police headquarters that suggested he might be innocent. I believe Valoni has asked the well-known detective, Joe Jenkins, to take on his case.

Ever your,
Kurt.

• • ● • •

November 30th.

My dear Clara,

I met somebody very interesting yesterday. For the first time since the night of the murder I went to the Rembrandt Theatre, which has been re-opened under a new management. I was particularly struck by the appearance of a man I saw in the foyer. He was tall and broad-shouldered, with a clean-shaven, square-jawed face, and very piercing grey eyes that seemed to be watching everybody and everything. I made discreet inquiries, and discovered that he was Joe Jenkins, the famous American detective. I was introduced to him afterwards by some theatrical critics I know. He knew my name from having seen my signed articles in *The Sensation,* and congratulated me on what he called my clear and concise grasp of the situation. A charming fellow, obviously a man of the world. He asked me, by the way, to help him in his investigations, and naturally I agreed. Mr Jenkins's photograph will appear in the next issue of *The Sensation.*

Ever your
Kurt.

• • ● • •

December 5th.

My darling Clara,

Joe Jenkins and I have become great pals. I sampled his methods of work yesterday morning. At ten o'clock he called for me at the office and took me along to the General Post Office, where he managed to verify that young Valoni did actually receive a telephone call at the theatre on the evening of the murder, at exactly ten minutes past nine. It was put in from a call box. And now comes the remarkable part of it—which call box do you think it was? One of those in the foyer of the theatre itself. Would you believe it! Most risky, I call it. There are two deductions to be made from this fresh discovery. Either Valoni is innocent, and someone did actually make use of a ruse to get him out of the theatre, or—it was all planned. Valoni, anticipating that the matter of the telephone call would be enquired into, got a confederate to ring him up. Jenkins is straining every nerve to follow up this clue, and trace the man who used the telephone box in the Rembrandt foyer.

With love,
Kurt.

• • ● • •

December 8th.
Dearest Clara,

Joe Jenkins has found another clue. It seems comparatively trivial, but may lead to something really important. Valoni left the theatre at nine-thirty in a heavy fur-lined coat, but when he returned he was wearing a mackintosh. Strangely enough the mackintosh, which was very long and light in colour, has disappeared since the night of the murder. Young Valoni declares he has not been able to find it. The commissionaire, the programme sellers, and the box attendant remember the mackintosh distinctly because of its pronounced light-yellow colour. The box attendant further added that he noticed distinctly the smell of a certain Russian leather perfume which young Valoni habitually used. He said it had been noticeable in the box, too…Things are getting hot, aren't they!

Love, yours,
Kurt.

• • ● • •

December 12th.
Darling Clara,

Really, Joe Jenkins is overwhelming me with friendly attentions, though to tell you the truth he gets on my nerves a bit at times. He seems to have taken a special fancy to me—very flattering, of course, but apt to be rather trying when it takes the form of calling on me at almost any hour of the day or night. Not long ago he knocked me up at seven in the morning. I wondered what on earth had happened. And what do you think he wanted? Simply to ask me if I had not noticed the Viennese actor's slip at the performance of 'Romeo and Juliet,' you know, on the night Valoni was murdered.

'Didn't it strike you,' he said, 'that there was an unsettled atmosphere about the whole theatre that evening?' When I looked at him in astonishment, he continued: 'Didn't you notice that Romeo missed his entrance in the Chapel Scene in the last act? The stage was empty for quite half a minute before he came on. Surely you remember?' 'Of course I remember,' I replied somewhat crossly. Whereupon Jenkins burst into a roar of laughter and cried: 'Ha!—caught you! It never happened at all.' Now don't you call that an extremely childish joke for a famous detective?

Then he played another practical joke on me. I got home at twelve o'clock the other night and found my landlady waiting up for me. She said that Mr Jenkins had called at about ten o'clock and told her I had promised to lend him my dress coat. I don't possess any such garment. My landlady told him so, but he would not be put off. He wasn't satisfied until she had taken him to the cupboard and shown him there was no dress coat there. When I met him on the following morning and asked him what the idea was, he threw back his head and howled with laughter. Just a little joke of his, he said…All I can say is, he has a very funny idea of a joke!

Then again he will be utterly charming and delightful. Yesterday evening for instance, he came round at about nine o'clock and brought a bottle of rum with him. He insisted that we should make some hot grog, and I was quite ready to agree. He swept the ash out of the stove with his own hands and lit a fire. Well, his idea of a joke may not be mine, but his grog was certainly great. I haven't had such a jolly evening for a very long time. Jenkins is an amazingly interesting companion. I don't know what we didn't talk about—I remember though that I told him all about you, and showed him your photograph. He asks me to send you his very special regards.

Well, we'd got to about our fifth glass, when Jenkins, who was leaning back in his chair looking up at the ceiling, said suddenly: 'Things are going to start moving, Harsfeld. Quite soon.' 'Do you mean the murder?' I asked him. He nodded. 'Then you don't think Valoni is guilty?' 'No,' he said. 'And are you on the track of the real criminal?' 'Yes,' he said curtly.

You can guess how curious I was to know more. But I didn't want him to think I was prying, so I tactfully refrained from further questions—not that they would have been much good with a man like Jenkins.

Best love from
Kurt.

● ● ● ● ●

December 17th.

Dearest Clara,

Jenkins came in to the office to see me this morning. 'Be prepared,' he said, 'by this time tomorrow he'll be in our hands.'

'Who?' I asked.

'The real murderer.'

'No, really?' I cried, in great excitement.

'At noon tomorrow.'

'Where will you find him?'

'In the Café Sirius. You must come along, too.'

'You want me to be there?'

'Yes,' he said. 'You have helped me in my investigations so far, you must be in at the death. Think of the article you'll be able to write up for *The Sensation*. Be ready by a quarter to twelve, I'll call for you at your house.'

Picture me like a cat on hot bricks, waiting for tomorrow to come. I'll write and tell you all about it.

Ever,
Kurt.

• • ● • •

December 18th.

Dear Clara,

I am in a great state of excitement, waiting for Jenkins to come and take me along to the place where we shall catch the real murderer at last. Who will he be?…It is a quarter to twelve already. Ah, I hear Jenkins's step on the stairs.

(*An hour later.*)

My darling sweetheart…This is saying good-bye to you. The game's up and I have lost. Forgive me, if you can find it in your heart to do so, and try to remember that I did it for your sake.

Joe Jenkins is outside the door. His footsteps as he paces up and down are those of a gaoler. For he has kept his promise and shown me the murderer…The clock struck noon, I looked at Jenkins, waiting…'I thought you were going to show me the murderer at twelve o'clock…?'

'I will do so,' he replied.

'Well? Where is he?'

Then Jenkins stepped up to me and laid a hand on my shoulder.

'Here, Herr Harsfeld.'

He was right. I did it. It was I who rang young Valoni up from the call box in the foyer, to lure him out of the theatre.

As soon as he was out of the way I went to his room, made up my face, and put on the mackintosh. Having transformed myself into his double I walked through the theatre, and entered his father's box, where I sat down beside the old man. He never for a moment doubted that I was his son, and for that very reason he never spoke a word to me—they were on bad terms. Then I strangled him…

You would ask me why I did it? There is only one answer. Ambition. Vain, vaulting ambition. I wanted a big story, a sensation, something that would lift me and my paper on to the crest of the wave, pitch us right into the centre of the public eye.

Jenkins, who is no mean student of human nature, suspected me from the first. I see now the reason for those practical jokes of his. It was the scent of Russian leather he was after when he went to my wardrobe, and he found it. The mackintosh was not there, but he found the remnants of that when he raked a couple of buttons out with the ash of my stove.

It was an experiment, and it nearly succeeded—but I must pay for it with my life.

In spite of everything, I say Jenkins is a gentleman and a sportsman. He left me to write this letter, and he did not take my revolver from me.

At half-past one he is coming in…I hear the church clock strike…Farewell. Forgive your unhappy

Kurt.

Postscript

The shot has been fired.

I am sending you this letter together with his watch and his photograph. I shall make it my business to see that his memory rests without stain. You must forgive me, too. It was my duty—God knows it was hard to do.

Joe Jenkins.

The Spider

Koga Saburo

Haruta Yoshitame (1893–1945), who wrote as Koga Saburo, was a contemporary of the legendary Japanese crime writer Taro Hirai (1894–1965), who adopted the pen-name Edogawa Rampo, a loose transliteration of Edgar Allan Poe, in tribute to the father of the detective story, and founded the Mystery Writers of Japan in 1947. Edogawa is credited as the author of the first detective story in Japanese, publishing 'The Two-Sen Copper Coin' in 1923. Shortly afterwards, Koga Saburo followed his lead, and Japanese detective fiction began to flourish. Koga is credited with coining the term *honkaku*, meaning 'orthodox', to describe Japanese Golden Age stories in 1930, the year in which the Detection Club was founded by Anthony Berkeley in London. Rather fittingly, the Honkaku Mystery Writers Club of Japan is to this day a thriving body, established in 1970, and modelled on the Detection Club.

Although unknown to British and American readers during the Golden Age, Koga's work was very popular in Japan. Traditionalist in his outlook, he contributed an essay about Conan Doyle to a book published in Japan in 1934, and favoured focusing on the puzzle element of a mystery, rather than on its literary aspects. 'The Spider' dates from 1930, and is not a conventional whodunit, but rather a pleasing fusion of elements from macabre fiction and the classic detective puzzle. The translation presented here was undertaken by Ho-Ling Wong and edited by John Pugmire.

• • ● • •

The bizarre laboratory of Professor Tsujikawa stood on top of a pillar towering at least nine metres high, as if competing with the surrounding *keyaki* trees which had lost their leaves. The laboratory was shaped like a cylinder about 4.5 metres wide and 2.7 metres high. It had a round ceiling and the windows, all of the same size, were spaced at regular intervals. The building had been unprotected from the forces of wind and rain for a whole year and the chalk-white walls had faded to a grey colour in several places; at first sight, the laboratory resembled a misshapen lighthouse or a time-worn fire watchtower. I gazed up at the building in awe.

The world was shocked when Professor Tsujikawa, a leading authority on physical chemistry, gave up his seat as a university professor and started research on a completely different topic: spiders. People thought the man had become mad when they heard the professor had built a laboratory shaped like a tube, nine metres above ground somewhere in the outskirts of Tokyo. I, too, was one of those surprised people who did not comprehend the professor's intentions.

But the professor was completely indifferent to the voices of critique and ridicule and devoted himself diligently to his research. He had over a hundred jars in his laboratory, in which he kept countless species of spider. He studiously examined the adaptability of spiders, among other topics. Within months of the professor starting his research, one could find the strangest spiders from all over the world inside his bizarre laboratory.

Half a year passed, and the world had forgotten about the professor cooped up in his strange laboratory, but then one night Professor Shiomi, a friend from the university who had come to visit, fell to his death from the laboratory and it became news again. There were even curiosity-seekers who came out of their way just to take a look at the laboratory. Professor Tsujikawa naturally didn't let just anyone in, so the gawkers had to be content with staring up at the circular tower ten metres above them from ground level.

But the world soon forgot about this incident, too, and Professor Tsujikawa was able to resume his spider research undisturbed. But that didn't last long either. Because, a month later, the professor was bitten by a poisonous tropical spider. He was brought to the hospital in critical situation, muttering incoherently, and lay in a coma for a week before finally falling prey to the poison. People started to talk about the professor again, of course, but this, too, didn't last long. Now there is almost nobody left who remembers the death of the professor, his bizarre laboratory, and the hundreds of spiders which crawled around in there.

I am an assistant at the university's zoology lab and have some knowledge on arthropods, so the professor occasionally asked for my help with his research. As I mentioned, Professor Tsujikawa was a world-class researcher in physical chemistry, but he was a relative amateur in zoology, so even someone like myself could contribute a little something to his research. Though I have to admit that was only true at the start; it was hardly surprising that someone with the professor's intellect was able to master the topic better than I in very little time. I asked the professor once or twice why he had abandoned his special field of physical chemistry for spider research, but he just smiled and gave no answer.

The professor's family had trouble deciding just how to dispose of the laboratory. The building itself was troublesome enough, but the real problem was the hundreds of spiders inside, among which were several species deadly enough to take a man's life. The family didn't dare come near the building, so they let me take care of it, as I have some specialist knowledge on how to deal with the creatures. And so it was that I found myself alone there on the appointed day.

Stepping on the fallen leaves, I walked towards the bizarre building. After staring in awe at its cylindrical tower for a while, I climbed the steep staircase of reinforced concrete. At the top was a small landing, slightly wider than one *tatami* mat and, leading from it, the only door to the laboratory. Although the staircase and landing followed the contour of the cylindrical tower, there was a very slight gap between, because they had been constructed separately from the tower itself. (This may appear to be a minor detail but it will prove to be important later on, so I mention it here.)

I entered the laboratory.

I had visited the place several times when the professor was alive, and I was also a student of zoology, especially arthropods, so I should have been quite used to the sight; nevertheless it still gave me the shivers and I was rooted for a moment to the spot. Inside hundreds of bottles lining the walls, eight-legged monsters were running around and spinning their webs. Big *Oni-gumo* and *Jorō* spiders, yellow with blue stripes; *Harvestmen* with legs ten times longer than their bodies; Cellar spiders with yellow spots on their backs. The grotesque *Kimura* spider and trapdoor spiders, *Ji-gumo, Ha-gumo, Hirata-gumo, Kogane-gumo:* all these different kinds of spider had not been fed for about a month and, having lost most of their flesh, were looking around with shiny, hungry eyes for food. Some jars had not been properly sealed, and the escaped spiders had spun their webs on the ceiling and in the corners of the room. Countless numbers of the ghastly creatures were crawling around on the walls and ceiling.

I plucked up courage and took a careful look at the jars. Fortunately, the fearsome tropical poisonous spiders were still sealed up safely in their jars. Professor Tsujikawa had been discovered in a critical state and had done little more than cry out incomprehensible curses, so I don't know how he was bitten, but I was pleased to note that the spider responsible for his death could not have escaped. I proceeded to check every corner of the room, the back of the bookcase, the desk, and even the cracks in the floor, in fear that some other venomous creature might be lurking there.

I didn't find any poisonous spiders, but when I examined the back of the professor's work desk, I did discover an electric switch on one of the desk's legs. It seemed to be a strange place for a switch for the lights or the heater, so I pushed it two or three times tentatively. As I had almost expected, the lights did not go on, and neither, apparently, did anything else, so I had no idea what the switch was for.

By then I was getting tired and decided to take a rest. I brushed the dust off the professor's armchair standing in the middle of the room, sat down and lit a cigarette. Through the broom-like branches of the *keyaki* trees outside the windows, I could see the clear blue sky. The sunlight of the winter day's afternoon poured into the room.

I looked at the cloud that rose from my cigarette as I thought about the professor when he was alive. I have to say that he was quite difficult in his dealings with other people. Although he enjoyed considerable fame in the academic world, he was disliked by his fellow researchers. By contrast, his colleague Professor Shiomi was a lively and amusing man. The glowering Professor Tsujikawa always seemed to be the butt of Professor Shiomi's jokes. Even though his colleague's comments didn't appear to be malicious, Professor Tsujikawa seemed to harbour resentful feelings towards him—although he never expressed his feelings openly.

Then my mind drifted back to the day that Professor Shiomi fell to his untimely death from the laboratory's staircase. It had happened six months ago, at the end of summer. Professor Tsujikawa had invited me over, and when I entered the room, the professor was sitting in the very armchair I was sitting in, talking with Professor Shiomi who was sitting opposite him. In contrast to his usual manner, Professor Tsujikawa was very talkative, and his loud laughter sounded like that of a different man. When the professor noticed me he offered me a seat and introduced me to Professor Shiomi (who was sitting with his back to the door, which meant that Professor Tsujikawa was facing the door, which is why he saw me entering the laboratory. The position of Professor Shiomi's seat will become important later on, so I mention it here.)

I joined in the pleasant conversation. Professor Tsujikawa was unlike the man I initially described. Usually, when I was alone with him, I'd often have trouble coming up with topics to discuss, but here he was engaging in lively discussion with the always talkative Professor Shiomi, and even I got caught up in the cheery chat. I was very impressed by Professor Shiomi's characteristically humorous banter and very surprised to see Professor Tsujikawa giving as good as he got. It appeared then that the rumours of bad blood between them were ill-founded (but this naïve conclusion turned out to be entirely wrong.)

The conversation went on and on. I think we talked for about two hours. It was then that Professor Shiomi suddenly jumped up from his seat. Surprised, I looked at the professor, who looked as pale as a ghost. Screaming, he flew to the door behind him and rushed outside. I had no idea what these sudden events meant, until I caught a glimpse of a rare spider crawling across the floor. The creature had probably gone close to Professor Shiomi's feet.

'That's a kind of trapdoor spider. Shiomi probably thought it was poisonous,' I seem to recall Professor Tsujikawa say, as he pointed to the creature on the floor (I also recall repeating the same observation to the policemen who came later to examine the body.)

But I had not really paid attention to the professor's words at the time, because as soon as Professor Shiomi had gone through the door we heard a cry and the sound of something falling. Startled, I ran towards the door, but Professor Tsujikawa stopped me. 'Look out! There's a steep staircase!' he said as he pulled me back. Then he himself went out.

What happened next was also reported in detail in the newspapers. Having rushed outside, Professor Shiomi had slipped and hit his head two or three times on the concrete staircase as he made a fall which turned out to be fatal. Because rumour had it that he and Professor Shiomi couldn't get along, the policemen in charge questioned Professor Tsujikawa quite aggressively. But I testified that the two had had an extremely peaceful and relaxed conversation, and Professor Shiomi had only rushed outside because he had seen a spider crawling on the floor, which he had taken to be venomous. But it was not venomous at all: it was Professor Shiomi's own mistake, as was his fall down the staircase, so no blame was attached to Professor Tsujikawa. Nevertheless, the newspapers had a field day with the story and once again reported on how Professor Tsujikawa had quit his university post to focus on his new field of spider research, and how he spent his days inside a laboratory on top of a nine metre high circular pillar. The news attracted quite a number of people and, for a while, onlookers would assemble beneath the laboratory—which annoyed Professor

Tsujikawa immensely, as I stated before. The professor didn't cease his spider research but sealed himself inside his laboratory; I had heard lately that he seemed to be acting rather strangely, so the whole ordeal might well have affected him.

Anyway, sitting inside this bizarre circular laboratory, surrounded by monstrous spiders, I reminisced on the late Professor Tsujikawa; before I knew it, a small forest of cigarette stubs had grown in the ashtray on the table. Surprised at how much time had passed, I took one last look at the spiders inside the jars, just to be sure, and made a plan in my head to dispose of them. With the object of my visit to the room fulfilled, I reached for the door (as I mentioned before, there was only one door,) opened it inwards and was about to step out, when I cried out and gripped the frame. I had nearly dropped nine metres down to the ground. It was impossible: there was no trace of the staircase and landing which should have been outside the door! Far beneath my feet, I could see the disk-shaped concrete foundation that formed the base of the nine-metre high pillar, which seemed to beckon to me.

I rubbed my eyes and took another look. But it was not an optical illusion. I looked over my shoulder at the room but, needless to say, there was no other opening. I closed the door, staggered back inside and looked through each of the windows. And, lo and behold, I found the landing and the attached staircase beneath the third window.

I was bewildered. If I climbed out of the window to the landing, I could make my way down to the ground. Even though I was relieved that there was a way down from this strange tower anymore, I was mystified as to how a staircase of reinforced concrete could have shifted position like that.

After standing there pondering for a while, the answer slowly dawned on me. I looked carefully at the sunlight streaming through the window, and at the big trees outside the window.

I had it! This circular laboratory was rotating silently, with the pillar as its axis! Then I remembered. I had found a curious switch at the back of the desk when I had arrived, and had pushed it a couple of times. I thought I was switching it off, but I had unwittingly turned the contraption on and the concrete tower 4.5 metres wide had started to rotate. I made an estimate of the rotation speed: the staircase had moved about 4.5 metres, which would be approximately 20 degrees. That had taken about one hour, so it would make a full 360 degree rotation in three hours.

I thought about switching the contraption off immediately, but it seemed better to let it complete a full rotation, so I let it run until it returned to its original position. Once again, I sat down in the armchair in the middle of the room, and silently pondered on why this room had been designed to rotate.

It suddenly came to me. The hideous idea made me shudder. I stood up in shock and walked around the room, feeling as if I were going insane. I started to pull everything in the room apart and search feverishly. I needed to know Professor Tsujikawa's secret, and I was convinced it was hidden here somewhere.

After going through the room in a frenzy, I finally discovered the professor's diary hidden away in a secret compartment behind a bookcase. With trembling hands, I turned the pages. Inside, I found the professor's secret.

● ● ● ● ●

19XX, XX, XX
It's been three months since I decided to kill S. I finally thought of a plan. My reasons for killing S. are strictly personal and there is no need for me to try to justify it

for my own conscience. I only need to fool everyone else. I don't need to fool my own conscience.

Whenever my intention to kill S. wavers, I only need to think of the countless times I have been insulted by him. On both private and public occasions, S. has kept mocking me, ridiculing me, oppressing me, abusing me, all under the guise of 'a joke.' Whether he himself is aware of it or not, to me this is an unforgivable affront. But, as I have a timid nature and am a poor speaker, I can never put up a fight against his sparkling eloquence and I am reduced to being just a mere clown. Captivated by his repartee and wit, everybody laughs along, but nobody notices me, the victim, grinding his teeth. No, there is no need for me to write about these events any more now. The conclusion is simple. I hate S. I hate him enough to want to kill him. That is an undeniable fact. The only problem is the method of murder.

I have looked at various methods over the last three months. None of them was both certain and undetectable. But I did find one interesting method in a mystery short story written by a foreigner.

In it, person A wanted to kill person B. He rented a room on each of the ground and top floors of a large building and had the interiors made completely identical, so if someone blindfolded were brought into either room, he would not know which floor he was on when the blindfold was removed. And so, one night, A brought B to the room on the ground floor, overpowered him and tied him up. Then he lied to B, saying a time bomb had been placed in the room and was set to go off at nine o'clock, in thirty minutes, which would blow B to smithereens. A then knocked B out with sleeping gas and carried him to the top floor room where he stopped the clock at five minutes to nine and left B in the room.

The clock had to be stopped in advance at the right time, because he could not know when B would wake up.

After a while, B woke up. He found his arms and legs were tied but, as the knots were loose, he managed to free himself. Then he remembered what A had said (naturally, he thought he was still on the ground floor.) Shocked, he looked at the clock. Five minutes to nine! Only five minutes until the explosion. B jumped to the door, but it wouldn't budge. Panicked, he tried the window. Luckily (he thought,) it was open. Thinking he was on the ground floor, he jumped out. And, as you can imagine, the next moment he was lying in a pool of his own blood on the ground.

This is an ingenious trick. But if you think about it, to rent two rooms in a building and have the interiors be identical without drawing attention to yourself is not so easy, and carrying an unconscious person from the ground floor to the top floor without anyone noticing is also quite difficult. But the method's fatal weakness is that it depends on chance and therefore lacks certainty. If B wakes up and does indeed panic according to plan—like placing your order with the waiter—then all is fine. But if he stops and thinks calmly, he may first notice that the clock is standing still. Secondly, he might realize he is not on the ground floor anymore when he opens the window. And, most dangerous of all, should B see through the plot, his testimony would leave A no room to escape a charge of attempted murder. That is why I thought of an improvement: B should not be forced into doing anything. If B isn't forced to do anything, then even if the plan goes awry, nobody will be able to blame A.

19XX, XX, XX

I quit the university as planned. The construction of my laboratory in the suburbs is also proceeding on schedule. I had thought about building the laboratory inside my own house, because it would be easier to invite S. there. But no matter how brilliant this plan is, I fear that if I attempt it in a populated area, someone will notice, so I decided to build my laboratory in the inconvenient suburbs.

19XX, XX, XX

The laboratory is finally complete. I knew just the man for the laboratory's secret and I have no fear of anyone finding out. The construction workers all think it's necessary for my research. Who would even suspect I need the device to kill someone?

19XX, XX, XX

I have decided my research will be on spiders. I had considered snakes, but very poisonous spiders also exist out there, so I will use spiders.

19XX, XX, XX

I did a test run in the middle of the night. The results were excellent. I was worried about the rotation speed. We humans don't notice uniform motion if there is no object of comparison. Among the lower animals, there are those who don't mind even if they have an object of comparison. Flies, for example can stay motionless even on the back of a running horse. Flypaper makes use of this behaviour. If you smear some substance flies like on a chip of wood, then they will land on it. But these same flies will not notice if the piece of wood starts spinning and finally falls into an inescapable pit, until it is too late.

But I was not sure if humans could notice uniform motion without perceiving the world around them—not true uniform motion, but artificial uniform motion. Because of that, I slowed the rotation speed down considerably. People can see the movement of a seconds hand on a watch. But if you glance at the seconds hand for just an instant, you don't see the movement. That is why when people want to know whether a pocket watch is still working, they listen to it instead of looking at it.

But it is almost impossible to see the movement of the minute hand. The face of a watch is divided in sections and if you stare at it for two or three minutes, you might notice that the hand is slowly nearing the next section, but if these divisions weren't there, you probably wouldn't perceive the movement. And the movement of the hour hand is practically undetectable. That is why I did a test run with a revolution speed of one complete rotation every three hours. The results were very promising.

19XX, XX, XX

I have made another improvement to my plan. At first I had planned to be alone with S. in the laboratory, but I feared I would be suspected of having pushed S. myself. I need a witness, but if I arrange for one to be outside, he might realize the laboratory was rotating. Furthermore, because I need to execute the plan at night-time, when there is nobody around and nothing can be seen through the window, my witness cannot be someone outside. That's why I have decided to have a witness inside the room. I will need to make sure this witness doesn't notice the laboratory's movement if S. really falls to his death as planned. People usually go into a state of shock when something violent and out of the ordinary occurs, so even if I move the laboratory quickly back to its original state, this witness will probably not notice it.

19XX, XX, XX

I finally succeeded. I invited S. over and entertained him. Not knowing he was about to die, poor S. chatted on just as he always did, making fun of me. I hid my intentions and told him gruesome stories of poisonous spiders and mentioned that I had unfortunately lost one of them recently. S. naturally looked horrified. After a while, K., an assistant at the university zoology laboratory, arrived as per my invitation. I switched the secret button on and let the laboratory slowly rotate. No one noticed. To make sure no one would detect the movement, I kept on chatting. S. and K. probably noticed I wasn't my usual, silent self.

When the appropriate time arrived, I released the trapdoor spider I had hidden beneath my foot. It made its way sluggishly to S.'s feet. Having heard my terrible tales of poisonous spiders, S. turned pale, jumped up and ran towards the door (perhaps S. thought I had set the poisonous spider on him to kill him: he probably knew I hated him and his flight seemed to be genuinely fearful.) At that particular time, the door was a short distance from the staircase landing. But even a little is fatal. He missed his step, hit the staircase halfway down, bounced off a second time and finally hit the ground. He died instantly. My plan had succeeded perfectly, but even if he had not died instantly, nobody would have suspected me of murder. My witness K., of course, had no idea of the malice within me. Crying out in fear of the spider, fleeing to the door and missing the staircase: all were S.'s own actions. I returned the laboratory to its original state while K. was still in shock. The rotation sped up, but K. didn't notice it at all.

19XX, XX, XX
Some idiots are making a ruckus beneath the laboratory. I wouldn't be surprised if someone eventually sees through my plan, but there is nobody like that here now.

19XX, XX, XX
S. died. That is a clear fact. But his death does not offer me as much comfort as I had expected and I even feel something is lacking. I had planned to stop my research on spiders after I killed him. I thought that with his death, the university would offer me a lecturer's seat, but there has been no such news. I am disappointed, but somehow I feel I can't stop my research on spiders.

19XX, XX, XX
Still no news from the university. I have started again with my research on spiders.

19XX, XX, XX
I have succeeded in obtaining a male and female pair of a tropical poisonous spider species.

19XX, XX, XX
I feel I might be cursed by these spiders. My spiders, they glare strangely at me with eyes like a detective.

19XX, XX, XX
I am cursed! I had not noticed that S.'s ghost was inside this tropical spider! Look at those eyes! Those are the eyes of S. as he lay at the foot of the tower covered in blood! He has become a poisonous spider!

19XX, XX, XX
I am not going to lose. Not to a mere poisonous spider.
S. is a fool too. As befitting of someone who got himself
killed, he returned to this world as a spider. Come and
try. I will crush you. I will pick you apart. But that
look…ah, lately, I have become afraid of spiders. Those
eyes, those eyes… The horrible eyes of that spider…

19XX, XX, XX
I am afraid of the eyes of the spider. I can't sleep anymore
in this room. Tomorrow, I will finish this. Wait for it,
spider S., I will crush you with my bare hands.

• • ● • •

The terrifying spider diary ended there. I shuddered as I
finished reading. Suddenly I was aware that within all the
jars around me, hundreds, thousands of spiders, right of
me, left of me, in front of me, in the back of me, were all
crawling slowly towards me. In a frenzy I ran for the door.
By a great stroke of luck the landing was right there. I flew
down the stairs without looking back.

I caught a fever and stayed in bed for several days. During
that time, a fire broke out in the bizarre laboratory, everything inside burned down and the hundreds of spiders all
burnt to death. The police believe a beggar or tramp sneaked
inside and started the fire. Without the fire, that peculiar
tower would have continued rotating in silence, but probably
nobody would have noticed, I think, even now.

The Venom of the Tarantula

Sharadindu Bandyopadhyay

Sharadindu Bandyopadhyay (1899–1970) has been described as Bengal's answer to Arthur Conan Doyle, although there were naturally significant differences between their approaches to crime writing. He was educated in Calcutta, writing poetry and studying law, before introducing his series detective Byomkesh Bakshi in 1932. Most of the Bakshi stories—which have evocative titles such as 'The Gramophone Pin Mystery'—are narrated by a writer called Ajit. Bandyopadhyay moved to what is now Mumbai in 1938 to write screenplays, and he continued to work in the film industry until the 1950s. A writer as versatile as he was popular, he also wrote stories of the supernatural (he created a ghost-hunter called Baroda), historical stories, and children's fiction. Films and television series based on his stories continue to be popular to this day.

Bakshi is a Satyanweshi, or truth-seeker, and he and Ajit form a pleasing duo, broadly in the Holmes-Watson tradition but distinctively portrayed. Pinaki Roy argues in *The Manichean Investigators: a Postcolonial Rereading of the Sherlock*

Holmes and Byomkesh Bakshi Stories (2008) that the Bakshi stories are 'generally aimed at solving principally social problems of the ordinary Indians in and around the subaltern metropolis of colonial Kolkata…Bandyopadhyay thus first of all negates the Eurocentric convention of granting primacy to the bourgeoisie.' 'The Venom of the Tarantula', first published in 1933, and translated by Sreejata Guha, is one of the most celebrated stories about Bakshi. This is another story in the 'impossible crime' vein, featuring an ingenious poisoning.

• ● ● ● •

It was almost under duress that I got Byomkesh to leave the house.

For the last month he had been concentrating on a complicated forgery case. He would sit with a pile of papers all day and try to conjure up the image of the criminal from it all. As the mystery thickened, so did his conversation trickle gradually to silence. I noticed that this endless ploughing through papers, sitting in the library day after day, wasn't doing his health any good. But every time I brought this up, he would say, 'Oh no, I am quite all right.'

That evening I said, 'I am not going to take no for an answer. We're going for a walk. You need at least a couple of hours' respite in the day.'

'But…'

'No buts. Let's go to the lake. Your forger won't give you the slip in two hours.'

'Oh, all right.' He pushed the papers away and set off, but it wasn't difficult to guess that his mind hadn't let go of the problem at hand.

While walking by the lake I suddenly spotted a long-lost friend of mine. We had studied together until the Intermediate class—then he had entered the medical college. I hadn't seen him since. I called out to him, 'Hey, you're Mohan, aren't you? How are you doing?'

He turned around and exclaimed delightedly, 'Ajit! It is you! It's been so long. So tell me, how is everything?' After exchanging excited greetings I introduced him to Byomkesh. Mohan said, 'So *you* are Byomkesh Bakshi? Delighted to make your acquaintance. I did suspect at times that the Ajit Bandyopadhyay who writes about your exploits is our old friend, Ajit. But I wasn't quite sure.'

I said, 'So what are you up to nowadays?'

Mohan replied, 'I have my practice here in Calcutta.'

We strolled about and spoke of this and that. An hour passed pleasantly. I noticed that during the conversation Mohan opened his mouth a couple of times as if to say something, but then stopped himself. Byomkesh must have noticed it too because at one point he smiled and said, 'Please go ahead and say what you want to say.'

Mohan said, a little shyly, 'There is something that I want to ask you, but I am hesitant. Actually it is such a trivial problem that it seems unfair to bother you with it. Yet—'

I said, 'That's all right, tell us. If nothing else, it will at least serve the purpose of delivering Byomkesh for a short while from the hands of that forger.'

'Forger?'

I explained.

Mohan said, 'I see! But perhaps Byomkeshbabu will laugh at what I have to say.'

'If it is amusing I shall certainly laugh,' said Byomkesh, 'but from your manner it doesn't seem to be a laughing matter. Instead it appears that a certain problem has kept you pondering—you are desperate to find a solution to it.'

Mohan said excitedly, 'You are absolutely right. Perhaps it is very simple—but for me it has become an irresoluble conundrum. I am not entirely stupid—I think I have my fair share of common sense; yet, you'll be surprised to know how an ailing old man, who is paralysed to boot, is duping me every single day. It isn't just me; he is defeating his entire family's attempts at strict vigilance.'

In the course of the conversation we had sat down on a bench. Mohan said, 'Let me tell you about it as briefly as possible. I am the family-physician in a very affluent household. The family goes back a long way to when the city was just coming up. In addition to other incomes and assets they own a market from which they earn a massive monthly amount as rent. So you can gauge their financial standing.

'The master of this house is Nandadulalbabu. He is actually my only patient in that household. In his heyday he was such a profligate that by the time he reached the age of fifty his health gave up on him. His body plays host to a plethora of diseases. He has long been rendered immobile from arthritis. Now there are signs of paralysis as well. There is a saying among us doctors that there is nothing strange about man's death; it is the fact he is alive at all that is a source of wonder. This patient of mine is a prime example of that.

'Words fail me in trying to describe the character of Nandadulalbabu to you. Foul-mouthed; mistrustful, crafty, malicious in brief, I have never seen a meaner nature than his. He has a wife and a family, but he isn't on good terms with anyone. He would like to continue along the same depraved lines as he did in his youth. But his vitality has sapped and his health doesn't permit such excesses any longer. Hence, he bears great bitterness and envy towards everyone—as if they were responsible for his condition. He is always looking for ways and means to pull a fast one on someone to prove his ability.

'His body is weak and he has a heart condition too— hence he cannot leave his room. He sits there in his den, heaping unspeakable indignities upon the entire universe with every sentence he speaks and filling page after page with writing. He has a misplaced notion that he is an unparalleled litterateur; so, now in black, now in red ink, he writes and writes. He is terribly upset with the publishers—he believes that they are in on the conspiracy against him and therefore refuse to publish his work.'

Curious, I asked, 'What does he write?'

'Fiction. Or it may even be autobiographical. Only once did I glance at a page of the stuff; never again have I been able to look at it. After you've read that filth, even a holy oblation won't cleanse you. I am certain that even today's young experimental writers would have a fit if they read it.'

Byomkesh gave a slight smile and said, 'I can see the character before my eyes. But what exactly is the problem?'

Mohan offered a cigarette to each of us, lighted one for himself and said, 'Perhaps you think that such a special character cannot possibly have any more qualities, right? But that is not so. He has another terrific trait—to add to his wonderful health, he has a dangerous addiction.' He took a couple of puffs on his cigarette and continued, 'Byomkeshbabu, you are always dealing with such people; the most inferior class of the society is regular fare to you. I am sure you are familiar with alcohol, marijuana, cocaine and many other such kinds of addictions. But have you heard of anyone being addicted to spider juice?'

I gasped out loud, 'Spider juice? What on earth is that?'

Mohan said, 'There is a certain breed of spiders from whose bodies a venomous juice is extracted—'

Almost as if speaking to himself, Byomkesh muttered, 'Tarantula dance! It used to be practised in Spain—the spider's bite would make people cavort! It's a deadly poison! I have read about it but I haven't come across anyone using it in this country.'

Mohan said, 'You are absolutely right—tarantula. The use of tarantula extract is very prevalent among the hybrid Hispanic tribes of South America. The venom of the tarantula is a deadly poison, but if used in small quantities it can provide a tremendous thrill to the nervous system. As you can guess, this venom is very tempting to someone who cannot live without a constant state of nervous excitement. But continuous use of this stuff can prove to be fatal. The user would be sure to die of a fit of palsy.

'I am almost certain that Nandadulalbabu had picked up this beautiful addiction at some point in his youth. Later, when his body became totally unfit, he couldn't let go of it. It was about a year ago that I came in as his family-physician and, at that time, he was a confirmed addict to spider venom. The first thing I did was to prohibit this; I told him that if he wanted to live he would have to give up the drug.

'There was quite a tussle over this—he wouldn't let go of it and I simply wouldn't let him have it. Finally I said, "I shall not let the stuff enter your house. Let me see how you lay your hands on it." He gave a sly smile and said, "Is that so? All right, I *shall* go on having it—let me see how you stop me." And thus, war was declared.

'The rest of the family was, quite obviously, on my side and so it was quite easy to set up a strong barricade system within the house. His wife and children took turns in guarding his room so that there was no means of the drug reaching him. He himself is practically immobile. So he is unable to go out of the house and collect it for himself. After making such rigorous arrangements to prevent him from getting at the drug, I began to feel a sense of immense satisfaction.

'But it was all in vain. In spite of all our precautions he continued to consume the drug. No one could figure out his means of gaining access to it. At first I suspected that someone within the house was secretly supplying the drug to him. So one day, I myself kept guard for the entire day. But amazingly, right under my nose he took the drug at least thrice. I could determine this by checking his pulse, but I could not figure out when and how he did it.

'Since then I have searched every nook and cranny of his room, I have stopped any outsider from coming into contact with him, and yet I have been unsuccessful in stopping him from getting his narcotic fix. This is where things stand.

'Now, my problem is that I need to locate how that man gets hold of the spider venom and how exactly he tricks everyone and consumes it.'

Mohan stopped. I couldn't tell if Byomkesh had become unmindful during the monologue but as soon as Mohan stopped speaking, he stood up and said, 'Ajit, let us go home. I have suddenly thought of something and if my guess is right, then…'

I realized that the forger was on his mind again. It was possible that the last part of Mohan's story had entirely slipped by him. A little disconcerted, I said, 'Perhaps you weren't paying attention to Mohan's tale—'

'No, no. Of course I have heard him carefully. It is a most amusing problem, and I must say I am also quite intrigued by it; but right now it will be difficult for me to make the time. It *is* a rather difficult case that I am handling now…'

Perhaps Mohan felt a little offended, but he concealed the emotion and said, 'Oh of course, in that case just let it go. It certainly isn't right to bother you with such trivial matters. But, you know, if this mystery could be solved, perhaps the man's life could be saved. What can be more frustrating than watching a man—albeit a sinner—die a slow death right before your eyes, simply by consuming poison?'

A trifle abashed, Byomkesh said, 'I didn't say I wouldn't look into it. It will take me at least a couple of hours' cogitation to solve this riddle. It would also help if I could see the man himself. But I may not be able to make it today. It will certainly be a crime to let an unusual man like Nandadulalbabu die. And I shall not let that happen—you may be sure of that. But I need to return to my room right now—I think I may have been able to pin down the forger—I need to take another good look at the papers. Therefore, let Nandadulalbabu continue to consume his poison in peace for just another night—from tomorrow on, I shall put a spanner in his works.'

Mohan laughed and said, 'That is fine with me. Please give me a time that's convenient for you and I shall arrange for the car to pick you up.'

Byomkesh gave it a moment's thought and said, 'I have an idea it may even help lessen your anxiety for now. Let Ajit accompany you and take a good look around. After hearing his report I should be able to give you the answer to your riddle either tonight or tomorrow morning.'

It was impossible not to notice the shadow of disappointment that crossed Mohan's face at the suggestion that I should go with him instead of Byomkesh. Byomkesh noticed it too and laughed, 'Since Ajit is an old friend of yours, perhaps you do not have much faith in him. But please do not lose heart; in the company of greatness his faculties have now become so unusually sharp that a few examples of his perceptiveness might astonish you. It may even happen that he will solve your problem all by himself and not need my assistance at all.'

But even such high praise couldn't convince Mohan. His face reflected the despondency of an angler who fishes through the day in the hope of hooking a big one and then manages to land only a lowly bluegill. He said, 'All right then, let Ajit come along. But if he isn't able to—'

'Most certainly, in that case you can count on me.' Byomkesh called me aside and said, 'Take good notice of everything—and don't forget to inquire about incoming mail.'

I had seen Byomkesh solve many a complex mystery and even aided him in some cases. Observing him over the years, I had even picked up some of his modes of investigation. So, I thought to myself, could it be so difficult to solve this simple problem? As a matter of fact, Mohan's mistrust of my capabilities had hurt my pride, and I felt a little headstrong urge to solve this mystery all by myself. My mind made up, I followed Mohan away from the lake with resolute steps.

A bus-ride brought us to our destination. It was already dark. The streetlamps had been lit. Mohan walked ahead, showing the way. We walked down a lane off Circular Road; after a few minutes he pointed to a big house with an iron fence around the compound and said, 'This is the place.'

It was an old house, built in the baroque style. In front of the iron gate a watchman sat on a stool. He saluted Mohan and let him through. Then he noticed me and, after casting a suspicious glance my way, said, 'Sir, you are not—'

Mohan smiled and said, 'It's all right watchman, he is with me.'

'Very good, sir.' The watchman stepped aside. We entered the courtyard of the house. As we crossed it and stepped onto the veranda, a young man of about twenty stepped out, 'Is that you, doctor? Do come in.' Then he raised questioning eyes at me, 'This is…?'

Mohan took him aside, said something to him and the young man replied, 'Certainly, of course, do let him come and see.'

Mohan then introduced us. The young man's name was Arun; he was Nandadulalbabu's eldest son. We followed him into the house. After passing two doors, Arun knocked on the third. At once a querulous, hoarse voice answered from within, 'Who's there? What is it? Don't bother me now, I am writing.'

Arun said, 'Father, the doctor has come. Abhay, please open the door.'

The door was opened by a youth—probably Arun's younger brother—who looked to be about eighteen. All of us filed into the room. Arun asked Abhay quietly, 'Has he had it again?' Abhay wanly nodded his head.

Upon entering the room my eyes fell first on the bed, which was placed in the centre of the room. Upon it, clutching a pen, slouched the gaunt Nandadulalbabu, leaning against a pillow and glaring at us with eyes burning with hostility. There was a fluorescent light overhead and another table-lamp was placed upon a bedside table; so I could observe the man very clearly. His age was probably on the right side of fifty but all the hair on his head had become grey and his skin had taken on a pallid hue. His structure was bony, with not an ounce of extra flesh on his angular face. The cheekbones seemed to be piercing through his skin, and his sharp, slightly crooked nose was jutting out over his lips. The eyes were glittering from an unusual excitement. But within them there lurked the obvious signs that the ebb of the excitement would turn them back into expressionless fish-eyes. His lower lip hung limply. All in all, the entire face had a famished, discontented expression stamped upon every single pore.

As I stared at this ghostly physiognomy for some time, I noticed that his left hand gave a jerk from time to time, as if it had a life that was independent of the rest of the body and had decided to tango all on its own. Those who have seen a dead frog's limbs jump up when they come in contact with electric current may perhaps be able to visualize this nervous twitch.

Nandadulalbabu was staring at me too with vicious eyes, and soon, in that sharp, cackling voice, he ranted, 'Doctor! Who is this with you? What does the man want? Tell him to buzz off—at once—now…'

Mohan glanced at me and nodded to indicate that I shouldn't take my host's profanities to heart. He then moved the pile of papers that lay scattered on the bed to make some space, sat down and took his patient's pulse in his hand. Nandadulalbabu sat with a perverted grin stuck on his face and alternated his gaze between me and the doctor. His left hand continued to jerk erratically.

Finally Mohan let go of his wrist and said, 'So you have taken it again?'

'You bet I have—what bloody business is it of yours?'

Mohan bit his lip and then continued, 'You are only doing yourself harm with this. But you wouldn't understand that. You have let the venom addle your brain.'

Nandadulalbabu made a diabolical face and mocked, 'Is that so? I have addled my brain, eh? But you still have a lot of grey matter in there, don't you? So why can't you catch me out? You have placed your guards all around me—so how is it that you can't get to me?' He laughed in a vicious and obscene fashion.

Exasperated, Mohan stood up and said, 'It is impossible to have a conversation with you. I suppose I should just leave you to yourself.'

Nandadulalbabu continued cackling in that irritating manner and said, 'Shame on you, doctor, you call yourself a man? Catch me if you can, or suck on one of these and let me have my fun.' And he waved both his thumbs right under our noses.

Such gross and crude behaviour in front of his sons began to seem unbearable to me. Mohan had probably reached the end of his tether too because he said, 'All right Ajit, look around and take whatever notes you need to take. This is becoming impossible to tolerate.'

All of a sudden the victory-dance of the thumbs came to a stop. Nandadulalbabu raised his reptilian eyes towards me and demanded sourly, 'Who the hell are you and what are you doing in my house?' When he got no answer from me, he continued, 'A smart alec, are you? Well, you better listen—your tricks won't work on me, you get it? Better get out of here as fast as you can or else I'll call the police. Bunch of rogues, scoundrels and thieves, every single one of them!' He included Mohan in his sweeping glance as well. Although he couldn't quite figure out Mohan's reasons for bringing me there, he was obviously deeply suspicious of my presence.

Quite embarrassed, Arun whispered into my ear, 'Please ignore all that he says. Once he consumes the drug, he is completely out of his mind.'

How terrible is the venom that aggravates and brings to the foreground all that is mean and ugly in a person's nature, I thought. And how would anyone check the moral degeneration of a person who consumes this venom willingly and of his own accord?

Byomkesh had instructed me to take note of everything carefully. So I tried to quickly make a mental inventory going round the room. The room was quite large and sparsely furnished. There was just the bed, a few chairs, an almirah and a bedside table. There was a lamp and some blank sheets of paper and a few other writing accessories on the table. The written sheets were scattered all over the place. I picked up a sheaf. But after reading a few lines I shuddered and had to put them down. Mohan was right. The writing would have made Emile Zola blush. To make matters worse, Mr Litterateur had actually underscored the 'juicier' sections of the material in red ink to draw attention to them. In truth, I could not recall ever having come into contact with a dirtier or a more repugnant mind.

Revolted, I looked up at the man and found that he had gone back to his penmanship. The Parker pen was rapidly filling up the sheet of paper with scrawls. In a little penstand which stood on the bedside table, another crimson Parker fountain pen rested, probably awaiting a lull in the writing when the underscoring would begin.

This is exactly what happened. As soon as he reached the end of the page, Nandadulalbabu laid down the black pen and picked up the red one, only to find that it had run out of ink. He filled it from a bottle of red ink that stood on the table, and went back to underscoring his sparkling gems with a solemn expression.

I turned away and began to inspect the other sections of his room. The almirah contained nothing except for a few half-empty bottles of medicine. Mohan said they had been prescribed by him. The room had two windows and two doors. We had entered through one of these doors and I was told that behind the other lay the bathroom. I inspected that too; there was just the usual bath-linen, soap, oil, toothpaste etc. My queries about the windows revealed that they did not open out into the courtyard; in fact, they remained shut most of the time.

I tried to visualize how Byomkesh would have gone about it had he been there, but I drew a blank. I was just wondering whether to knock on the walls or not—might there be a secret vault or something?—when I suddenly noticed a silver essence-holder in one corner of a shelf in the wall. I examined it eagerly; it held some cotton wool and *attar* in some of the tiny compartments. I asked Arun in a whisper, 'Is he in the habit of using essence?'

Hesitantly he shook his head and said, 'I don't think so; if he had, we would have smelt it on him.'

'How long has this been here?'

'Oh, for as long as I can remember. It was Father who had it brought.'

I turned around and noticed that Nandadulalbabu had stopped writing and was gazing in my direction. Excited,

I dipped some cotton wool in the *attar* and dropped it in my pocket.

Then I took one last look around the room before walking out. Nandadulalbabu's eyes followed me; he had that mocking, grotesque smile pinned on his face.

We came out on the veranda and sat down. I said, 'I would like to ask you all a few questions. Please give me honest answers without hiding anything.'

Arun said, 'Certainly, please go ahead.'

I asked, 'Do you keep a constant vigil on him? Who are the ones on guard?'

'Abhay, Mother, and I take turns in staying with him. We don't let any of the servants or outsiders go near him.'

'Have you ever seen him consume the stuff?'

'No, we haven't seen him actually putting it in his mouth; but we have found out every time he has ingested it.'

'Has anybody seen what it actually looks like?'

'When he used to take it openly, I did see it—it is a transparent liquid which used to be kept in a bottle for homeopathic medicine. He used to dilute a few drops of it in a glass of fruit juice.'

'Are you certain that no bottles of that kind are still there in the room?'

'Absolutely certain. We have turned the place upside down.'

'Then it obviously comes in from somewhere. Who brings it?'

Arun shook his head, 'We don't know.'

'Is there anybody else other than the three of you who enters that room? Please think carefully.'

'No, there's nobody else. Just the doctor.'

My inquisition ended. What else could I ask? As I sat there trying to come up with something else, Byomkesh's advice came to my mind and I started afresh, 'Does he receive any letters?'

'No.'

'Any parcels or anything else like it?'

Now Arun said, 'Yes, once a week he receives a registered letter.'

I leaned forward eagerly, 'Where does it come from? Who sends it?'

Arun hung his head in embarrassment and spoke softly, 'It comes from within Calcutta. A woman called Rebecca Light sends it.'

I said, 'Oh, I see. Has any one of you seen what it contains?'

'Yes,' Arun said, looking towards Mohan.

I asked impatiently, 'Well, what does it contain?'

'Blank paper.'

'Blank paper?'

'Yes—just a few blank sheets of paper are stuffed into the envelope—there's nothing else.'

Dumbly, I repeated, 'Nothing else?'

'No.'

I was speechless for a few moments and then asked again, 'Are you absolutely sure that the envelopes contain nothing else?'

Arun gave a slight smile and said, 'Yes. Although Father signs and takes the letters from the postman, I open them myself. There is never anything but white sheets inside.'

'Do you open the letter each and every time? Where do you do this?'

'In Father's room. That is where the postman brings the letter.'

'But this is extremely strange. What is the meaning of sending empty sheets of paper by registered post?'

Arun shook his head and said, 'I don't know.'

I sat there a little longer like a dimwit and finally, with a great big sigh, I rose to leave. The first mention of the registered letters had raised my hopes to think that perhaps I had hit upon the solution; but no, that particular door seemed locked and sealed. I understood that although the problem appeared to be quite simple, it was beyond my acumen. Appearances can be very deceptive. It was beyond my capabilities to take on the old geezer with his body riddled with poison and paralysis. What was required here was the razor-edged, crystal-clear intelligence of Byomkesh.

As I was leaving with a crestfallen look, promising to report everything to Byomkesh, something else occurred to me. I asked, 'Does Nandadulalbabu write letters to anyone?'

Arun said, 'No, but he sends a money order every month.'

'To whom?'

With shame writ all over his face, Arun murmured, 'To the same Jewish woman.'

Mohan explained, 'Once she was Nandadulalbabu's...'

'I see. How much does he send her?'

'Quite a hefty sum. I don't know why, though.'

The reply drifted to my lips, 'Pension.' But I held my tongue and quietly walked out. Mohan stayed back.

It was almost eight o'clock when I reached home. Byomkesh was in the library. He answered my knock immediately and held the door open, saying, 'How was it? Is the mystery solved?'

'No.' I walked into the room and sat down. Byomkesh had been examining a piece of paper through the thick lens of a magnifying glass. He gave me a piercing look and said, 'Since when have you become this fashionable? Are you using *attar* nowadays?'

'I'm not wearing it, merely carrying it.' I reported every-thing to him in great detail. He listened attentively. In conclusion I said, 'I couldn't solve it, my friend, so now you have to have a go at it. But I have a feeling that an analysis of this *attar* may reveal something—'

'Reveal what—the spider venom?' Byomkesh took the piece of cotton wool from my hands and held it to his nose. 'Ah, wonderful essence. Pure, unadulterated amburi *attar*. Yes, you were saying something,' he continued as he rubbed some of the *attar* onto his wrist. 'What may be revealed?'

A little hesitantly I said, 'Perhaps under the pretence of using *attar* Nandadulalbabu…'

Byomkesh laughed out loud, 'Is it possible to hide the use of something that, by its smell alone, can alert people for miles around? Have you got any indication to believe that Nandadulalbabu actually wears this *attar*?'

'Well, no, I haven't—but…'

'No, my dear, you're barking up the wrong tree; try looking elsewhere. Try to think about how the stuff is smuggled into the room and how Nandadulalbabu consumes it in everyone's presence. Why do blank sheets of paper arrive by registered post? What is the reason for sending money to that woman? Have you figured that out?'

Dejected, I said, 'I have thought about all these things, but the solution is beyond me.'

'Think again, harder—nothing will come from nothing, you know. Think deeply, think intensely, think relentlessly,' and so saying, he picked up the lens again.

I asked, 'What about you?'

'I am thinking too. But it is going to be impossible to think intensely. My forger…' He leaned over the table.

I left the room and stretched out in the armchair in the living room and started to think again. For God's sake, this couldn't be all that difficult to solve. I was sure I could do it.

To begin with, what was the significance of sending blank sheets by registered post? Was there something written on the sheets with invisible ink? If that were so, how would Nandadulalbabu benefit from it? His quota of venom could not be reaching him that way.

All right, let us assume that the venom somehow managed to get smuggled into the room from outside. But where did Nandadulalbabu hide it? Even a bottle of homeopathic medicine wasn't easy to conceal. He was constantly under surveillance by vigilant eyes. There was even the occasional raid on his room. How then did he do it?

All this intense thinking heated up my brain; five cheroots were burnt to ashes; but I still could not find an answer to even one of these questions. I had almost given up hope when suddenly a marvellous idea occurred to me. I sat up straight in the armchair. Could this be possible? And yet—why ever not? It did sound a bit odd, but what other solution could there be? Byomkesh always said that if there was a logical inference that could be made, even if it appeared improbable, one had to take it to be the only possible solution. In this case too, this had to be, absolutely, the only possible explanation.

I was just going to go to Byomkesh when he himself came in. He took one look at my face and said, 'What is it? Have you figured it out?'

'I just may have.'

'Good. Tell me about it.'

When it came to spelling it out, I felt some pangs of hesitancy, but I brushed them aside and proceeded, 'Look, I just remembered seeing some spiders on the walls of Nandadulalbabu's room. I believe that he—'

'Just grabs them off the wall and gobbles them down?' Byomkesh burst out laughing. 'Ajit, you are an utter— genius. You are matchless. Those house spiders on the wall—if someone ate those there would be some abrasive rashes on the body, but no addictive surges. Understand?'

A little huffily I said, 'All right then, why don't you explain?'

Byomkesh took a chair and put his feet up on the table. Indolently, he lit up a cheroot and asked, 'Have you understood why blank sheets come by post?'

'No.'

'Did you figure out why the Jewish woman is paid every month?'

'No.'

'Haven't you at least worked out why Nandadulalbabu needs to underline his obscene stories?'

'No. Have you?'

'Perhaps.' Byomkesh took a long drag on the cheroot and said, his eyes closed, 'But unless I am absolutely certain about one fact, it will not be fair to make any comments.'

'What is that?'

'I need to know the colour of Nandadulalbabu's tongue.'

It looked like he was pulling my leg. Brusquely I said, 'Are you trying to be funny?'

'Funny!' Byomkesh opened his eyes and saw my expression. 'Are you offended? Honestly, I am not joking. Everything hinges upon the colour of Nandadulalbabu's tongue. If the colour of his tongue is red, then my guess is right, and if it is not—you didn't happen to notice it, did you?'

Irritated, I said, 'No, it didn't occur to me to notice his tongue.'

Byomkesh grinned and said, 'Yet, that should have been the first thing to look at. Anyway, do something—call Nandadulalbabu's son and ask him about it.'

'He may think I am being facetious.'

Byomkesh waved his arms and recited poetically, 'Fear not, oh fear not, there is no need for thee to quail—'

I went into the next room, located the number and dialled it. Mohan was still there and it was he who answered. 'I didn't tell you about it because I hadn't thought that piece of information mattered,' he said. 'Nandadulalbabu's tongue is a deep crimson in colour. It seems a bit unusual because he doesn't take much paan either. But why do you ask?'

I called Byomkesh. He asked, 'It *is* red, right? Well then, it is solved.' He took the phone from me and said, 'Doctor, it's good that I got hold of you. Your riddle has been solved. Yes, it *was* Ajit who solved it—I just helped him a bit. I was so busy with the forger…yes, I've got him too…You don't have to do too much, just remove the bottle of red ink and the red fountain pen from Nandadulalbabu's room…Yes, you got it. Please drop in sometime tomorrow and I shall explain everything. Goodbye. I shall certainly convey your gratitude to Ajit. Didn't I say that his intellect has grown really sharp nowadays?' Laughing to himself, Byomkesh put the receiver down.

After returning to the living room, I said a trifle bashfully, 'I think I am beginning to get it in bits and pieces, but please tell me in greater detail. How did you work it out?'

Byomkesh glanced at the clock and said, 'It is time for dinner. Putiram will be here at any moment to announce it. All right, let me go over it briefly with you. You were on the wrong track from the very beginning. It was important to find out how the stuff entered the room. It doesn't have limbs of its own, hence obviously it was being brought in by someone. Who could that be? Five people have access to the room—the doctor, the two sons, the wife, and one other person. The first four people would not deliberately bring the poison to Nandadulalbabu. So this was the work of the fifth person.'

'Who is the fifth person?'

'The fifth one is—the postman. He comes in once a week. It was through him that the poison entered the room.'

'But the envelopes contain nothing but blank sheets of paper.'

'That is the trick. Everyone thinks that the envelope might contain the stuff and so nobody pays attention to the postman. The man is smart; he switches the red inkpot with ease. The point of sending blank sheets of paper by registered post is to give the postman access into Nandadulalbabu's room.'

'And then?'

'You made one more error in your judgement. The money that is sent to the Jewish woman—it's not a pension: that custom doesn't prevail anywhere. It is payment for the drug; the woman supplies it through the postman. So now you see, the venom comes into Nandadulalbabu's hands and nobody even suspects how. But the room is under surveillance at all hours, so how would he consume it? This is where his writing comes in useful. The paper and ink is always at hand and there is no need to get up in order to take in the drug—the task can be accomplished from his seat on the bed. He writes with the black pen, highlights with the red one and at every chance, sucks on the nib of the fountain pen. When the ink runs out he refills the pen. Now do you understand why the colour of his tongue is red?'

'But how did you know it would be the red one? Couldn't it be the black one too?'

'Oh no, can't you see? The black ink is used much more profusely. Would Nandadulalbabu want any superfluous use of that precious stuff? Hence the highlighting—hence the red ink.'

'I get it. So simple—'

'Of course it is simple. But the brain that has come up with such a simple plan is not to be slighted. It is because of its simplicity that all of you were fooled.'

'How did you figure it out?'

'Very easily. In this case two facts seemed to stand out as entirely unnecessary and therefore suspicious. One, the arrival of blank sheets by registered post, and two,

Nandadulalbabu's excessive writing and highlighting habit. When I began to mull over the real reasons for these two, I stumbled upon the solution. You see, my forger too—'

The telephone shrilled into action in the next room. Both of us hurried to it. Byomkesh picked it up and said, 'Yes, who is it?...Oh, Doctor, yes, tell me...Nandadulalbabu is creating a racket?...He is ranting and raving? Well, well, that is inevitable...What was that? He is cursing Ajit? He is using the "f" and "b" words?...That is very wrong...very wrong indeed. But if he cannot be shut up, it can't be helped... Of course Ajit doesn't take it to heart, he is well aware that good deeds seldom go uncriticized in this world! You have to take the brickbats with the bouquets...such is life...all right then, goodbye!'

Murder à la Carte

Jean-Toussaint Samat

Jean-Toussaint Samat (1865–1944) was born in the Camargue to a family with literary connections; his grandfather founded *Le Petit Marseillais*, and he too was heavily involved with the newspaper, both on the business side and as a journalist. Although little-known today, he wrote crime and adventure novels with considerable success. A notable example is *The Shoes That Had Walked Twice (L'Horrible Mort de Miss Gilchrist)*, a mystery concerning the death of a female English landscape artist, which was translated into English in 1933, a year after becoming the third winner of Le Prix du Roman d'Aventures. The prize was inaugurated by the Librairie des Champs-Élysées in 1930 to stimulate interest in detective fiction in France, and pre-dated the establishment of the Mystery Writers of America's Edgar Allan Poe Awards (1946), and the Crime Writers' Association's Dagger Awards (1955).

Samat's other novels included *The Dead Man at the Window* (1934), which again was among the handful of translated French mysteries published by Lippincott in the US in the Thirties, perhaps because of heightened interest

arising from creation of the prize. His principal series character was a detective called Levert. This story was first translated
into English in 1931 for the magazine *Living Age.*

• • ● • •

'If I tell you the truth, you will not listen to me…
You will listen to me only if I say, "This is a story."'
Kalamatra to his disciple

His voice had such a profound ring of truth in it that when
he stopped talking the rest of us could not help staring at
each other. Then one of us—I do not recall which—said
aloud what we had all been thinking: 'You've got to tell
people about this. If you really know such things to be true,
you can't let it go at that. It ought to be published, at once.'

His only reply was a shrug of the shoulders.

Then someone else asked: 'Why don't you want to?'

He pushed back his chair, blew a smoke ring toward the
ceiling. 'Bah. What's the use? No one would believe me!'

Immediately we all started talking at once, loudly, like a
crowd of people gathered about a street accident, each trying
to make his opinion heard without a thought for what the
others were saying. Then we realized what idiots we must
seem, and with equal abruptness fell silent.

He went on smoking his cigar and watching the blue smoke
drift quietly toward the ceiling. He seemed detached from us,
detached from everything save those bluish smoke clouds and
the smoke rings that he was conscientiously blowing.

I stepped forward—we had by this time all risen from
the table save him—and said: 'All right. If you don't want
to do it, I will. If *I* publish it, they'll *believe* me!'

He was a scholar and a man of profound human understanding. He spoke twenty languages, and never once used
a false word.

Since he continued to look at me with doubt in his eye, I stamped my foot and shouted—yes, shouted in what must have seemed a ridiculously loud voice, 'I tell you they *will* believe me!'

Finally he laughed and murmured, 'Poor man!'

Well, here is the story.

Last night I dined at the home of my friend Georges Rainfort, the traveller. There were six of us altogether, six globe-trotters come to honour the One who was the Great Globe-Trotter, the eldest of us all and our acknowledged master. He knows all the highroads and bypaths of all the world. He has examined the seven continents, forged through the seven seas. There is not an island in any ocean that he has not picked up with a curious hand, turned over, studied, felt, weighed, only returning it to its native waters when he was certain that it concealed nothing from him. One of those men of whom one can honestly say that what they do not know of this earth is not worth knowing.

During the course of the meal he said almost nothing. Our own conversation he followed with an air of abstraction; his mind was elsewhere. We tried in vain to find the note that would set him vibrating in sympathy with us. Whether through pride or through disdain or through mere coquettishness, he refused to give in.

Then someone said: 'Queer, wasn't it, that Montblanc case? Do you suppose strychnine is at the bottom of every poisoning? How did it happen that *all* the guests at *both* weddings were taken ill? How do you explain that? A monstrous plot against them all, or mere coincidence? Poisoning? But with what?'

At this point he raised his eyes. His hands were still occupied in mechanically twisting and crushing a crust of bread. Suddenly he set it down on the table, brought his fist down with a sharp, decisive blow, and began to speak. His tone was even and low, as in a monologue, which was really what he was about to deliver.

• • ● • •

'Poisoning? What with? With anything you choose! *Or with nothing whatever!* I mean just that. People don't realize it, that's all. They think they know; they really don't know anything about it. They think that you have to use a *poison.* Strychnine? Obviously strychnine is a poison. A killer. But the symptoms of strychnine poisoning are too well known. And besides, you have to *get* strychnine. But why bother with strychnine? You talk about poisons. There are hundreds of effective poisons. Ah, but their symptoms, too, are all known? And even those whose symptoms aren't known reveal themselves in the autopsy? Well? There are things which are poison, and things which are not poison. Poison and nonpoison. There's no trick about murdering with poison; any fool can do it, provided he has the killer instinct, or the desire, or the need. There are so many people, and they commit murder for so many different reasons: vengeance, jealousy, cupidity, ignorance, hate, love, to see what will happen, or never to have to see again. Imbeciles!

'We want to murder someone. We haven't the courage to walk up to him and attack him, or for that matter to strike him from behind. So we go to the corner drug store, buy a penny's worth of rat poison, and give it to the son-in-law, the rich heiress, the man across the street, the husband, the lover. Then we have only to wash the cup carefully and wait until death strikes. But—there is a gauntlet to run: the family of the dead man, the coroner, the police, the judge, the jury, the jailer, and, at the end perhaps, the executioner.

'Our only chance of escape is that somewhere in that line is a man who will not do his duty, or will not realize it, or will do it badly—or who has better things to do. But there is always the chance that they will all do their duty, and then…?

'All in all, not a very clever method. But there is a possibility that the crime will not be discovered? Of course. Out of every ten cases of poisoning, four are due to carelessness. To drinking or eating poison by error. These four cases are banal, uninteresting. Five cases have criminal intent at their origin. Of these five, three are never suspected of being crimes, two are prosecuted as such. Only one of these two results in a conviction. A conviction, I said—not punishment. Four cases plus three cases plus two cases; that makes nine. Nine deaths due to poison. Banal, all nine of them. But the tenth? Ah, *there* is something worthy of real admiration! Yes, I mean admiration. For the tenth case is one of poisoning by a nonpoisonous substance!

'A poison which is not a poison! Ah, the man who discovered *that* I consider to be a genius. A criminal genius, perhaps, but a genius nevertheless. An expert. A man who *knew.* And I know what I'm talking about. Poisoning without poison? What with? Why, with the best dishes you ever ate in your life. With a whole series of them. In short, with a menu. A delicious little menu—or, if there is no hurry, a whole series of delicious little menus! Ah, gentlemen, that is art! Criminal, perhaps. Cowardly. But art! And I have known artists…

'One was a cook. An Annamite cook. Name was Nug-Hyen. Thû-Nug-Hyen from Phô-Vân-Nhoc. There was a man who knew how to plan a "menu" like no one else! I can tell you his name because he is dead now—poisoned. He had it coming to him. Another—Abbas-Ilahim, a Batavian innkeeper. He too knew his "menus"—those delicious-meals-that-strike-you-dead. He, too, died of poison—indirectly. And then there was Randriajafy, concession-holder and governor at Tsifory in Madagascar. His speciality was a "banquet for the inspector general." And a beast named Pitacunca, the sorcerer on the upper Amazon. He died early in his career. And an old scoundrel named Dolorès-Maria-Virgine Alvarez, who kept an inn (my God, what an inn!) in the Andes, on the highroad to Cuzco, over which the gold prospectors passed on their way back home, after two or three years of successful mining. And—there were so many others! Bah. Gone, all gone! In the long-run, they were all stricken down by the same hand with which they had struck so many others—and no one can say that they didn't richly deserve it. The hand of God—with a good bit of human assistance.

'Still, what masterpieces they were—those marvellous, deadly meals, dish after delicious dish that the host himself was the first to eat and enjoy! What reason is there for suspicion when the cook, or one's host himself, one's delightful, attentive host, eats as heartily as you?

'What reason for suspicion? None, of course. Naturally. One never thinks of it, never realizes what is happening—unless one *knew.*

'Take milk, for instance. Delightful drink, isn't it? Finest example of a healthy food, isn't it? And then the artichoke! Is there any more delectable vegetable (is an artichoke a vegetable or a flower?) than the artichoke, especially when it is young and tender? Healthy, too. Good for you. Milk is good for you. Artichokes are good for you. Of course. But if you eat a French artichoke *after* having drunk a glass of milk, the milk curdles in your stomach and you are ill. Milk plus artichoke means something harmful. Now do you follow?

'Nature contains quantities of foods that are all excellent if eaten alone but that have a reacting mate, another food that acts as a catalytic agent which, if allowed to enter the stomach at the same time, brings about the formation either of a harmful substance or of a deadly poison. Nearly any food, given the proper catalytic, may decompose into a dangerous acid or salt. It all depends on the proper constitution of the menu.

• • ● • •

'Sometimes the deadly menu is positive, so to speak; sometimes negative. We may call positive those menus that include certain dishes whose combination provokes a chemical reaction in the stomach or intestines which in turn brings about the formation of a poison. When the poisoner uses such a "positive" menu, he has merely to avoid eating one of the dishes in the mortal combination. Let us say, for example, that we have Ramon, José, and Josélita at table together. José and Josélita wish to kill Ramon. The two dishes which, when combined, will form the poison are, let us say, a stew (often it is a stew) and a salad. Ramon is on his guard, watches his hosts suspiciously. José passes the stew by. But Josélita eats hers heartily, takes a second helping—and naturally Ramon eats his. He doesn't know how these things are done. Then comes the fish and the roast; all three eat fish and roast. The salad is brought on. Josélita says: "I've had enough. I can't eat any more." "You're making a mistake," answers José, and plunges into his salad with a will. Why should Ramon be suspicious? He helps himself to the salad also. Now the two necessary elements are together. Stew plus salad equals death. He dies—almost immediately, or after a long interval, depending on the requirements of the case. But the meal was *excellent*, throughout!

'On the other hand, we may call "negative" those menus arranged in such a way that if one *fails* to eat a certain dish, the combination of the others is fatal. Let us say, for example, that Pierre is stopping for the night with Paul and Julie, on his way back from a successful season's gold washing. He is tired and hungry. They sit down to supper together. Pierre, vaguely suspicious, watches the others and says nothing. Hors-d'œuvre, entrée, fish—all are brought on and all are partaken of heartily. Then comes the roast—a tender young monkey. Paul says in an offhand manner:

'"Curious how much it looks like the corpse of a newborn baby!" Pierre's appetite disappears. "I don't believe I'll have any," he says, disgusted. "Don't force yourself," says Julie kindly. "Paul and I are used to it; you're not. Let me get an antelope steak for you instead." *They all eat some of the antelope.* Pierre has eaten *nothing* which the other two have not eaten also. In fact they have eaten even more than he—the monkey. There was where he made his mistake. He should have tasted the monkey in spite of his revulsion, for in the sauce or in the stuffing was the saving substance that would have prevented the poison from being formed. Neat, isn't it?

'There would be fewer unexplained deaths in Europe if the people in so-called "civilized" countries would only realize that such reactions can occur in the human stomach or intestines, and that you don't have to use poison to poison people with.

'The day they killed Thû-Nug-Hyen of Phô-Vân-Nhoc (he *had* to die) he blubbered like a child because they tied him to the chair so tight, but for a long while he refused to confess. "Is it my fault," he wept, "is it my fault if the chief engineer's wife did not eat the fish with the caper sauce? That meal was the best meal I have ever served. It was *perfect.* You ate every bit of it yourselves and nothing happened to you. Why are you torturing me now? Was it my fault?"

'Thomas, the chief engineer, whose eyes were red from weeping for the wife who lay quiet and cold in the next room, said nothing. He merely kicked the candlestick gently along the floor and under the chair to which Nug-Hyen was bound until the flame began to lick the seat on which the Annamite was sitting.

'Nug-Hyen blubbered and swore, then said in a weak voice: "Take it away, M. Thomas! For God's sake, take it away! The seat is burned through! Yes, I *knew* that Mme. Thomas hated caper sauce!"

'So they killed him. But before he died he had time to tell me what he knew—gave me the menus for those delicious-meals-that-strike-you-dead. And Abbas-Ilahim and all the others—they told me, too. Dolorès-Maria-Virgine was the hardest to persuade, but she was the best of all. An artist! A real genius!

'Forty-five menus they gave me altogether—but Dolorès-Maria-Virgine alone told me in addition her eleven incomparable dishes and her five delicious ways of brewing ordinary coffee. If you eat any one of those eleven dishes with ordinary coffee—or any other dish with coffee brewed in any one of her five ways—pftt! It's all over.

'There you are. All those people *knew. I know.* But who else does? They all *think* they know, but they are all, or almost all, completely ignorant. And if I were to tell them that people can die from perfectly innocent dishes, and do die—they'd laugh me out of Paris.

'Yet there is always the example of the milk and the artichoke. And the forty-five menus. And the five ways of brewing coffee.

'Now will you have a brandy? Come, a brandy can't do you any harm! Never? Well, I won't say that...'

The Cold Night's Clearing

Keikichi Osaka

In the course of his short life, Suzuki Fukutara (1912–1945) produced several notable crime stories under the pseudonym Keikichi Osaka. Among them was 'The Monster of the Lighthouse', published in 1935, which is included in Arisugawa Alice's *An Illustrated Guide to the Locked Room*, a beautifully presented book which offers readers a visual treat, even for those who do not understand a word of Japanese, in the form of graphic illustrations of each crime scene. Arisugawa lists twenty 'international' novels and short stories, including classics by Carr, Chesterton and Zangwill, and twenty Japanese stories, such as the Osaka tale, which he identifies as outstanding examples of the form.

Equally impressive is 'The Cold Night's Clearing', which dates from 1936, and is a classic example of the 'tracks in the snow' type of impossible crime puzzle. Both stories are included in *The Ginza Ghost* (2017), a collection of Osaka's mysteries published by Locked Room International. The stories were published from 1932 onwards, translated by Ho-Ling Wong, and edited by the owner of Locked Room International, John Pugmire.

• • ● • •

The season of snow has arrived once again. And snow reminds me of that tragic figure, Sanshirō Asami. At the time, I was working as a simple Japanese language teacher at an academy for girls in a prefecture far up in the north: let's call it H-Town. Sanshirō Asami was an English language teacher at the same school, and also my best friend at the time.

Sanshirō's parental home was in Tokyo. His family had made a fortune as trade merchants, but, as the second son, he wouldn't inherit and trade didn't really suit him anyway. So, after graduating from W University, he became a teacher, moving all around the country. He originally wanted to write literature, but he'd had little success, and by the time we became acquainted in H-Town, he was already in his thirties and had become the caring father of an eight-year-old child. Sanshirō could be a bit quick-tempered, but he was also a frank and lovable person, and we quickly became friends. And it wasn't just me: there wasn't a person around who didn't become friends with him. This might have been because of his wealthy family, but he was also very easy-going with his fellow teachers and likeable in his dealings with his fellow man, with nothing calculating behind his actions. So he wasn't really suited to walking the dark path of literature writing—which might explain his lack of success. I quickly noticed this as I became friends with him.

Sanshirō at home was a joy to see. His deep love for his beautiful wife and his only child was evident, as was the respect he enjoyed from his girl students, albeit tinged with envy. In fact, even though every teacher is destined to be given a nickname at a girls' academy, I have to admit I've never heard one for Sanshirō. That was almost a mystery in itself. Yet, in hindsight, what occurred may have happened precisely because of his beautiful nature.

At the time of the horrific event I was living in a house very close to the Asamis, in the outskirts of H-Town, which is probably why I was one of the first to hear about it. Sanshirō himself was away at the time and I was unsure what I should do. He had been sent by the Ministry of Education to a newly-opened agricultural school in the mountains, as a temporary teacher for the last month of the semester. The school vacation was supposed to start on December 25th, so Sanshirō was expected to return home that night, but the incident had occurred the night before, on the 24th.

The cousin of Sanshirō's wife, Hiroko, had been staying with her since the start of the month; his name was Oikawa, and he was a student at M University. I didn't know much about him except that he seemed to be a good, bright lad; that he belonged to his university's ski club; and that he had been in the habit of visiting his cousin here in the north every winter. (The snowfall here in December is so heavy, it's possible to ski from the rooftops.) Oikawa, Hiroko, and her son Haruo, who had just entered elementary school this spring, kept watch on the house during Sanshirō's absence. So Oikawa was Sanshirō's hired guard, in a way, yet the bizarre and horrific incident had occurred despite his presence.

Clouds had started gathering in the morning of the 24th, and the grey skies finally gave away around the evening, so by nightfall snow had started to fall. At first it was just dancing down gently, but by six o'clock it was falling quite heavily. Yet at eight, as if the show's final curtains had fallen, the snow just stopped, and a bright, star-filled sky could be seen from between the breaking clouds. Such sudden meteorological changes are pretty common in these parts. During the coldest thirty days of winter, the weather behaves strangely: by day the sky becomes more and more overcast and then at night, as if it had all been just a dream, the clouds part and the moon and stars shine coldly in the clear blue night sky. Local people call it *Kan no Yobare*: Cold Night's Clearing.

I had finished a late dinner around eight. Because vacation had already started at the girls' academy, I was preparing for a trip somewhere to the south. Suddenly Miki, a student in Sanshirō's refresher course A, arrived at my door, bringing me the bad news of what had happened at the Asami home. Despite feeling a shudder because of the cold weather, I immediately grabbed my skis and hurried there with Miki. As I was leaving, I could hear the Christmas Eve bells of the town church ringing, so it must have been around nine o'clock.

• • ● • •

Miki was a tall and lively girl, one of the early-maturing ones you see in every girls' academy. She had already mastered the secrets of make-up, the length of her skirt was always changing, and she was always filling the corners of her class-books with the names of poets in very small print. Miki often went to visit Sanshirō at his home. 'Mr Asami is teaching me literature,' she would say, but she also visited the home during Sanshirō's absence, so it might have been Oikawa, and not Sanshirō, who was 'teaching her literature.' Anyway, that night Miki had gone to Sanshirō's house, but it seemed as though nobody was home, even though the doors and windows weren't locked. Thinking this was a bit strange, she opened the front door and went to the back, as she always did when visiting. When she discovered the abnormal state inside the house, she hurried to my place, it being one of the closest.

I lived less than ten minutes away from the Asami residence by ski. Their house was stylish, like a timbered lodge. It was the right-most house in a block of three. The people of the house on the far left seemed to have gone to sleep already, as the curtains were already drawn. The house in the middle was also dark; a notice said it was for rent. When we stopped in front of Sanshirō's house, Miki was trembling and seemed as if she didn't want to go inside, so I told her to go to the house of Tabei, a physics teacher at the academy, who also lived close by. Finally, I got a grip of myself and entered the house.

● ● ● ● ●

Haruo's room was near the front door. A child's crayon drawings of 'a general' and 'a soldier with tulips' were pinned to the wall. In the middle of the room stood a potted fir tree, with braids of golden wire and chains of coloured paper threaded between the branches, topped by snow made of white cotton. It was the Christmas tree Sanshirō had bought for his son just before he had left for his temporary assignment.

But the first thing I noticed as I entered the room was the empty bed of the little master of the Christmas tree standing in front of a small desk in one corner. The blankets had been thrown back and the child who should have been sleeping there was nowhere to be seen. The silver-paper stars of the Christmas Tree that had lost its master sparkled as they started to turn and sway in the cold currents of air.

It was then that I found the other, temporary, inhabitant of the room. Oikawa was lying in the opening of the door leading to the living room in the back, face down towards me. I recoiled, but when I saw the chaotic state of the living room through the door, I pulled myself together, cautiously sneaked to the opening and looked at both the man lying at my feet and the occupant of the living room.

Sanshirō's wife, Hiroko, was lying with her head leaning on a stove which was standing on a galvanized plate. The awful stench of burnt hair hung in the room. I stood there for a while, trembling in shock, but finally pulled myself together, crouched and carefully touched Oikawa's body. It was not the body of a living person.

• • ● • •

From the disorder around their fallen figures, it seemed as though both Oikawa and Hiroko had put up a struggle. They seemed to have been beaten, as I could see countless purple welts on their foreheads, faces, arms and necks. I quickly found the weapon: the stove's iron poker, slightly bent, had been thrown near Oikawa's feet. The room was in chaos. The chairs had been overturned, the table pushed away and a big cardboard toy box, which had probably been on top of the table, had been thrown in front of the sofa. It was wet and crushed. A toy train, a mascot figure, a beautiful big spinning top and more had been thrown out of the box, together with caramel, bonbon, and chocolate animal candies. You could almost sense a childish purity from these toys which had lost their master.

If I'd been a witness to this kind of scene in the house of a total stranger, I probably wouldn't have stayed to take in so much detail of what I saw. I'd have been so shocked at finding dead bodies that I'd have run to the police immediately. But at the time I was less troubled by what I'd seen than by what I hadn't seen. It dawned on me that I hadn't seen the son ever since I'd entered the house. It might seem strange, but I felt more anxious about the missing child than about the dead people in front of me. Just like Oikawa and Hiroko, I, too, had been responsible for his safety during Sanshirō's absence.

The house was divided into four rooms. I quickly searched the other two as I tried to keep my fearful heart in check, but even after going through the whole house, I couldn't find any sign of the child.

Then a thought suddenly occurred to me: the sliding window of the room where the tragedy had happened was open. That was strange: nobody would normally leave a window open on such a cold night. I imagined that the individual who had beaten two people to death and taken the child must have fled through the window, failing to shut it in his haste. And so, with some trepidation, I returned to the living room. Inching slowly round the wall, and ready to take on the invisible enemy if necessary, I peeked out of the window, which looked out on a garden and hedge at the back of the house.

I saw exactly what I'd expected to see, there in the snow below the window. The chaotic prints of someone putting on skis were clearly visible, even in the dark. From those prints, two long lines went through an opening in the hedge and disappeared into the darkness beyond. Beneath the star-filled sky, I could clearly hear the tolling of the Christmas bells. They sounded eerie, like the whisper of the devil.

Without hesitation I returned to the front door, strapped on my own skis, and went round to the back of the house, to the open window of the living room. There were two parallel lines there in the snow, so one person must have skied there. Making sure not to erase the tracks, I went through the opening in the hedge and followed them. I'd only just started my chase, when I found an important clue: even though he was skiing on a flat surface, the kidnapper hadn't used both of his ski poles. On the left side of the tracks, I could see the snow being scattered around by the ring at the end of the ski pole every three or four metres, but there were no such marks on the right side. I felt anxiety in my heart. I was right: the skier was using a pole in his left hand, but couldn't use one with his right hand. That meant he was holding something else in his right hand. In my mind's eye I could clearly see the image of the child struggling in the arms of his kidnapper. I grew more tense as I followed the tracks, which seemed to continue forever.

• ● ● ● •

The tracks went through the hedge, across an open field, and towards a silent back road. This was a new residential area of H-Town. Here, there were houses with a lot of green space, spread far apart, and snowy fields. I couldn't tell whether they were farm fields or just open ground.

The snow had fallen from dusk till eight and almost no ski tracks had touched the fair snow skin. Besides some tracks crossing in front of people's houses, and dog tracks, nothing had disturbed the tracks I was chasing. But I had to watch out for my prey. I shuddered and continued to glide carefully beneath the silent night sky.

The ski tracks turned right at the back street and entered a wide snowfield. On the other side of the field was the main road that passed in front of Sanshirō's house, going towards the town. The ski tracks crossed the field diagonally, going in the direction of the town and looked as if they might get back onto the main road at some point. If so, I might be able to ask for help from a policeman on the way. My spirits rose at the thought, and I hurried across the large field towards the road. But my hopes were dashed in the most surprising way.

It had been a mistake in the first place to assume the tracks would continue on the main road. When I reached a point halfway across the field, I suddenly realized I had lost sight of the ski tracks. Shocked, I looked about me. But there was nothing there except my own meandering tracks! Cursing myself for my inattention, I hurriedly retraced my own tracks, looking from side to side as I went. But no matter how much I went back and looked around, there was no sign of those tracks. I felt perplexed.

But near the entrance to the field, I did finally manage to find the tracks again in the pale snow. Relieved, I went near them and followed them carefully like following a piece of thread, making sure I would not lose them. Once again the tracks appeared to cross the field diagonally, heading towards the road on the other side. I wondered how I had managed to lose them the first time. I cursed myself again, and proceeded very cautiously with my eyes locked on the tracks. This time I noticed something truly unexpected.

The tracks became less deep near the centre of the field. They hadn't been deep in the first place, but they became shallower and shallower with every metre, every centimetre I proceeded forward. Finally, to my utter surprise, when the track reached the middle of the field, they disappeared completely, as if the person who had been skiing here had flown right into the sky above.

Judging from the way he disappeared, the owner of the skis had to have grown a set of wings, or fresh snow had to have fallen on top of the tracks; there could be no other explanation for such a strange disappearance.

Still perplexed, I thought as hard I could. But, as I said before, the snow that had started at dusk had stopped completely by eight, and it had been the Cold Night's Clearing ever since; snow had not fallen since then. Even supposing it had, why would it only have erased the tracks here and not the tracks back at the house? Snow would have fallen everywhere, and all the tracks would have been erased. Well then, could a strange wind phenomenon have happened here on the field, with the snow carried by the wind erasing the tracks just at this spot? But no wind able to do that had been blowing that night. I stood still in the field, feeling like I had seen a ghost. The eerie bells had not stopped tolling and the sound carried across the field, seeming like the sneering of the devil himself.

But I couldn't afford just to stand there. The kidnapped child's safety was at stake. Two people had died in the house and I had to contact the police at once.

I went straight towards the town. Locating the closest police box, I reported the crime. But, even as I went back with a young policeman, I still couldn't fathom the disappearance in the field.

When we finally arrived back at Sanshirō's house, we found a couple of people from the neighbourhood there who had just learnt of the incident and were just about to go to the police. Amongst the people in front of the house was also a shocked Miki, who looked as if she would cry at any moment. Mr Tabei, whom I had sent Miki to fetch, was in the house, loudly opening and closing the doors of the rooms in search of the child, just as I had done.

• • ● • •

Entering the house and taking a look around, the policeman told us not to tamper with the crime scene until the detectives from the precinct arrived. Then he called us into the room Sanshirō used as his study, Miki included, and started questioning us. Both Miki and I talked feverishly about how we had discovered the crime and about the inhabitants of the house, occasionally interrupting each other. Tabei, however, was very calm and talked little.

Finally a stout, apparently high-ranking policeman arrived, together with several of his subordinates and started investigating the crime scene. I could hear the sound of a shutter several times, as they took photographs. When they had finished with the room, the police officers went back outside the house and gathered by the open window. The stout official was listening to the young policeman's report and looking at the bodies, while the policemen outside the window started following the tracks through the opening in the hedge towards the open field. The stout officer couldn't stay still either and, leaving the rest to the young policeman, went outside as well.

• • ● • •

I wrote a telegram to Sanshirō and asked Miki to take it to the post office. When I finally regained my composure, I turned to Tabei.

He had been calm while I was explaining the events to the policeman, but now he wasn't looking calm at all, more as though he was thinking very deeply. What was he thinking about? Had he discovered a clue?

'Mr Tabei,' I began resolutely, 'what are your thoughts about this case?'

'My thoughts?' Tabei replied, raising his head and blinking.

'What I mean is,' I said as I turned towards the other room, 'you probably saw it too. The tracks of the man who committed those violent crimes and abducted a child just disappeared into thin air. It's a very strange case.'

'That's true. It's really strange. But then everything about this case is strange.'

'I don't quite…'

'The toys and candy lying around here, do you think they had been here from the start, I mean, before any of this had happened?'

'Well, they had probably been there already, with the kid playing and eating, I think.'

'I don't think so. If he'd been eating here, there should also have been silver wrapping paper or paraffin paper here and there. I took a look before the police arrived, but there's nothing at all. And those toys lying there, they're all brand new. And the fact that the crushed cardboard toy box lying in front of the sofa is all wet, even though nothing—not even a drop of tea—has been spilt, is very strange, too…I think it might have been snow from the top of the cover, which melted because of the room temperature. But even without those trifling details,' Tabei continued, changing his tone and looking me straight in the eye, 'the ingredients for a mystery have been gathering here from the start. It's Christmas Eve...skis in the snow...going in and out of the window...and returning to the sky...'

Tabei suddenly stopped talking and, gazing into my eyes, asked:

'Who do you think it was...?'

'Hmm,' I groaned. 'Do you mean...are you suggesting it was Santa Claus?'

'Yes. To put it simply, Santa Claus appeared in this room.'

I was very surprised. 'It must have been a very violent Santa Claus.'

'Precisely. A Santa Claus such as you've never seen before...maybe the devil himself turned into Santa Claus and paid a visit here.' Tabei suddenly took a serious tone and stood up. '...but I'm starting to see through the masquerade...I've already solved more than half of the puzzle. Let's track this Santa Claus down.'

Tabei went to the door of the living room and told the policeman, who had eagerly been taking notes of the crime scene there, that he was going outside. Giving me a meaningful look, he left through the front door. I didn't really understand what was going on, but, impressed by his confident attitude, I stood up too, rather uncertainly. As I went out after Tabei, the image of the tracks I was about to follow again, and the image of the stout officer probably looking up into the night sky with his arms folded, appeared in my mind's eye.

But Tabei didn't go to the window in the back. Instead, he went to the hedge at the front, looking at the road there. In the snow were the tracks of the people who had entered and left the house, and some of the people from the neighbourhood were standing there with pale faces. What was he doing?

'Mr Tabei, the tracks are at the window in the back.'

'Oh, those tracks,' he said as he turned around. 'I don't care about them anymore. I'm looking for another set of tracks.'

'Another set of tracks?' I repeated.

'Yes.' Tabei laughed grimly, and continued: 'There was just one set of tracks outside the window, if you recall? You can't come and then go again leaving just one set of tracks. If someone entered back there, there should be tracks leaving here.'

He looked at the roof of Sanshirō's house and grinned. 'Even if he was Santa Claus, he wouldn't have been able to enter through that small chimney…because this murder case isn't just a fairy-tale.'

I saw it now: there had to be tracks entering the house, too. Realizing my own carelessness, I felt ashamed. But suddenly, a thought entered my mind.

'Mr Tabei, I see what you mean. It was snowing before eight. Santa Claus came here before eight, and went out after the snow had stopped. That's why the tracks of him arriving have been erased, and why only the tracks of him leaving remain.'

But, to my surprise, Tabei silently shook his head.

'You're gravely mistaken there. True, that's one way to look at the case. When I first took a look at the tracks outside the window, I myself thought so too for a while. But when I heard about the disappearing tracks from you, I understood I was wrong. The problem lies in the tracks that suddenly disappear.'

'By which you mean…?'

'So you think snow had fallen on top of the tracks?'

'Yes.'

'Then why had the snow fallen in such an uneven, irregular way?'

Tabei placed his hand on my shoulder. 'The starting point of your deduction is wrong, you see. Inside, people have been murdered and a child has been abducted. The window has been opened, and in the snow outside are ski tracks with just one ski pole; indeed as if someone had been carrying a child. But as you were observing this, you deduced that the fiend had abducted the child and gone out through the window. That was your mistake.'

Tabei changed his tone and added hand movements.

'So let's think about this situation…Let's suppose a man is walking in the middle of a heavy snow fall…but during his walk, the snow tapers off and the sky clears. How would the man's footprints appear then?…You see, while the snow was falling, the footprints would be obliterated by the snow immediately, but if the snow started to taper off, his footprints would gradually appear deeper and deeper as they were less and less filled by the snow. But if you now think about ski tracks and follow them in reverse—unlike footprints, you can't tell which direction ski tracks are pointing in—the tracks in the snow would become shallower and shallower until they were gone completely, just as if a man had disappeared…So the snow didn't fall after someone had arrived here, nor did someone leave here after the snow had stopped: the snow tapered off just as someone was skiing…So now do you understand the mystery behind those disappearing tracks? The man who made them didn't go out through the window, he came in. Tonight, the snow stopped falling at eight, so Santa Claus must have come from the town and entered the house shortly after eight.

'Now I get it.' I scratched my head and asked:

'But what do you make of the tracks of just one snow pole?'

'That's easy. It was just as you thought from the beginning. Santa Claus was carrying something in his arms. Not a child, but that big cardboard toy box that was wet from the snow. It was a present from Santa...'

Tabei then said seriously: 'So now most of the case is clear to you, too. The tracks outside the window were made when entering the house and there are no tracks leaving the house from there. As there are no signs of either Santa Claus or the child inside the house, the two of them must have left through the front door...by the way, when you first arrived here, were there tracks like that at the front?...They should have left here before you arrived.'

'That's a difficult one...don't forget, I was in a panic then...'

'It can't be helped. It might take a while, but let's search for tracks with one snow pole amongst all these here.'

Tabei crouched down and started to look for such tracks. I did the same, of course, and started the hunt in the pale snow light. The onlookers on the road looked puzzled, not sure what was going on.

The snow had become messy because of all the different tracks, including ours and those of the police, and we couldn't find any ski tracks with just one ski pole. The policemen who had gone to the end point of the disappearing ski tracks, had returned and it had become crowded inside the house.

It was then that Tabei suddenly asked:

'Miki of class A arrived before you, didn't she? Was she wearing adult skis?'

I nodded.

'That means it must've been the child's skis,' Tabei mumbled mysteriously and he led me to where the hedge followed the road, and pointed to two sets of tracks that were still visible there.

'Of course we couldn't find a set of tracks with one ski pole. Santa Claus wasn't carrying the child. The child was wearing his own skis as he was being led away by Santa.'

Indeed, there in the snow were the tracks of narrow skis, next to an adult's skis, going towards the main road.

'Let's hurry and follow these tracks before the police call us in for questioning.'

We set out immediately.

• • ● • •

A lot of time had passed since the incident, so we had no idea how far the owners of those tracks could have gone. Or so I thought at first, but after having gone about fifty metres parallel to the hedge, the two tracks, as if to evade something coming from the opposite side, suddenly made a sharp turn to the right. I felt a shiver. It was the empty house in the nearby block. The two tracks went through the front side of the small hedge, turning away from the entrance, and going round the side to the back of the dark building. I held my breath.

'That was unexpectedly close by,' said Tabei with a pale face, as he followed the tracks. 'It seems likely there's a bad ending ahead…By the way, who do you think Santa Claus is? You probably already know, don't you?'

I shook my head vigorously as I scratched my head. As Tabei reached the rear of the empty house, he said: 'It's difficult to say it, even if you do know, isn't it?…Who's the person who dressed like Santa Claus and came through the window with presents?…And the child followed him on his skis, without any resistance…I believe there's a train which arrives at half past seven every day here in H-Town…I think that Sanshirō Asami arrived by that train, one day earlier than expected.'

'What? Sanshirō!?' I cried. 'That's ridiculous…even if Sanshirō had come back, why would he have done such a dreadful thing?…No, someone who loved his family so much would never do something like that!'

But then Tabei discovered a large and a small set of skis beneath an open window, through which he too entered a pitch-dark room. I started to follow suit and it was then that I heard Tabei's quavering, painful cry.

'We're too late...'

When my eyes got used to the darkness, I could see the cold, dead figure of Sanshirō hanging from a curtain cord attached to the ceiling. At his feet was his child, strangled with a belt, lying there as if he were asleep. Some chocolate candies lay on the ground. A neatly folded piece of paper lay beside them. Tabei picked it up, looked briefly at it and then handed it to me. There were Sanshirō's last words, addressed to me. It seemed to have been written in a rush with nothing but the snow light, but as I stood trembling near the window, I could just make out the words.

Dear Hatano,

I have finally fallen down to hell. But I want you to be the only one to know the truth. Because of a snowslide, the agricultural school started vacation one day early. I arrived back in town by the seven-thirty train, when I remembered it was Christmas Eve and I bought some presents for Haruo and headed home. I think you know I am just a simple man, and how much I loved my wife, my child, my family. Thinking of how happy my wife and child would be with me coming back one day earlier, made me even happier and that's why I thought of Santa Claus. Bursting with joy, I went all the way to the back of the house, and silently sneaked up to the window. I removed my skis there and imagined the surprised look of my family as I went to the glass window and opened it.

But then I saw something I should never have witnessed. I entered the room to find Oikawa and my wife locked in an intimate embrace on the sofa. I threw the toy box, together with my happiness, at them.

But Hatano, do you think that would be enough to quell my overflowing rage? You probably know what I did with the poker I grabbed as I was crying with grief. Haruo, who had been sleeping in the room next door had woken up, so, making sure he wouldn't know what had happened, I lied to him and fled with him through the front door. But I have nowhere left to flee now. Even if I did, nothing can save my broken heart anymore.

Hatano. I go with the joy that my beloved Haruo will be beside me as I leave on this dark voyage.

Farewell.

Sanshirō

Outside, snow blown by the night wind which had just started, seemed like a funeral wreath. The church bells stopped ringing then, but their lingering sounds weighed heavily on my trembling heart.

The Mystery of
the Green Room

Pierre Véry

Pierre Véry (1900–1960) was one of several French mystery writers of the Golden Age—Noel Vindry and Marcel Lanteaume were others—whose clever detective stories were ignored by British and American publishers. Véry also wrote children's fiction and screenplays with considerable success. His first crime novel, *The Testament of Basil Crookes* (1927) satirized the classic mystery; it brims with youthful verve, and was the first winner of the Grand Prix du Roman d'Aventures. In *Great French Detective Stories* (1983), T.J. Hale quoted Véry as saying: 'My dream is to renew detective fiction by rendering it poetic and humorous…hence my decision to write a series of mystery stories…with characters who will no longer be mere puppets in the service of an enigma to resolve, but human beings fighting towards their truth.' Hale argues that: 'It is difficult to communicate Pierre Véry's uniqueness to an audience which has never been favoured with translations of his work—briefly they are detective stories but they are also fairy stories for grown-ups.'

Written in 1936, this story pays homage to Gaston Leroux's *The Mystery of the Yellow Room*, and is translated by British-born, US-based locked room mystery expert and publisher John Pugmire. Leroux is now remembered primarily as the author of *The Phantom of the Opera* (1910), but *The Mystery of the Yellow Room* (1907) was one of the most popular detective novels published before the First World War. An ingenious locked room whodunit, it introduced the youthful journalist and amateur detective Joseph Rouletabille, who proceeded to become a popular series detective. The story's enduring appeal, coupled with its historic significance as a milestone in the evolution of the detective novel is illustrated by the Folio Society's recent decision to republish the book as one of a collectors' edition of three 'locked room' classics. John Dickson Carr himself rated it the greatest locked room mystery of all time.

● ● ● ● ●

Dedicated to the memory of Gaston Leroux

The colour of the wallpaper was old pink.

The salon wallpaper, of course—for in the bedroom it was green, an exquisite Trianon green.

'Yes, gentlemen,' declared Madame Emilienne de Rouvres, 'it was about two in the morning. I was sound asleep. But suddenly…'

Upset by the recollection of her adventure, Madame de Rouvres shuddered at the word 'suddenly.' The two listeners seated opposite her shuddered as well, out of respect and with perfect tact. One was Inspector Jean Martin of the local detective squad; the other was a private investigator, Marcel Fermier, under contract to Sirius, the company with whom

Madame de Rouvres had taken out an insurance policy against fire and theft.

It was ten o'clock in the morning. The only sounds to disturb the peace and quiet of Rue Sablons in Paris came from the squealing brakes of the delivery tricycles ridden at breakneck speed by butchers' or grocers' assistants.

'Suddenly,' continued Madame de Rouvres doggedly, 'I am woken with a start by creaking noises in the corridor. I turn on the light. "Who goes there?" I ask. No reply. "Who goes there?" I ask again. Silence. I live alone, gentlemen, and there are no firearms here. Still, I get out of bed and get as far as the bedroom door. A masked individual is standing there in front of me, blocking my path. Before I have time to cry out, he throws himself on me…'

The expressions on the faces of the policeman and the private detective underwent a series of almost comically synchronized changes: admiration for the boldness Madame de Rouvres had shown, anxiety about the risk she had run, and horror at the thought of the barbaric treatment she might have received.

Madame de Rouvres's face, powdered and pampered, was coloured by a retrospective anguish and, it must be said, by the reflection from the salon wallpaper. An irreverent Anglo-Saxon might have described the lady as a 'dear old thing.'

Not that she was old. She *confessed* to being forty. *Maybe* just a little bit more. Well, *scarcely more* than fifty.

She was from the top drawer, of ample charms, and had been extremely seductive around 1910—the same year that her salon had been the most ravishing example of Louis XVI, thanks to a happy choice of furnishings.

Alas, the auctioneers had come and gone, and the Aubusson-covered armchairs and the rest of the inlaid rosewood furniture had finished up under the hammer. Only the old pink wallpaper remained as a reminder of the opulent past. And Madame de Rouvres' features had, alas, also been marked by time, that pitiless auctioneer of beauty. Only the sparkle in the eyes and the carnation-coloured cheeks remained—enhanced by kohl and make-up, it must be admitted.

'So, madame,' prompted Marcel Fermier, 'the frightful individual comes at you and knocks you down—.'

'No, detective,' corrected Madame de Rouvres with an ambivalent pout, 'he didn't knock me down! He gagged me and bound me to a chair from the corridor.'

'Then,' suggested Jean Martin, 'he went into the green room?'

'No, inspector,' corrected Madame de Rouvres again, 'he didn't go into the green room, but into the dining room, where he helped himself to my silverware. Then he went into the salon where we're sitting and helped himself to a small clock and two silver chandeliers. After that...'

Madame de Rouvres got up, moved a screen aside and pulled back a curtain to reveal a small safe. It had been forced open.

'In addition to family papers, this safe contained three thousand francs. The thief took them, naturally.'

'What about your jewels?'

'I don't keep them here, as a precaution. I imagine safes attract burglars like bears to honey. I keep my valuables in the drawer of a bedside table.'

'Just like Edgar Allan Poe's *The Purloined Letter*,' murmured Fermier. 'The best way to hide something is not to hide it.'

He asked:

'So after he left the salon the thief went into the green room and made off with your jewels?'

'My jewels, thank God, are safe,' replied Madame de Rouvres, with a deep sigh.

'The thief didn't go into my bedroom. The fool just poked his head in from the doorway, then left with the clock, the chandeliers, the silverware, and the three thousand francs. I had to wait until eight o'clock in the morning, when my maid arrived, before I was untied and the gag removed.'

• • ● • •

Madame de Rouvres had now retired to the green room, leaving the rest of the apartment to the two men and their investigations.

'It's completely against all the rules!' muttered Fermier.

'What?' said Martin. 'What's against all the rules?'

'This break-in! Why didn't the thief go into the green room?'

Martin made a vague gesture.

'I don't see what's so surprising. The green room *had been* Louis XV, just as the salon *had been* Louis XVI. But apart from the divan, the bedside table, and the chairs, there's nothing left but the wallpaper.'

'But what about the jewels? It's public knowledge that Madame de Rouvres owns a very valuable pearl necklace and a string of diamonds. They're estimated to be worth eight hundred thousand francs!'

'A tidy sum,' replied Martin.

'Those valuables are all that remain of her fortune. She's so attached to them that, rather than sell them, she preferred to let everything else go—her furniture, her carpets, and her paintings—and lead a more modest way of life. Everyone knew that. The thief must have known that as well!'

'All right,' muttered Martin, becoming irritated. 'We're dealing with a beginner, that's all there is to it. Obviously he couldn't have imagined the jewels would be in the drawer of the bedside table.'

The methods of the policeman and the private investigator differed profoundly. Martin, a big man with a large moustache, applied the principles drilled into him by his police training. He studied the furniture and the surface of the mantelpiece, examined the safe and the dresser, scrutinized the parquet floor, and probed the front door-lock. He searched methodically for prints and other clues.

Footprints, fingerprints, cigarette butts, gobs of spit. He even sniffed them like a retriever. And it certainly wasn't the violet fragrance that permeated the apartment, so beloved by Madame de Rouvres and so redolent of 1900, that his olfactory senses were seeking. It was an infinitely more vulgar odour, far removed from perfume—except for the canine species. Inspector Martin had learned, during his police classes, that many burglars could not resist the temptation to leave an excremental 'signature.' But nowhere could he detect such a Gallic visiting card. He reasoned: no excretions, so the man is of a reasonably elevated social level; no fingerprints, so the fellow had worn gloves to work.

Fermier, planting himself in the middle of each room, confined his activities to pivoting slowly on one heel and taking note of all the objects in there.

He was a frail, bespectacled young man. Weaned on a diet of specialist reading, his methods were of a more literary nature, modelled on those of Poe's gentleman detective Auguste Dupin.

While the policeman looked for clues, Fermier tried to determine the motive. For it was ridiculous to think that the theft of the clock, the chandeliers, the silverware and the three thousand francs was the objective of the expedition.

From time to time, Martin would cast sardonic glances at the investigator, then thrust his hand into his jacket pocket to caress the cold bowl of his beloved pipe. He was refraining from smoking, not so much out of deference towards the lady of the house seated in close proximity, but more out of the respect that the prestigious Louis XV and Louis XVI furnishings—long gone, no doubt, but with the old pink and Trianon green wallpapers still there to stand testimony—inspired in a common man like himself.

Abruptly, Fermier approached him.

'You've read Gaston Leroux's *Mystery of the Yellow Room*, of course?'

Martin shook his head.

'If you think I've got time to waste reading that stuff—'

'It's not always a waste of time.'

Martin shrugged his shoulders.

'In his book,' continued Fermier, 'Leroux posed what's called a "locked-room" puzzle.'

Martin sneered.

'I saw that one coming. The business about the hermetically sealed room, under constant surveillance, where it's impossible to enter or exit without being seen—which doesn't prevent the murderer getting in and out, nevertheless. That kind of poppycock is all very well in fiction, but in reality…Anyway, what has that to do with the case?'

'Well, what strikes me about the green room puzzle is that it's exactly the same as the yellow room puzzle in the sense that it's the precise opposite! The problem that's posed is, if I may use the expression, an *open-room* puzzle. In actuality, the thief could very easily have gone into the green room and come out again.'

Martin burst out laughing.

'And he spared himself the trouble. If that's what's bothering you, it doesn't take very much.'

Moments later, while Fermier was pursuing his meditations, Martin expressed the desire to examine the diamonds. They were splendid. The inspector was dazzled. Next to the window, in the bright light of that June morning, Fermier, too, admired the jewels before handing them back to their owner.

The inspector and the private detective left shortly thereafter. Martin was sullen. This business didn't interest him at all; what interested him were real crimes, bloody crimes, investigations that were worthy of his talents, that could demonstrate his gift for detection for all to see. Not this vulgar burglary. An exercise for beginners, maybe not even that. Fermier, on the other hand, seemed particularly agitated.

He said, in that emphatic tone that is so often used for quotations:

'The necklace has lost nothing of its charm and the diamonds none of their brightness.'

Martin looked startled.

'What are you talking about?'

'Nothing. I was just amusing myself by paraphrasing a vital message from the *Yellow Room,* involving a presbytery and a garden.'

Martin's shoulders shook uncontrollably, while the inspector looked at the private investigator with pity.

'You poor fellow. I'm starting to worry about you.'

Fermier looked at his watch.

'Eleven-thirty. What would you say to a drink?'

They found a table on the terrace of a nearby café.

The Pernod slowly changed colour as the sugar cube melted, helped on its way by a gentle stream of ice water from above. Transparent dresses went by, inhabited by pretty young girls that made them worthwhile. Martin was all in favour of the free street show.

'One *could* think of an explanation to the mystery of the green room,' announced the private detective suddenly. 'Suppose that Madame de Rouvres' jewels are fake.'

'Sorry?'

'I said: suppose…Let's suppose the jewels, at sometime in the past not yet determined, and without Madame de Rouvres' knowledge, had been replaced with almost perfect copies. And, while we're at it, let's also suppose that last night's burglar, at some point, had found out about the substitution. Given those two assumptions, it's easy to see *why he didn't bother to go into the green room*. What would have been the point, since he knew the jewels were just paste?'

'You're letting your imagination run away with you,' was all the inspector would say.

Fermier gave him a dirty look from behind his horn-rimmed spectacles. He looked at his watch.

'Gosh! Almost an hour already. It's time to go and *eat red meat*.'

Not having read *The Mystery of the Yellow Room*, Martin couldn't know that, once again, Fermier had paraphrased a well-known text from Leroux's celebrated novel. He took the witticism at its face value and replied in all seriousness:

'You're lucky. As for me, it's white meat in perpetuity, I'm afraid.'

And he started to talk about stomach pains, flatulence, etc. Fermier listened with half an ear.

They parted ways. After a short distance, the inspector turned round: he spotted the detective in front of a second-hand book store. Yielding to his favourite pastime, Fermier was fingering the dirty, dog-eared books, perfect hiding-places for microbes.

'Too much reading will drive him crazy,' thought Martin.

That afternoon, the policeman had a number of appointments in town that had nothing to do with the de Rouvres case. As he walked, he passed by numerous shops: hatters, furriers, tailors, milliners, almost all empty of customers.

'There it is,' he thought. '*The problem of the open room*, where nobody feels like going in…'

• • ● • •

But inspector Martin was quickly made to realize that the private detective was more subtle than he had previously thought. Indeed, the affair of the Rue Sablons burglary took a sudden and unexpected turn.

Worried, Madame de Rouvres had decided to take her valuables to the jeweller who had sold them to her many years ago. The response almost caused her to faint: the jewels were fake.

Madame de Rouvres filed a complaint against persons unknown and put the Sirius company on notice to pay the indemnity.

'I'm afraid the company is going to balk at paying out,' Fermier confided to Martin.

'Why so?'

'Because,' the detective said comically, 'this business resembles the *Yellow Room* more and more, in the sense that it's exactly the inverse.'

'The best jokes are the shortest,' replied Martin gruffly.

'I'm not joking.'

'Well, then, explain yourself.'

'It's very simple. I find a *parallelism of opposition* between the two cases quite striking. Thus, in Leroux's imaginary adventure the villain gets into the yellow room despite all the difficulties. But in the present case, the villain—'

'—takes great care not to enter the green room despite the open invitation. You've already told me that. Now what?'

'The parallelism continues. In the case of the yellow room, the villain uses his cunning to make us believe that the attack, executed beforehand, actually came later. Conversely, in the case of the jewels, I get the impression that someone wants us to believe that the job, executed afterwards, was done beforehand.'

'Someone? Who the devil do you mean?'

'Madame de Rouvres, for heaven's sake!'

'Are you mad?'

'Inspector, think about this: Madame de Rouvres is far from being rich. In fact she's in desperate need of money. Little by little, armchair after armchair, table after table, she has had to relinquish her Louis XV bedroom and her Louis XVI salon. But now, once again, she needs money. There's only one option left: sell her valuables. That, Madame de Rouvres does not want. She cannot bring herself to do it.

'So, discreetly, she has a copy made. Then, later, she creates a burglary, a complete fabrication: she breaks into her own safe, steals three thousand francs from herself, a clock, a couple of chandeliers, and some knives and forks. After that, when we arrive on the scene, she draws her attention to the fact that the burglar didn't go into the green room. What was the point of that manoeuvre? *To make us think that the thief spurned the valuables. To lead us to suspect they might be false, and from there to conclude that the real jewels had been stolen a long time ago.* And, speaking personally, I must admit I fell for it.

'The rest follows as night follows day. Visit to the jeweller. Discovery of the fake jewels. Complaint filed against persons unknown. *Indemnity claimed from insurance company.* An indemnity of four hundred thousand francs. Well worth a few hours tied up—not too tightly—on a stool.'

'Pretty complicated, but not so dumb, your theory,' murmured the inspector. 'That stage production would constitute a kind of moral alibi for Madame de Rouvres.'

He thought about it.

'Unless...'

'Unless?'

'I can see another possible suspect: the jeweller who previously sold her the valuables. He was in a better position than anyone to create copies. Let's suppose he organized the burglary. All he has to do afterwards was to wait for Madame de Rouvres, anxious because the thief had *scorned* her jewels, to bring them to him to be examined. He swaps them, and the deed is done. Who'd suspect him?'

'That's possible, too,' conceded Fermier. 'But, in either case, how do we prove it?'

● ● ● ● ●

Four days later, Inspector Martin found the proof. In the course of a search of the jeweller's premises he discovered, in a corner of the cellar under a pile of empty cartons, Madame de Rouvres's clock, chandeliers, and silverware.

As expected, the jeweller protested his innocence, claimed he had no idea how the objects had found their way into his cellar, and swore he was the victim of a plot.

He was arrested nevertheless. Even so, it proved impossible to find the real jewels.

Fermier, meanwhile, didn't hide his opinion from the inspector. He remained unconvinced of the jeweller's guilt and continued to suspect Madame de Rouvres.

'She could quite easily have hidden the clock and the chandeliers in the jeweller's cellar.'

'Come off it! You've been reading too many detective stories.'

Two weeks went by.

Fermier diligently watched the area around Madame de Rouvres's home; he followed her every time she went out.

Even though nothing came to light as a result of his tenacity, he kept going.

Finally, one afternoon around three o'clock, as he was again lying in wait at the Longchamp roundabout, he ran into Martin.

'Not discouraged yet? You certainly don't give up.'

'As long as the valuables have not been found, my friend, I feel we must give the jeweller the benefit of the doubt.'

Martin, full of himself, smiled condescendingly. He took the private detective's arm.

'I didn't come here by accident. I came to relieve you of your duties.'

'What do you mean?'

'The jeweller is indeed innocent; he's just been released. And it turns out that Madame de Rouvres is innocent as well.'

'Do you have any proof?'

'Cast iron! I laid my hands on the valuables—the real ones.'

'Where did you find them?' asked Fermier, alarmed.

'Come now, you must be joking. They were in your bedroom, carefully hidden under one of the parquet blocks.'

The detective went as white as a sheet.

Martin hailed a passing taxi.

'Police headquarters, please.'

The two men sat down in the back.

'You see, Fermier, you made a big mistake in drawing my attention to the parallelism of this affair and the *Yellow Room*. I finally bought the book and—I who never read—read it.

'That's when I had an idea. A crazy idea. "*Suppose the parallelism applies all the way through?*" I said to myself. "*Suppose the mystery of the green room turns out to be the exact opposite of the* Yellow Room, *even at the very end?*" I wanted to see what would happen.

'And, my goodness, the result was pretty intriguing.

'In the *Yellow Room*, there's a private detective and a professional policeman. The latter is the guilty party. In order for the parallelism of opposition to be perfect in Madame de Rouvres's misadventure, the policeman—that's me—has to be the honest man, and the amateur detective—that's you, Fermier—has to be the scoundrel.

'That conclusion made me laugh out loud for a start. Then I started thinking: why not, after all? It was all very feasible. You carried out the theft of the clock and the chandeliers. The next day, while pretending to examine the real jewels, you pocketed them under my very nose and substituted the fakes. After that, you pronounced the mysterious phrase: "*The necklace has lost nothing of its charm and the diamonds none of their brightness.*" Then you directed my suspicions, first to a theft in the distant past, then to Madame de Rouvres herself. For my part, I raised the possible guilt of the jeweller. You went round straight away to hide the stolen goods. Then, just for appearances, you started tailing Madame de Rouvres.

'I wouldn't have worked it out so soon if your incessant talk of the *Yellow Room* hadn't driven me to buy the book.

'Let it be said in passing that, thanks to me, the parallelism of opposition of the two affairs will be perfect.'

'What do you mean?'

With a hearty laugh, Martin explained:

'In the *Yellow Room*, at the end of the book the amateur detective allows the policeman to avoid the reach of the law. Therefore, today, the opposite must happen: the policeman mustn't let the dishonest detective escape. You can count on me for that.'

The handcuffs clicked firmly on Fermier's wrists.

'And to think I told you,' said the latter disconsolately, 'that reading wasn't always a waste of time.'

Kippers

John Flanders

Ghent-born Jean-Raymond-Marie De Kremer (1884–1967) published, it is said, more than 1500 short stories and novels as well as at least 5000 articles. Not surprisingly for a writer with such a prodigious output, he used a variety of pen-names, most notably Jean Ray and John Flanders. He was evidently a colourful character with a vivid imagination and a taste for the fantastic. In a fascinating article for *Weird Fiction Review*, Antonio Monteiro says that Flanders variously claimed to have been 'a smuggler of weapons, pearls, ivory, and liquor (during the American Prohibition era), chased wild animals in distant jungles, been an executioner in Venice, a pirate in the Atlantic Ocean, a gangster in Chicago...'

His career as a smuggler came to an abrupt end with a prison sentence, which at least gave him plenty of time to write. An admirer of Conan Doyle, he produced Sherlockian stories, although—like Maurice Leblanc—he fell foul of claims of breach of copyright, and had to modify his approach, creating Harry Taxon, 'the American Sherlock

Holmes'. The 1971 film *Malpertuis*, which has the more lurid alternative title *The Legend of Doom House*, starred Orson Welles and Susan Hampshire, and was based on a horror novel published in 1943 by Jean Ray. Monteiro highlights Flanders' fictional preoccupation with food and drink, which is again evident in 'Kippers'. The story, originally written in Flemish, and published by Albin B. Young, has also appeared under the names of Jean Ray and John Flanders. This is a new translation by Josh Pachter.

• • ● • •

That day, they served us kippers…

> *Pilot Hauser considered how best to proceed with his narrative: he was not a good storyteller, but he was something of a gourmet, and anything smoked—be it ham or sausage or herring—was all right in his book.*

Kippers, delectable salmony kippers, smoky as a chimney, dripping with fat, one for each of us, of course, the real thing.

Even Bertie the cabin boy got one. That was only fair, for although he was but a lad of thirteen summers, he did the work of a grown sailor: he polished the brass, reefed the sails, clambered up the shrouds like a cat in times of wind and heavy seas, swabbed the decks, did the washing up, served the Old Man in his cabin, sometimes even helped out the cook in the galley.

The boy, possessed of a hearty appetite, was about to take his first succulent bite when the fish was ripped from his hands.

It was Meesy the halfblood who did it, and the rest of the crew eyed him angrily, but none of us dared say a word, for Meesy was a giant of a man, strong as a tiger, evil as a snake.

'That's *my* kipper!' cried Bertie, furious.

Meesy unleashed a backhanded slap that flung the lad

to the deck, and sat there, calm as you please, devouring the boy's treat.

We were underway, heading for Kingston on the island of Jamaica, to take on a cargo of sugar and rum. After a few days there, we set out across the Caribbean Sea, a strong wind in our sails.

And that's when our luck turned against us. As the first of the Lesser Antilles came into sight, the air suddenly blossomed with all the colours of the rainbow. The sky turned slate grey, and the sea glowed as if a fire raged far below her surface.

Our sails went slack, and we came to a dead stop in the water.

'This is bad', the captain growled. 'We're in for it now. Look, the inkwell has begun to spill'.

And truly, it was as if a flood of jet-black ink poured out of the heavens, staining the sea with heavy, silent strokes.

'We'll have plenty to do soon enough', the Old Man went on. 'For now, we may as well make use of the rest period we've been afforded to smoke a pipe and drink a glass of whisky. Who knows? This may be the last chance ever we get!'

The poor man, he knew not how prophetic those words would be, but when the wind kicked up again it was as if the gates of Hell had flung themselves open wide.

Our masts shattered like panes of glass, and there was no question of being able to steer a course. No matter where we *desired* to go, we went wherever the storm condescended to carry us.

'We'd best pray', said I, and then our old keel cracked like a dried walnut and I swallowed a gallon of salt water.

'Abandon ship!' I stammered. "Tis food for the sharks we'll be...though praise God the filthy beasts won't reach us till we're long drowned and dead and drifting with the waves. But a man may just as well lie buried in the belly of a shark as beneath a thousand leagues of ocean'.

It was at that point that I fell unconscious.

And you can imagine my astonishment when I reawakened.

I must be dead, I thought, *and my soul has beached on some distant Heavenly shore*. But I was curious to know why my soul was still dressed in my dirty, ragged sailor suit instead of a pure white sheet like any normal spirit.

At that moment, I suddenly heard a voice call my name and spied Bertie the cabin boy running toward me across a broad stretch of sand.

'Well, then, Bertie', said I, 'so you're dead, too, then, same as me? Do ye know where we are, lad?'

'We're on an island', replied Bertie, 'and we're not dead, sir. For quite some time I feared that *you* were, for you never moved a muscle, but now I see as I was wrong, and I couldn't be better pleased. I would hate to be stranded in this strange place all by myself'.

'Where are the others?' I enquired.

'The others? They're all gone, sir, we're the only ones left. But luckily some of the barrels and chests from the ship have washed ashore with us, so we won't go hungry'.

'How long have I lain here on the sand?' I asked.

'It's a day and a half since I dragged you out of the water. I was just now thinking to dig you a hole and drop you in it, and tonight I was of a mind to take a few bits of driftwood and make you a nice cross in remembrance'.

'That's very kind of you, Bertie', said I with a bit of a shiver, 'but I believe that plan can wait a while longer'.

'There's a crock of tobacco stopped tight enough to keep it dry', the cabin boy announced with pride, 'some matches and a couple of pipes. Here they are! Would you care for a smoke, sir?'

'Indeed I would', I cried, delighted, taking a pipe from his hands. 'Oho', I added, a moment later, 'I know this one. Surely it's Meesy's!'

'It must have fallen from his pocket when he drownded', Bertie opined. 'I found it atop a pile of shells just over there'.

When once I had Meesy's pipe filled and lit, we set off to take inventory of all the useful items the sea had spared us, and that was a considerable store: tins of biscuits and milk, syrup and salmon, barrels of corned beef, crocks of wine, drums of flour.

'A pity', said I, 'that we don't have that chest of kippers!'

Bertie laughed so heartily that the tears rolled down his cheeks. 'Pilot', he cried, 'what a rogue you are, sir! A chest of kippers, indeed!'

I understood not why he found this so amusing, but truth be told it mattered little.

A week went by. All was well. It was hot as a furnace, there on our island, but not far from the beach flowed a little stream of cool spring water, which we mixed with a splash of wine to enhance its flavour.

One day, Bertie asked, 'Do you still have a taste for kippers, Pilot?'

'Indeed I do', I acknowledged, 'especially as we have no need to worry about thirst'.

'Kippers do make a man thirsty, do they not?' said the lad.

'Powerful thirsty', I agreed.

That evening, he brought me a half a chest of kippers, which he informed me he had that very afternoon discovered washed up on the west coast of the island.

We enjoyed them thoroughly, and doused the thirst they provoked with our usual mixture of water and wine.

On our fifteenth or sixteenth day, as I sat quietly smoking my pipe on the beach, I spotted a three-master's sails on the far horizon.

'Bertie!' I shouted. 'We're saved, lad! A ship!'

But he had gone inland to scavenge and heard me not. I set off along the path I had seen him take, and some time later spied him standing at the edge of a ravine, staring into its depths with great solemnity, so consumed by his thoughts that he failed to observe my approach. I reached his side and gazed down into the abyss.

How I screamed! For there below us lay the body of a man...and what a body it was!

Tied up like a Westphalian sausage, the man had been unable to move a muscle. His face was twisted into a tortured grimace, and his blackened tongue protruded from between his lips.

When Bertie at last noticed my presence, he started, then spoke with supreme calmness: 'Do you recognize him, Pilot? It's Meesy. I found him on the beach, unconscious, same as you. I dragged him here and bound him hand and foot. When he awoke, I came to see him. He was hungry, of course, and I fed him—kippers, stuck on the end of a long stick, so as not to have to come too close to him. I returned often, two or three times a day, and gave him all the kippers he could eat. You remember how much he loved them, sir, so much he stole the one was meant for me. But not a drop of water did I allow him. And when he looked as you see him now—dead of thirst, like an animal—I brought the rest of the kippers back to you'.

With that, Pilot Hauser fell silent. A few moments later, he concluded his tale in a whisper:

And from that day to this, gentlemen, I have never eaten another kipper.

The Lipstick and the Teacup

Havank

Havank was the pseudonym of the Dutch author, journalist, and translator Hendrikus (Hans) Frederikus van der Kallen (1904–64), who along with Ivans (another contributor to this anthology) was one of the two people generally considered to be the fathers of the Dutch detective story. His main series characters were two French police officers, Bruno Silvère and Charles C.M. Carlier, the latter also being known as 'the Shadow'). He translated into Dutch novels by such diverse crime and thriller writers as Raymond Chandler, E. Phillips Oppenheim, and Leslie Charteris. He spent most of his life in France, Spain, and England, and set many of his stories abroad, but died in Leeuwarden, the town of his birth. After his death, an unfinished novel was completed by journalist Pieter Terpstra, who subsequently produced further Havank titles under the name Havank-Terpstra.

Over six million copies of Havank's books were sold during his lifetime, but his work has not been widely translated. The Dutch national forensic biometric system which enables searches to be made for criminals' finger and palm prints is known as HAVANK. 'The Lipstick and the Teacup', translated by Josh Pachter, comes from a 1957 collection, *Havank and Co.*

• • ● • •

'It was in fact only thanks to an unusual circumstance that was nearly overlooked that I was able to unravel the truth regarding the notorious murder in the Rue St Didier'.

> *So Chief Inspector Silvère of the Sûreté began his story as he sat that balmy spring evening with his inseparable companion Manon and his friend Haro Aberdeen on the terrace of Le Triomphe, gazing out at the busy night life that flowed along the Champs-Élysées.*

> *After screwing a fresh cigarette into his long silver-and-ebony holder and setting it alight, he continued.*

• • ● • •

The case began rather strangely.

The telephone in my office rang. The caller would not give his name, and spoke in a voice that was obviously disguised. If the police would go to such and such an address, he claimed, they would discover there something of considerable interest. Immediately upon the delivery of this cryptic message, the connexion was broken. Later investigation revealed that the call had been placed from a public telephone box.

Well, Inspector Charles Carlier—who, as you know, is referred to in the press as 'the Shadow'—and I proceeded without delay to the indicated address, and we arrived simultaneously with an individual who spared us the trouble of having to break down the door of the fourth-floor flat. A sort of servant. Carlier questioned the man closely, but he knew nothing—or at least *appeared to* know nothing—and his dismay upon hearing of the mysterious call which had summoned us seemed genuine.

Meanwhile, I entered the flat. The foyer, which gave onto several rooms, was in darkness. The only illumination was a narrow stripe of light that spilled from a door that stood slightly ajar onto the grey carpet. I pushed that door further open and, from the threshold, shouted, 'Don't move, or I'll shoot!'

My threat proved completely unnecessary. Within the chamber—a comfortably furnished library—there was but a single person, and he would surely never move again.

He was dressed in evening clothes. A tall, well muscled man. But the position in which he lay left little doubt of the veracity of the telephonic message I had received. He was apparently lying as he had fallen, upper body stretched across a low divan, head thrown back, one leg extended, the other folded at an awkward angle. The right arm dangled, the left arm—its fingers balled into a fist—was half-hidden beneath the body. A red blossom stained the chest of the dead man's stiff-fronted shirt.

But my initial conclusion proved false, as I saw when I examined his wound more closely. There had been no gunshot here. The murder had indubitably been committed with that most deadly of blades, the stiletto. The work of a Corsican, I suspected. And the victim had not been dead for long.

From behind me, I heard Inspector Carlier murmur the single word, 'Remarkable'.

I turned to see him bent over the smoking table which stood beside the divan. 'Yes, remarkable', he said again, and I watched him pick up a still-lit cigarette end, stub it out and carefully place it in a plasticene envelope he withdrew from one of his capacious coat pockets and redeposited upon the table.

There was more than one reason for him to bless that solitary cigarette butt with his patented ejaculation. In fact, there were—if I remember correctly—*three* reasons for him to do so.

Firstly, the cigarette had been lit but not smoked, as evidenced by the long, unbroken ash that remained on the silver candy dish where the Shadow had found it.

Secondly, the cigarette was of a rare and rather expensive Yugoslavian brand, a Drina.

Thirdly, the crepe filter at the unlit end of the cigarette was red, quite a bright shade of crimson, the colour unmistakably a popular shade of lipstick.

An additional point of interest was the half-empty teacup which stood beside the candy dish.

'Remarkable', came Carlier's voice yet again, this time from the foyer, to which he had absented himself. 'Did the gentleman have more than one head?'

As past experience has proven conclusively that Inspector Carlier is anything but a fool, I suspended my investigations for a moment to consider what he might have meant by this apparently nonsensical remark.

The Shadow re-entered the library with two hats in his hand—hats he had apparently found on the coatrack in the foyer. They were of clearly different sizes: one, I estimated, was a 48, the other a 45.

The servant was able to resolve this riddle without delay.

No, he assured Carlier, his master did not have two heads. And thank heaven for that, as—according to the servant—the whims and vagaries that rattled around within his single head were quite troublesome enough. Why, then, the two differently sized hats? 'Ah, that's dead simple, sir. The 45 belongs to my master, it does, and the 48 to his friend who shares the flat with him'.

The obvious questions followed: Who was this friend? What work did he do? And, of the utmost importance, did the servant know where he could be found at this moment? Yes, indeed, he did. Most likely in a well known club in the Boulevard Malesherbes.

The Shadow went to telephone, and I questioned the servant further. At what time had he gone out? Approximately four in the afternoon. His master was expecting a visitor, and on such occasions the servant was inevitably sent for a walk. On this particular afternoon, he had strolled to the cinema—the Madeleine, to be precise. He could offer thus no alibi, or at best an alibi that would be difficult either to confirm or disprove.

And the visitor…?

The answer to that vital question was slow in coming. When it did, it boiled down unsurprisingly to a case of *cherchez la femme*.

Who was she? The servant could not reveal her name. *Could* not or *would* not. But the dead man's wallet brought me a significant step closer to an answer. It held a photograph of a woman. Was that her? Yes. And a letter, signed 'Mathilde', provided another piece of the puzzle, since the sprawling feminine handwriting spoke of a rendezvous scheduled for that very afternoon. A rendezvous which had indisputably been the victim's last.

Mathilde's full name and address were on the envelope, and I made a brief call to the Sûreté, requesting that two officers should ask for Mademoiselle Mathilde Fournier at the Hôtel St George and, upon finding her, should bring her to me as expeditiously as possible.

We continued our investigation of the crime scene, though there was little else to be investigated, and discussed the case while awaiting word from the Sûreté. The Shadow did much of the talking—almost all of it, to be honest. As he droned on, his voice seemed to fade into the background, like the sound emanating from a loudspeaker when the volume control is turned anti-clockwise. In reality, of course, the fault was my own—my thoughts were fixed involuntarily on that red-smeared cigarette end and the half-consumed cup of tea. Indeed, those two simple objects quite fascinated me.

My thoughts extended like a collapsible telescope—to use a cliched image. It took perhaps a second, possibly two…but in that brief span of time the key to the solution revealed itself to me.

I examined the stubbed-out cigarette butt under my glass, studied it closely and could not hold back a smile. What, the Shadow wanted to know, was I grinning about? Rather than explain, I sent him off to the Sûreté with the plasticene envelope and its contents and a drinking glass I found in one of the bedrooms.

He left, for once deprived of his usual bonhomie, muttering imprecations over some people and their secretive folderol.

I scarely heard him, for at that moment the detective I had charged with fetching the dead man's flatmate from his club returned, his mission successful. I steered the man, whose name was Popewitch, directly to the salon, without giving him any opportunity to glance through the library door. He was in quite a state, upset at being dragged away from his bridge game. I let him vent his anger, then posed a series of questions, confronting him at last with the information that a murder had been committed. I had the impression that the man was shocked by this news.

The other detective, who had been sent to enquire after Mathilde Fournier, followed, accompanying a woman who, after the usual game of questions and answers, delivered a performance which might be described as bordering on hysteria. She acknowledged, however, that she had indeed visited the flat that afternoon and that she smoked Drina cigarettes.

It was noteworthy that neither suspect had a tenable—or perhaps I should say a verifiable—alibi.

• ● ● ● •

'That makes three without firm alibis', Manon commented at this point in the story. 'Popewitch, Mathilde, and the servant'.

Chief Inspector Silvère smiled and nodded. He lit yet another cigarette and resumed his narrative.

• ● ● ● •

That was not as important as you might think. I waited impatiently for a call from Inspector Carlier. Perhaps five minutes after I had finished with the very charming Mathilde, it came. And the good inspector's message provided the last piece of evidence I needed. When I wrote my report on the affair, the reasoning behind the arrest was as follows:

It struck me immediately as bizarre that the cigarette had been abandoned within seconds of being lit. I also noted that, while its filter was smeared with red lipstick, the rim of the half-empty teacup, which had obviously been used by the same person, was not. From these details I drew a series of conclusions which culminated in the discovery I made when I examined the cigarette butt with my glass. The lipstick had been applied to the filter with a finger, not a pair of lips, and that finger had left a faint impression in the crimson paint. Quite small, but large enough. For that reason, I had directed Inspector Carlier to the fingerprint service, which had identified nine distinct points of correspondence between the print in the lipstick and those on the drinking glass—quite enough, according to international agreements, to classify them as identical.

And so I arrested Popewitch, for the glass had come from his bedroom.

• • ● • •

A brief silence ensued.
Then came Manon's voice.
'Next case, bailiff'.

The Puzzle of the Broken Watch

Maria Elvira Bermudez

'The detective story has been regularly, although not extensively, cultivated in Mexico since the 1920s,' said Amelia S. Simpson in *Detective Fiction from Latin America* (1990). Maria Elvira Bermudez (1916–88) was one of the pioneers, and J. Patrick Duffey, in an essay included in *Latin American Mystery Writers: an A-Z Guide* (2004), said that during her lifetime she was 'the most prolific female detective fiction author in the Spanish-speaking world, one of the most innovative practitioners of the genre in Mexico and one of its most perceptive critics.' She also put together a landmark anthology, *The Best Mexican Detective Stories* (1955); all the stories were set in Mexico, and written by Mexicans.

Bermudez created two major series characters. Armando H. Zozaya was in the mould of the American detective Ellery Queen. Maria Elena Moran is an enthusiastic reader and writer of detective fiction. Donald A. Yates, an expert on Latin American crime fiction, has praised the quality of Bermudez' characterization, while Duffey argues that Bermudez' work 'has not received the critical attention it deserves'—a fate common, at least until recently, to far too many authors of classic crime fiction. This story dates from 1960; translated by Donald A. Yates, it appeared in his excellent anthology *Latin Blood: the Best Crime and Detective Stories of South America* (1972).

• ● ● ● •

Comfortably reclining on his divan, he was absorbed in reading the short stories of Arkadio Averchenko. He smoked slowly, absently, the smile that appeared and reappeared on his lips causing him to forget his cigarette. Suddenly, a man somewhat younger than he entered the room. It was his good friend Miguel Prado, the lawyer.

'*Quiúbole!*' greeted the newcomer. 'Are you busy now?'

'Very busy,' replied Armando Zozaya.

'Very busy?' exclaimed Miguel. 'If all you're doing is reading—'

'So you think one can't be busy with a book?'

'Well, I suppose so, but I have to talk with you.' He took the book from Zozaya's hands and sat down before him. The latter gave a sigh of resignation and retrieved his book. He found his place, carefully folded over a corner of the page, and settled back to listen to his friend.

'I'm defending a person who's charged with murder,' explained Prado. 'And I'm convinced of his innocence. The problem is I haven't been able to find a way to prove it. That's why I—came to see you.'

'What is it that you want me to do?'

'Well, it's clear to me that the only way to get my client acquitted is to find the real murderer.'

'Nicely put. But I question whether this is possible. You understand, of course, that it's one thing to find yourself at the scene of the crime, in possession of fresh facts, and another to investigate a crime committed Lord knows how long ago.'

'Naturally. All the same, I think you can help me.'

'I'll do what I can, Miguel. Go ahead and tell me what it's all about.'

'My client, Juan García, is charged with having murdered his sister-in-law, an attractive young girl who lived with Juan and her married sister in the García home together with the couple's seven-year-old daughter. On the day in question, Rosa, the victim, stayed at home because of a bad cold, and she was left alone when her sister and the latter's daughter went out shopping. Juan, as usual, was at work, but unfortunately that day between eleven-thirty and noon he had left work without telling anyone where he was going. Juan's wife and daughter were at the market longer than usual. I think they went to get medicine for Rosa, or something of the sort. At any rate, what happened was that when they returned they found the girl dead. She had three bullet wounds in her chest. There were signs of a struggle. The murder weapon was found at the scene. It was a gun that belonged to my client.'

'None of the neighbours heard the shots?'

'No. The murder occurred on the third of May, the day of Santa Cruz, which is celebrated by construction workers. There's a new building going up nearby, so it's very possible that the gunshots were taken for part of the racket made by the fireworks. What's more, these same circumstances explain why the neighbours, entertained by the festivities of the construction people, failed to observe closely who entered and left the girl's home.'

'I see. And what does your client have to say about all this?'

'He didn't deny that he left work. Actually, he had to secure permission from his boss at the match factory to get time off. He claimed that he left work because he had received an anonymous message in which he was told to be at a spot near the factory at eleven-thirty. The place indicated was in Atlampa, there where Vallejo Street begins. The spot, you realize, is out of the way and usually deserted. The message he received insinuated that there was something of great importance he should know about the conduct of his wife. Juan's wife is a good soul, and never had he had cause for doubting her loyalty. But, as you can imagine, Juan was intrigued, then disturbed, and ended up keeping the appointment. He couldn't have spent more than five minutes passing under the Nonoalco Bridge and covering the few blocks that separated him from Vallejo Street. He says he arrived precisely on time and waited half an hour, but that no one showed up to give him the slightest information on the matter suggested in the message. The only people he saw were a ragpicker and an old woman beggar, who were more than a little surprised when he asked them if they had called him. He was furious by this time and returned immediately to work. His obviously agitated manner which his fellow workers subsequently observed has since been interpreted as the nervousness to be expected in a man who has just committed a crime.'

'How did the anonymous message come to him? Has he shown it to you?'

'Unfortunately, he tore it up when he realized he had been the victim of a cruel joke. The message had been delivered into his hands that same day when he arrived at work by a small boy who had said merely, "A gentleman sends you this."'

'Haven't they been able to find the lad?'

'Impossible. The authorities maintain that the boy doesn't exist, that he's a product of my client's imagination, created in an attempt to establish an alibi for himself. And, as you know, I have neither the time nor the means to devote myself to the search for a little urchin lost in the streets of a city of four million people.'

'Of course. Tell me, at what time has the murder been fixed?'

'Now that's the strangest thing in the whole case. Unquestionably, the murder had to have taken place during the period when Rosa's sister was absent—a space of two hours. However, according to a watch that belonged to the deceased, which was found in the possession of my client, the precise moment of the crime was eleven forty-five. The watch had been smashed, and the hands had stopped at that time.'

'Very strange, very strange.' Armando meditated a moment. Then he pursued the point. 'I accept the fact that the smashing of the watch during the struggle that took place would leave the hands indicating the time of the victim's death, but what I don't understand is why Juan, if he killed the girl, carried off the watch and kept it on his person.'

'That's precisely what bothers me. What you might expect is that he would change the time indicated if he happened to notice it. Or that he'd leave it behind, not considering it a piece of evidence that could incriminate him. The District Attorney proposes that Juan carried it away and later lost his wits and forgot to get rid of it.'

'That could be, but I don't believe so. For the time being we can arrive at the following conclusion: the fact that the day of Santa Cruz was selected for the crime so that the reports of the gun would be lost amid the noise of the fireworks, the delivery of the anonymous note to Juan with the object of strengthening his guilt through his absence from work, and, above all, the puzzling detail of that watch, strongly suggest that we are faced with a premeditated crime. One other thing, Miguel. Had the girl bought the watch for herself?'

'I don't know. It didn't occur to me to ask about that.'

'It's very important. And, too, why were the sister and her little girl gone so long on their errand?'

'Do you believe that this has something to do with the problem?'

'I don't think any detail should be overlooked.'

'All right, then. Why don't we go and speak with the sister?'

'A very good idea,' said Armando Zozaya. 'I was about to suggest the same thing to you.'

• • ● • •

The tenement house where Juan's wife and daughter lived was one of the many tenements which characterized the older, poorer Mexico. It was located on Venus Street, near the highway to Laredo, in the heart of the Atlampa quarter. The greyish brick walls, ravaged by the years, opened onto a long, narrow entrance hall which greedily imprisoned the daylight. In the broad, open patio the light regained its freedom and joyfully poured down on the cracked paving tiles and glimmering pools. Blocking the path before them were countless little children, sombre pigeons, and drying clothes scattered about like so many gay pennants. Against the walls, geraniums and rue, daisies and a carnation here and there emerged from the flower pots placed along the stairways and lay claim to a place in the sun. Armando and his friend entered the courtyard of the tenement house escorted by a dozen curious glances. Lupe, Juan's wife, lived in number 19. She came to the door in response to the lawyer's knock, and when she recognized the man who was defending her husband she politely invited them to come in.

The home consisted of a kitchen and two rooms, the smallest of which was crowded with tables, assorted junk, several unpainted pine chairs, and a number of earthenware utensils. The other room, which was a little larger, was divided into two parts by an improvised partition of bedspreads and sarapes. On one side was the couple's double bed and the child's crib, and on the other a cot and a small dressing table that had apparently belonged to the deceased Rosa. Still hanging on the wall were the girl's clothes, in the corner was a wooden trunk, and placed about the room were religious images together with pictures torn from old calendars, all of which had represented the girl's worldly belongings. Lupe explained:

'This is where poor Rosa slept. I haven't been able yet to make myself pack up her things. I just can't believe that she's gone.' And she dried a pious tear with her apron. She was about to add something more when she became aware of the sudden appearance of her daughter.

'Rosita,' she ordered, 'go out and play in the patio. Go on now, *ándale*!'

The child went out slowly, making a sad face. The mother added:

'I've told her that her father and Aunt Rosa have gone away on a trip, poor thing. She adored my sister. She was her godmother.'

The two visitors took seats around a humble table. Lawyer Prado explained to Lupe that *señor* Zozaya who accompanied him wanted to help in his defence of Juan and that he needed to know certain facts. Lupe said she was more than willing to tell him everything that she knew, but first she declared:

'God knows my Juan is a good man. I'm not saying that he didn't drink a little, or didn't—stray occasionally, like all men. But as far as what they say about him and my sister... that's pure lies. Neither my poor sister—may God bless her—nor Juan were capable of doing anything that—that would reflect on my honour, or that of my little girl. They are also whispering behind my back that Juan may have killed her because she failed to respond to his attentions. But I know that can't be true.'

'Who do you think might have done it?' asked Armando.

'I don't know. Only God can say. Perhaps someone who broke in intending to steal something.'

'Did you find any things missing?'

'No. They might have carried off the radio. It's the only object of value. But no, it wasn't touched.'

'Haven't you considered that it might have been someone who knew Rosa who…who committed the crime?'

'Well, I just don't know.' And she looked oddly at the lawyer.

'What just occurred to you, *señora*?' asked Armando. 'Tell me what it is.'

'Well…you see. Oh, God forgive me, but—'

'Go ahead. There's nothing to fear.'

'Well…Rosa had a boyfriend, you understand. And recently they had been quarrelling. The neighbours wouldn't tell me anything, but the other day I'm sure I heard *doña* Chona, the woman from number 10, tell Tula, who lives in 5, that she'd seen Tomás come here that day.'

'Tomás was Rosa's boyfriend?'

'Yes. I asked Tula what *doña* Chona had told her, but she refused to tell me. They are very close, you know. When it comes to gossip they're unbeatable, but—'

'When it comes to giving help in something like this,' interposed Miguel, 'they're worthless. I haven't been able to get a word out of them either. I forgot to tell you, Armando, that the *señora* had told me about this before. I tried to make the women understand what was at stake, but they flatly refused to go and testify in court. And if I ask that they be subpoenaed, I run the risk of making things worse. You understand.'

'Uh huh. But we must keep this point in mind,' commented Armando. And he added, 'Tell me, *señora*, why were you longer than usual at the market that day?'

Lupe responded to the question with surprise. It was evident that she hadn't been expecting it. She replied:

'I? Well...that is. I had to go and pick up a prescription for my daughter, and...'

'The pharmacy, is it far away?'

'No, it's just a little ways away, at the corner of Heroes and Neptuno.'

'I understand that you left at ten o'clock and that you returned at twelve...'

Lupe was confused. For the moment she was saved from the question by the appearance of her daughter.

'Mama, the men are here to talk with you about Rosa, aren't they?'

'*Muchachito esa!* Didn't I tell you to go out?'

'Let her be,' intervened Zozaya. 'Come here, little one. You love your Aunt Rosa a lot, don't you?'

'Oh, yes. She buys me lots of caramels. And I play with her. And I wear her clothes, too.'

At this point, the child, bent on showing the visitors how she played with her aunt, disappeared into the other room and returned laden with clothing and trinkets. She put a kerchief on her head, explaining that this was the way her aunt wore it, she threw on a dress and dragged it about the room with genuine grace, as if she were a princess at a royal ball. She made several trips to and from the other room, exhibiting one gewgaw after the other. Zozaya observed her good-naturedly while Prado and the wife looked on without comprehending why Zozaya was interested in the child's treasures. The latter, in one of her trips from the other room, brought out the most cherished article—her aunt's watch. Zozaya examined it with interest and asked:

'Is this the watch that was found in your husband's possession?'

'Yes, it is,' replied Lupe. 'They say he had it with him. What I think is that he took it away with him that day to have it fixed because it's broken. But at the police station they don't believe me.'

Armando looked fixedly at her and asked:

'Had Rosa spoken to you about having broken the watch?'

'No,' the woman replied, dropping her glance. 'But that must have been what happened.'

Armando interpreted the woman's theory as a feeble effort to clear her husband of the guilt of the crime. He took the watch in his hands and examined it at length.

'How is it that you happen to have this, *señora*?'

Miguel explained:

'Although it actually ought to be included as part of the evidence in the case, the *señora* expressed a desire to keep it as a memento of her sister, and one of the members of the police force who is a close friend of the Garcías arranged to have it returned to them before the trial was over.'

'How about that!' exclaimed Armando. 'The history of this watch gets stranger by the minute!'

As Armando was speaking, the little girl came to his side and, shaking her head, regarded the timepiece very seriously. Suddenly she took it from Armando's hand, turned it about in every direction, and exclaimed emphatically:

'This isn't Aunt Rosa's watch!'

'What are you saying, child?' murmured her mother in astonishment.

'It isn't, it isn't, it isn't!' repeated the little one with conviction.

'How do you know it's not?' asked Zozaya gently.

'Because it doesn't have the little hole.'

'What little hole?' asked the three members of her audience simultaneously.

'A little hole here,' the child explained. 'Aunt Rosa made one for me because when I wore it, it was too big.' And she indicated, beyond the normal series of perforations on the watch band, the unmarked expanse of leather.

'A child's nonsense. Pay no attention to her,' said Lupe.

'It's *not* the watch, it's *not* the watch,' the little girl insisted. Her mother, now exasperated, gave her a rude shove and obliged her to leave the room. Armando did not intercede. An eyebrow arched, and he appeared to be in deep reflection. At length he asked:

'*Señora,* did your sister buy the watch for herself?'

'No, *señor.* Our good friend Ismael, the one your friend spoke to you about, gave it to her for her birthday.'

'I see.' After some thought, he returned to his earlier question. 'Please excuse my insistence, but what kept you so long at the market on the day of your sister's death?'

Lupe stirred uneasily in her chair. She regarded the lawyer helplessly. Miguel returned her glance with interest and urged:

'Try to remember.'

'I've already told you,' she replied. 'I went out to get some medicine…' Suddenly her face brightened. 'Now I remember! That was the day when two women got into a fight in the marketplace, and I stood around watching the excitement. I even remember now that our friend Ismael arrived on the scene with the other officers and sent the women off in the police wagon. Afterwards—yes—afterwards he bought some ice cream for my little girl…'

'Excellent!' exclaimed Armando. 'That explains perfectly your delay. Now please, give me a bit more information about this Tomás, your sister's boyfriend.'

'Well, he didn't seem like such a bad fellow. They'd been going together for quite some time, but several days ago they had a quarrel. I don't know what piece of gossip fell on Rosa's ears, but she was very burned up.'

'Tomás customarily visited her here?' asked Armando.

'He used to come sometimes, but only when Juan wasn't here, because my husband didn't care much for the boy's informality towards the family.'

'Did Tomás know that Rosa wouldn't be leaving the house on the day she died?'

'Let me see…yes. Yes, he knew. I remember that the day before when I was going shopping, I ran into him over in Nopal and told him that Rosa had a bad cold and that I wouldn't be letting her go out for several days.'

'You had come across him by chance?'

'No. Tomás used to come and talk with me nearly every day with the hope that I'd be able to help him win over Rosa. Since he worked as a delivery boy, he was almost always around the streets. That day he told me that he had won on a lottery ticket and that he wanted to get married to Rosa… Just think of that!'

She began to cry. After a few moments, when she had calmed down somewhat, Armando asked her:

'Did Tomás know where your husband Juan worked?'

'Certainly. Tomás worked at the same place with him. That was how he met Rosa. It's a match factory, and one day when we all went to a party there, the young people met.'

'Very well. Thank you very much, *señora*. I think for the time being we'll not have to bother you anymore.'

The lawyer and his friend said goodbye and left. In the patio they found Rosita busily plucking feathers from a pigeon which she had tracked and caught. Armando gave her an affectionate pat and put a peso into her hand. The child promptly abandoned her captive and ran off in search of her mother.

• • ● • •

Back at Zozaya's apartment, the two friends were discussing the matter.

'It would be advisable,' Armando was saying, 'to check and see if on the day in question there actually was a disturbance in the market of the sort that Lupe mentioned.'

'It's already been checked and established,' replied Miguel. 'Juan called me to the police station immediately after they had arrested him and while I was there, I recall that Ismael Flores, the García's friend who is on the force, commented that on that day, the third of May it was, he had seen Lupe a *second* time after having chatted with her in the marketplace, when he received the call from the García's tenement.'

'Who called the police?'

'One of the neighbours. As a matter of fact it was the woman in 10—*doña* Chona...'

The lawyer suddenly stopped speaking, as if a startling thought had struck him.

'What is it?' Zozaya asked.

'I just remembered what the other neighbour, Tula, told me.'

'What's that?'

'She was at the market that day, too. And Lupe, she said, left the little girl with her while she went to the pharmacy...'

'Aha! So Lupe doesn't have an alibi after all!'

Zozaya burst out laughing when he saw the troubled expression on his friend's face. He said:

'Now you've really got yourself in a fix. In order to save the husband, you've got to implicate the wife. And the poor little daughter...Just imagine.'

Miguel regarded him sorrowfully. 'Do you actually think...'

'You're the one who's thinking it,' replied Zozaya. 'The wife suspects that her husband and her sister are deceiving her, jealousy blinds her, and she plans to dispose of her rival and, in the process, gain her revenge on the unfaithful husband. She goes to the market, leaves the child there with her neighbour, returns to the house, kills her sister with her husband's gun, takes the watch and hides it in Juan's clothing, and then hurries back to get her daughter. The family friend who invites them for ice cream is the ideal witness for establishing her alibi since, at the time the broken watch indicates, she is far away from the house in the company of a police officer.'

'You're right,' murmured Miguel, sadly, 'it all checks.'

'Everything, including the anonymous letter that she sends to her husband which arranges for him to go to a spot not too far from the house and leaves him looking mighty guilty.'

'I never dreamed that Lupe might have been the murderer...'

'Well, not too fast, my friend. Notice that everything fits *except* the little detail that the watch that showed up in your client's pockets was not actually the dead girl's watch.'

'You think, then, that the child is telling the truth?'

'Obviously.'

'But isn't Lupe's attitude a strong argument against her? You saw how upset and confused she was when you asked her why she had delayed in the market that day, and how she became disturbed when the child claimed that the watch wasn't the right one.'

'These arguments only have value when you can demonstrate a complete and convincing connection between them. Lupe's attitude in itself is not enough on which to base the assumption that she is the murderer. It could be that she actually was unable to recall the events of that morning; it could also very well be that she was nervous and impulsive owing to the difficult period she's going through. Attitude alone is not enough. You must prove that only the suspect, and no one else, could have committed the crime under each and all of the known circumstances.'

'Well, then?'

'Consider this: the murderer has to be a person who knew the habits of the family, who knew that Juan worked at the match factory, who knew that Lupe went to the market, taking the little girl with her, every day at more or less the same time—a person who chose the day of Santa Cruz so that the shots wouldn't be noticed, and who knew, moreover, that that day Rosa would be home alone...'

'Then it's...'

'Wait a moment. The murderer, to be sure, planned the crime in advance. He sent an unsigned note to Juan and made an appointment for a place where there would probably not be witnesses who might testify on Juan's behalf. Notice that the contents of the letter reveal a man as its author, since a woman, even in self-defence, would scarcely accuse herself—though her mind might be plagued by jealousy and indignation—of being deceived. Besides, the message boy spoke of a "gentleman." So we have the murderer, as I was saying, arriving at the house shortly after Lupe had left. He was, without doubt, someone known to Rosa, since otherwise she wouldn't have opened the door to him. Then there was a struggle and during it the watch was shattered, probably by the gun when the girl raised her arm to protect herself. When the murderer saw the watch smashed beyond value, there was nothing he could do but hurry to a jewellery shop and buy another. He needed the watch, you realize, to establish the time of the murder. He bought another, carefully broke the crystal, and jammed the hands at the hour desired. Then he waited for the chance to slip it into Juan's clothing. Notice that Lupe, aside from not having the time to go out and buy a watch during the crucial period, didn't have the *money* to buy one.'

'Of course. It all figures perfectly. Then it's Tomás who's the murderer. Really, he must have been seen entering the house.'

'He might have been seen. He probably went between ten-thirty and eleven to see Rosa. Unquestionably, the crime had been committed by then, and...'

'What did you say?'

'...he found the girl dead. He has said nothing about it for fear of being accused himself.'

'But what do you mean. Haven't we determined the fact that Tomás is the murderer?'

'We haven't determined anything. You're the one who's suggesting it. Tell me something. Was Juan arrested at home or at the factory?'

'At the factory. The police went first to the scene of the crime at the tenement. Since the gun was Juan's, he was immediately a suspect, and they went to the factory for him. His absence from work during the morning naturally served to place suspicion on him and they arrested him.'

Armando Zozaya said calmly, 'Then the real murderer is Ismael Flores.'

'The García's friend?'

'Precisely.'

Miguel gazed in bewilderment at his friend. Armando explained with patience:

'Lupe could have had a motive, but she didn't have money to buy another watch and, what is most important, she couldn't have placed the new one in Juan's pocket, since Juan never came back home. Tomás fills almost all the requirements, and moreover he had the money necessary since he won on a lottery ticket, but he has no known motive and also had no opportunity of leaving the watch with Juan since he was not at the factory. Remember that as a delivery boy, his work was away from the factory. Flores, on the other hand, fits perfectly into the picture. He gave the watch to the girl which suggests he had more than a passing affection for her. Rosa had a boyfriend which would indicate that she had rejected Flores. And there we have the motive. But what irretrievably condemns him is the fact that he is the only person among the suspects who had the opportunity to transfer the watch into Juan's possession.'

'When?'

'Obviously when he arrested him or when he took him to the police station. You know that it is customary to search all prisoners. This same Flores surreptitiously slipped the watch into one of the poor fellow's pockets and afterward ordered one of the other officers to finish the search of the prisoner. In this way, no one could ever suspect him. On the contrary, he was very kind, very good-hearted, he only wanted to help. Remember, too, that he kept Lupe in the marketplace with the enticement of the ice cream for the child so that Lupe would arrive home after the time indicated by the hands on the broken watch. The squabble between the women at the market was only a coincidence which happened to favour him, although it obliged him to hurry a great deal in his search for the new watch. The "good friend of the family" was a sharp number, without a doubt.'

'But how in the world am I going to prove his guilt?'

'Look for a jewellery shop where a man purchased two identical watches within a relatively short time, and who, when he bought the second, brought along a broken one as an indication of what he wanted. The jeweller will doubtless remember. The child's declaration regarding the watch will be a fragile bit of evidence, but perhaps confronting Flores with the jeweller will produce something substantial. This is a classic case of circumstantial evidence. It will all depend on your ability and luck in convincing the judge to withdraw the charge against Juan and reinstituting it against Flores.'

Miguel left in a hurry for the Penitentiary. He scarcely mumbled a '*gracias, hermano*' before disappearing. Zozaya bade him farewell with a friendly wave of the hand. Then he lit a Raleigh, and contentedly smoothing his moustache, took up once again his reading of the short stories of Arkadio Averchenko.

To see more Poisoned Pen Press titles:

Visit our website: poisonedpenpress.com/
Request a digital catalog: info@poisonedpenpress.com